COPYRIGHT © 2024 ANNA P.

All rights reserved. No part of this book may be reproduced or used in any manner without the prior written permission of the copyright owner, except for the use of brief quotations in a book review.

LOVE SONG, TAKE TWO is a work of fiction. Names, characters, places, and incidents either are the product of the author's imagination or are used fictitiously. Any resemblance to actual persons, living or dead, events, or locales is entirely coincidental.

Copy editing by Kristen Hamilton at Kristen's Red Pen

Cover Illustration by @wiggedwonder

Cover Design by Jordan Burns Designs @joburns.designs

Interior Formatting by Taylor Epperson

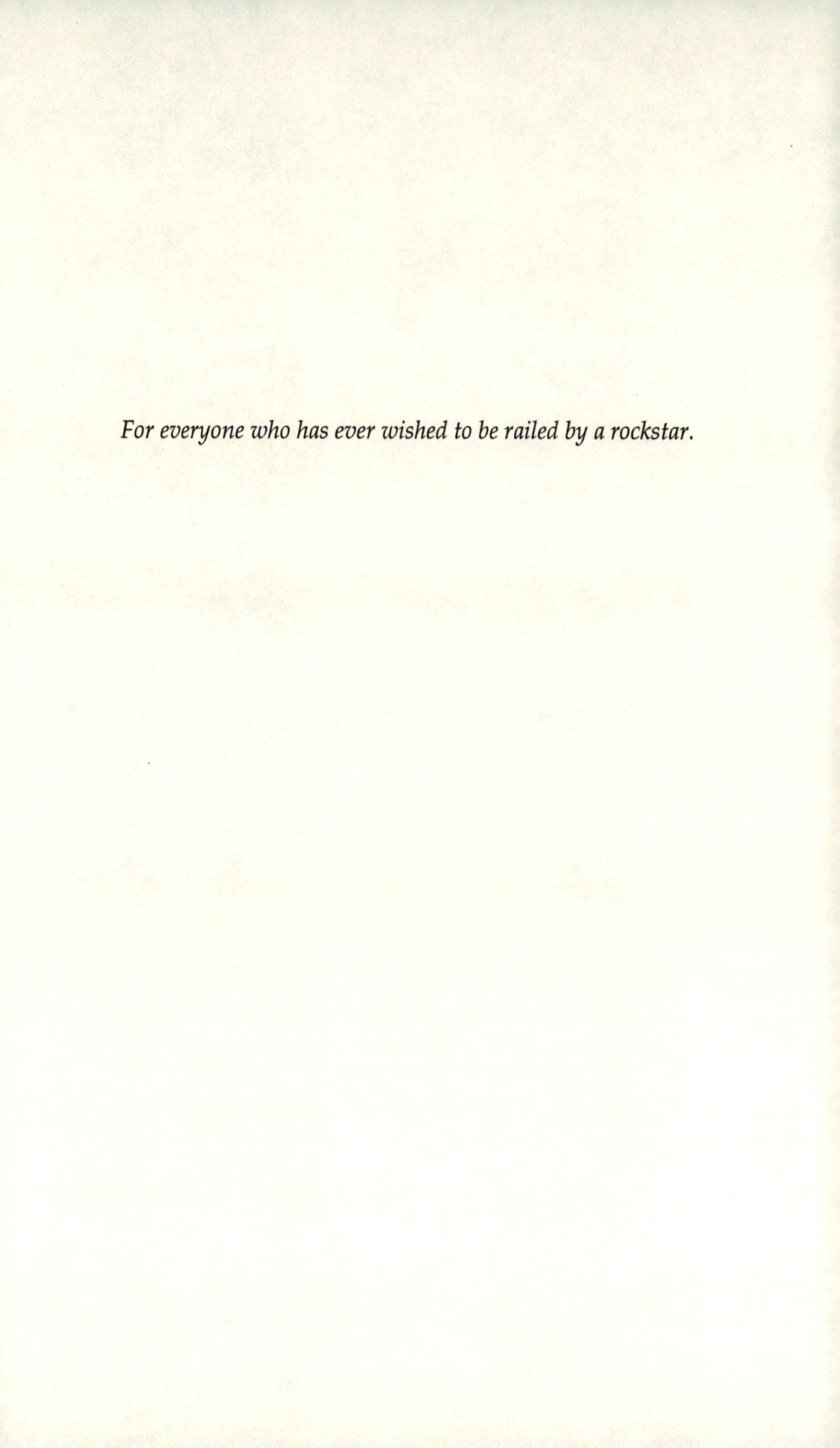

For everyone who has ever wished to be railed by a rockstar.

author's note

As a lifelong Foo Fighters fan, I was devastated when Taylor Hawkins passed away. I couldn't listen to any of their music, but found comfort in the pages of Dave Grohl's memoir—*The Storyteller: Tales of Life and Music*. It was such a heartfelt peek into his life, his journey to becoming the man we all know him to be and it also pushed me to start listening to Foo again.

This book was born from that rediscovery. They are my absolute favorite band and I would give anything to see them live again, especially with Taylor Hawkins behind the drums. Instead, I wrote this romance where a woman like myself falls in love with a rockstar in her early twenties, only to lose him and find him again sixteen years later.

Simply put, I wrote this book because I wanted something happy in my life. As authors, we write books for ourselves a lot of the time. There are also instances when we write for everyone else.

This book was written entirely for me.

Love Song, Take Two is a soft, low-angst, zero drama book. I wouldn't classify it as a romantic comedy, but you might! It has funny moments, it's swoony and charming. Both characters are 30+ (Micah's 38 and Fletcher is 47), there's tons of found family vibes, food and music.

However, there are a few things to be aware of going into the book.

Content & Trigger Warnings below.

There's mentions of divorce, child neglect and abandonment. There are also references to unsupportive and toxic parental figures. Micah (the FMC) grew up with a speech impediment that led to bullying and is addressed a few times through the book. As a speech therapist, she has clients who also have speech impediments and there are two or three scenes depicting this.

My brother grew up with a speech impediment that was oftentimes difficult for him to overcome. He struggled a lot as a kid and as his big sister, I always thought I needed to protect him. While he now presents as fluent, there are situations and instances where his stutter comes out. His journey and how he's handled it over the years inspired me to write this into Micah's history.

I had the incredible help of a fellow author, Julia Goodwin, to make sure that I was portraying the stuttering accurately. I am forever indebted to her for taking the time to help me with this. Any mistakes in the representation are my own.

The book also contains coarse language, consumption of alcohol and of course multiple wide open door scenes with explicit sexual content that include sensation play and use of food—all of which comes with eager consent.

If you have further questions and concerns, you can email me at
hello@annawriteshere.com

playlist

The full playlist has forty songs and didn't want to include them all here, but by scanning the above image, you can access the full playlist!

ALMOST (SWEET MUSIC) | Hozier
SKY FULL OF SONG | Florence + the Machine
LOWERCASE LETTERS | Noah Richardson
8TH WONDER | The National Parks
LINE BY LINE | JP Saxe and Maren Moore
BUTTERFLIES | Kacey Musgrave
ONLY YOU | Parmalee
FALLING LIKE THE STARS | James Arthur
I'LL NEVER NOT LOVE YOU | Michael Bublé
CONVERSATIONS IN THE DARK | John Legend
LUCKY | Jason Mraz ft. Colbie Caillat
EVERYTHING | John K
LET'S FALL IN LOVE FOR THE NIGHT | FINNEAS
IF I DIDN'T HAVE YOU | BANNERS
YOU ARE THE REASON | Calum Scott
LOVING YOU IS EASY | Ben Rector
I CHOOSE YOU | Sara Bareilles
YOUR SONG | Elton John
I AM YOURS | Andy Grammer
MADE FOR YOU | Jake Owen

*love
song,
TAKE
TWO*

prologue. fletcher

Will you think of me after tonight?

Then, 2008 | New York City, New York

"SO, what you're saying is, you have a bucket list."

She snorted, shaking her head. "Less about me kicking the bucket and more about me wanting to live my life a little better."

"All right, what's on the list?"

"Fuck a rockstar, for one. Looks like I can cross that off right now."

Fletcher gestured to himself with a smirk. "What else?"

She pursed her lips, eyes narrowed as she considered his question. Wearing only his T-shirt, this woman had all of his attention. They'd been at this for hours—talking and fucking and eating—and he was still desperate for more.

"Go on tour with Stevie Nicks."

"Just Stevie, not the whole band?"

She lifted her shoulder in a shrug, his T-shirt sliding down slightly to expose her collarbone and the mark he'd left there not too long ago.

"*Stevie,* huh?"

"We've hung out a few times, sure."

Her eyes widened, twinkling at him as she sat up fully. "What's she like?"

"Badass. Tiny, but an absolute force to be reckoned with."

"She's the best female rockstar in the world."

He hummed and fought back a smile as her eyes narrowed to slits. "I think I might have to disagree."

"I knew there had to be something wrong with you."

"Stevie's great, but we've also got Patti Smith, Grace Slick and Kim Gordon."

"You forgot Karen Carpenter."

"Cyndi Lauper too."

A smile played on her lips as she said, "Ann Wilson and obviously Alanis."

"Should have known you'd be an Alanis fan."

"What can I say? I like badass women who follow the beat of their own drum."

Just like you.

Their moment was interrupted by a knock on the door and he slid out of bed to pull on another T-shirt. A tray was pushed into the room, the tip was paid and then the door was pressed shut again. When he turned to face his companion, she was already digging into the food, her fingers and lips covered in bacon grease. She was the most unexpected part of the night, but the one element he wouldn't change or trade for anything else right then.

Life as Fletcher Kelley, drummer and founding member of The Rescuers, wasn't anything to sniff at. He played music with his best friends, sat in recording studios with some of the best music producers, and performed to sold out crowds. It's what other musicians only dreamed of and he got to do it.

He knew how lucky he was, how fortunate that he was able to follow this path and get paid to do it.

Leaving home hadn't been as hard people would think. His family expected him to follow in their footsteps, but that was never going to be Fletcher's life. So when his father told him to pick between music and the family business, he left them and their carpentry business behind to become a well-known rockstar. And damn, being respected by a group of his peers and being touted as 'drummer of the year' was a fantastic feeling.

The sudden shot to fame changed their lives. Everything was either cheap or free—food, alcohol, drugs, women—and rubbing shoulders with their heroes was startling. They adjusted to it pretty quickly though, but unlike the rest of his band, Fletcher didn't get too caught up in the world of groupies. Sex was great, having someone want you like that was even better, but that wasn't the life he wanted. Instead, he hung around with the roadies and crew members, learning about things behind the scenes, watching them set up and pull apart at venues. He asked questions and soaked up every bit of information they were willing to part with. To him, music was not only about the songs. It was about the experience, about each instrument and finding something you related to in every element. It was also about the feeling you got when standing in a bar with a hundred strangers singing along to your lyrics.

That's how he felt when he saw her earlier that night. Truth be told, Fletcher had felt that way about her every night for the last three weeks. The Rescuers were on the final leg of their sold out tour and they'd made the decision to do slightly smaller, more intimate shows on the East Coast. After big stadiums, being that much closer to the audience was intoxicating. Especially when his eyes had moved through the crowd and he spotted *her* headbanging not too far from the mosh pit. She'd flipped her thick curly hair back at the end of the song and her gorgeous brown eyes had stopped his heart. When she'd turned to her friend, laughing and attempting to smooth down her wild hair, Fletcher found himself smiling.

It was one thing to be horny for a random woman, but another to be besotted by her on sight alone. Then he saw her the next night and the one after that, and every night until their last show a few hours ago.

"Otis, I need you to find someone for me," he told their large mountain-sized security guard as he came off stage, rubbing the towel against the back of his head. "Brunette with thick curly hair, wearing a tee from the 2000 tour, prettiest girl you've ever seen."

Otis gave him a flat look. "Soren asked me to find him the prettiest girl he'd ever seen too, so I need more."

Fletcher rolled his eyes and focused on everything he could remember about this woman. He couldn't see the rest of her clothes, so he was basing all of this off what he had been able to see. A flash of red popped into his mind and he grinned. "Bright red streaks."

"All right." He headed towards the exit. "What do I tell this girl?"

"Ask her if she wants to come backstage."

"And if she says no?"

"Give her a T-shirt from this tour and thank her for being here."

Otis shook his head and vanished out of sight. Turning around as his bandmates, best friends and brothers from other mothers bounded off stage, he smiled. The four of them had been making music, traveling the country and meeting people for the last ten years. The only thing they had in common was their love for music, but that's what held them together as they navigated this new part of their lives.

"Was looking for you after the curtains went down," Jack said, whipping his towel at Fletcher.

"Needed to find someone."

Soren came up on the other side, sweaty arm slung over his shoulder. "Someone? Tell me more."

"Fuck off." He laughed and attempted to push Soren away, but his friend held on.

"Good for you, man. About time you participated in a little post-show fun."

Fletcher rolled his eyes and let his friends drag him back to the green room. He had nothing against groupies, but they weren't as fun as movies or other rockstars made them out to be. He often felt like the women were hooking up with them to brag about it to their friends later. Sure okay, fucking a random stranger and getting all your energy out with someone else was a good way to have fun. But that was no longer how he looked at sex. Maybe he was an old man, hoping to make a deeper connection with someone. Or maybe he had higher standards.

Jack had already filled up glasses with tequila someone had gifted them a few days ago, so Fletcher knocked back his shot and hissed as the alcohol burned its way down his throat. Grabbing a bottle of water, he twisted it open and took a swig as the doorway to the green room was filled with Otis's giant body.

"There's some people who want to see you boys," Otis said, stepping to the side to reveal a group of scantily clad women. Shaking his head at the way the women squealed and rushed for Jack and Soren, Otis added, "Be safe, kids."

Fletcher started to ask about *his girl* when Otis moved out of the way and she appeared. Her eyes were wide, bottom lip tucked between her teeth as she surveyed the green room. He didn't give a shit what the space looked like, because all he could see was her. Her extra large T-shirt stopped mid-thigh, revealing cut-offs layered over fishnet stockings. Her thick thighs and strong legs ended in well-loved red Chuck Taylors. His eyes dragged back up her body and found her watching him with an amused smile. Her full lips were pink giving them a soft and biteable look, her brown eyes were surrounded by thick lashes and dark liner. She was the opposite of every woman he'd ever known or hooked-up with, instantly making her the most interesting person around him.

She moved into the room, every step bringing her closer to him and Fletcher was certain he'd stopped breathing. When she stopped in front of him, he finally allowed himself to inhale—the heady scent of sweat and cookies wrapping around him.

"Was I wrong to assume that rockstars only hydrated with alcohol?" she asked, her voice was smooth like velvet and husky—probably from all the shouting and singing along she'd been doing—and fitting for a woman like herself.

"You missed the tequila shots."

Her soft lips curved into a pout. "Think I could get some too?"

He nodded, but didn't move. He was so captivated by this woman. Looking at him right then—ripped jeans, baggy sleeveless T-shirt, unkempt shaggy hair, patchy scruff and dopey look on his face—nobody would think that Fletcher Kelley was thirty.

"Fletch?"

He blinked, shaking his head as sounds and lights came back into focus. *Fletch.* Nobody called him that. Not even his bandmates, not his parents or siblings. Just this woman. And fuck if he didn't like it.

"Sorry, shouldn't have assumed I could call you that," she quickly corrected, a pretty blush spreading over her cheeks.

"You most definitely can." He tucked his sweaty hair behind his ears and added, "Seems unfair that you'd know my name but I don't know yours."

She smirked. "Pour me a shot and I'll consider it."

This time, he didn't stop the smile that tugged at his lips. Instead, he grabbed the tequila, poured out two shots and handed one to her. Her eyes stayed on his when she clinked their glasses and knocked the tequila back. His eyes were drawn to her neck, to the way her throat bobbed as she swallowed, to the dip between her clavicles.

"Wanna get out of here?" she asked, wiping the back of her hand over her mouth.

Fletcher's heart dropped. Maybe she was a groupie and he'd misjudged her because she wasn't dressed like the others. Nodding slowly, he set his untouched shot on the table and asked Otis for a car. They were ushered through the back exit into a blacked out truck and he finally found his voice again.

"Are you sure you want to do this?"

She tilted her head at his question, all that dark hair tumbling over her shoulder. "Get food and hang out with my favorite drummer?"

"What?"

"Okay, yeah, fucking you is not off the list, but I thought we could hang out too."

"So you're not..." he fumbled, not sure if the term *groupie* was offensive, but the woman shook her head, the most incredible smile lighting up her face.

"I am a *huge* fan of The Rescuers, been to every tour since you guys started out. If that makes me a groupie, then so be it. But nope. I'm only a fan and honestly? Being noticed by you might be the coolest thing that's ever happened to me."

He blushed, looking away from her to instruct the driver to take them back to the hotel. "I saw you every night on this leg of the tour."

"I know," she said, grinning at his shocked expression. She scooted across the seat to sit closer to him. "I was looking at you every night too."

"Is your list entirely music related?" he asked as they collapsed back into bed after inhaling every bit of food that was ordered. It was a miracle he was still able to breathe.

"Fuck no. There's a lot of sex stuff on there."

Lifting his head, he arched an eyebrow and Mick—"yeah, like Jagger"—grinned at him. "And did we do any of it?"

She nodded, wide grin still in place, as she swung one leg over his hips and pressed their bottom halves together. "That thing in the shower, your magical tongue, whatever you did with your fingers." She rattled them off, making Fletcher laugh.

"All right, what else can we cross off tonight?"

"Let's see…" He propped himself up on his elbows as she slid out of bed. His eyes followed her, watching the way the T-shirt slid up her ample bottom as she bent down to rummage in her bag. When she held up a rumpled piece of paper, he arched an eyebrow. "It's my list."

"You carry it around with you?"

"Never know when you'll need to mark things off." Pencil in hand, Mick returned to bed and resumed her position in his lap. "Okay. I've do—done, um…oh, we sh—should try something else."

If he wasn't watching her so intently, he would have missed the way her eyebrows dipped as she spoke. A soft hum-like sound accompanied the words. But he couldn't tear his eyes away as she swallowed and mouthed words, the sounds coming out in soft whispers.

"Tell me what you've crossed off so far."

Mick smiled and straightened her spine, like she was ready to give him a speech. "We already talked about me wanting to fuck a rockstar. Also shower sex, receive and give oral, uh…order room service and eat all of it. Then there's stuff from before we met."

"Tell me everything, Mick."

"Go on tour with my favorite band," she admitted, her eyes flicking to his briefly. "Get a tattoo, horseback riding, drive a truck, skinny dipping, keep a plant alive longer than a week."

Fletcher brushed his thumb over the dandelion tattoo on the side of her hip that he'd kissed an hour or so ago. He felt her shiver slightly and looked up to find her watching him curiously. "What's wrong?"

"If you had a list, what would be on it?"

"You."

Mick rolled her eyes. "Obviously. What else?"

"I can't think of a single other thing off the top of my head."

"Not even anything sexual?"

He laughed and pushed himself to sit up, one arm sliding around Mick's waist. "I'm pretty sure I did more sexual things with you than I have in my thirty years of existence."

"I fucking love that," she whispered, brushing her nose slowly against his.

He hummed, cupping her jaw with his other hand and tilted her head slightly so he could press a kiss to her mouth. She giggled softly, kissing him back before pulling away to stare into his eyes.

"Will you think of me after tonight?"

"What do you mean?"

Mick shrugged, list forgotten as her fingers brushed through his freshly washed hair. "The tour is over, we're both going back to regular life, so…will you think of me?"

"Regular life?"

"College, graduation, finding a job, making my parents proud."

Nodding slowly, he let that realization settle into his bones. He'd never see her after this. All he would have with this incredible woman was this one night, one night that he hadn't made the most of. Fletcher wondered if he would have done things differently if he'd known that this was the first and last night he'd get with her.

"What's your regular life look like, Fletch?"

"Jamming with the guys, maybe even back into the studio."

Mick's eyes widened. "Another album?"

"If we're lucky," he said, chuckling as he leaned in to bury his face in her neck. "I'm gonna miss you, Mick."

Her fingers moved through his hair slowly, the tips brushing against the back of his neck. "The night's not over, Fletch. Don't say goodbye yet."

He slipped his hands under her T-shirt, mapping her body slowly. The dip above her perfect ass, the arch of her spine. Then around to her soft belly and down to her thighs that no longer had the indents from her fishnet stockings. He *was* going to miss her; miss the way she didn't treat him like a famous musician, miss the way she called him *Fletch* and mostly miss how whole he felt when he was with her.

"Take it off," she whispered, her lips finding his in a slow kiss.

He bunched the T-shirt in his hands and tugged it upwards, breaking contact long enough to tug it over her head. Their mouths were drawn back to each other, like magnets as hers arms wrapped around his neck. The kiss was slow, a deep exploration of tongues and teeth, moans and groans echoing between them. He pressed his hands flat to Mick's back and held her flush against him, her hard nipples rubbing against his bare chest.

As her hands slid down over his shoulders and chest, Fletcher deepened the kiss, needing to imprint himself on her soul forever. She was young and beautiful, so when she returned to her 'regular life', some lucky asshole would get to love her. While he pondered all the ways he could have made her stay.

"Underwear," she said against his mouth and he grunted at the thought of being separated from her for even a few seconds. But Mick whipped off her blue underwear faster than he expected, a laugh bursting out of him at the way she tossed it aside. "Your turn."

Not to be left behind, Fletcher followed suit and made a dramatic show of getting rid of his boxer-briefs. At least it made Mick giggle, her face lighting up with a big smile.

"Come here, beautiful," he mumbled, tugging her back into his lap.

As his hands slid down to her ass, pulling her against him, her hand dipped between them to wrap around his dick. The contact made them both moan into the kiss. She nipped at his bottom lip as her body lifted off his briefly and then before he could catch his breath, she was sliding down on him. Their eyes met as he filled her to the hilt and Fletcher knew in that moment that nothing in the world would ever compare to this feeling—of being surrounded by a woman so beautiful, everything else lost its potency.

micah

Watch it, kid. I'm still plenty cool.

Now, 2024 | Sirena Beach, California

"MOM! WHERE ARE MY SUSPENDERS?"

Micah closed her eyes and focused on the way her luke-warm cup of coffee made her feel instead. It had been piping hot at some point, but raising a teenager meant that even though she started one thing, she ended up doing a million other things. Not to mention spending most of her life with undiagnosed ADHD and it was a miracle that she did any of the things on her list. Sure, she had her medication now and it helped a lot, but her teenager was still the biggest source of distraction.

"Mooooooooom!"

They'd done this enough times that she knew there was no point responding or even offering to help her daughter find what she was looking for. She sipped on her coffee and found her mug empty. Pouting, she rinsed it out and set it in her dishwasher before letting it slam shut.

"I found them! Was with my socks!"

"Where they always are," she whispered and moved

around the kitchen wiping down counters and putting things away. She started packing their lunches, keeping one ear focused on the movements upstairs. For all her complaints and concerns about her daughter, Micah was beyond grateful that she existed. Emery was the one thing she did right in her marriage, which was doomed from the start.

Geoffrey only proposed when they found out she was pregnant.

That entire relationship had been such a mess and every time she looked back on it, she winced. Fresh out of college, Micah and Geoffrey met at a friend's birthday party. He was a little punk rock and a whole lot boring, but he'd indulged her need to mix ridiculous drinks, humored her when she cracked bad jokes and listened intently when she talked about her 'life list'. She hadn't crossed a single thing off it since her night with Fletcher, but she kept it with her at all times. Geoffrey—never Geoff—had offered to help with a few of the items, but she politely declined. Instead, she slept with him that night and found out she was pregnant a few weeks later.

Her South Indian parents were less than pleased about the development, reminding her that was exactly why they'd been hesitant about sending her to another state for college. She moved home to Sirena Beach, California during her pregnancy, Geoffrey followed and *insisted* they get married. Three months later, with both sets of parents and her two best friends present, they were pronounced husband and wife at city hall in San Diego.

Emery Asha Mathis was born a few months later.

Three years into the marriage, Geoffrey drunkenly confessed that he hated being a father and husband. Then promptly forgot about those damning words when she filed for divorce.

Unfortunately for Geoffrey, he had to pay child support

and alimony because she didn't have a job since he'd all but demanded that he be the primary breadwinner of their family.

In the ten years since then, Micah and Emery had made a life for themselves. She used her savings and borrowed money from her parents, plus money from Geoffrey, to find the perfect home. She put all of her attention and love into raising her daughter, ensuring that Emery never once felt like Micah did when she was young—which was proving harder than she realized. Especially since her very opinionated mother always had something to say.

"Tie or no tie?"

She looked up at the staircase where her daughter was dressed like a punk rocker from the early 2000's—think Avril Lavigne's classic look—in a crisp white shirt tucked into baggy black pants, with black and red suspenders. Her once light blonde hair had dark tips and her eyes were drawn with the blackest eyeliner she could find. If Micah herself hadn't dressed the same at some point in her life, she would have been horrified by the sight.

Emery had gone through millions of phases in her short fourteen years. Starting at eight, she got Micah into a lot of trouble with the other parents at school. Instead of curbing her daughter's creativity and confidence, she did her best to keep it a little less in people's faces. She'd been raised with strict rules in place for what she could wear, what she could say and how she was meant to present herself. Micah didn't want that for her daughter, she wanted Emery to make mistakes and learn from them.

She'd gone through the expected princess and Disney phases, both were the shortest lived for a few months each. Then there was a Vikings phase, which had been hard for Micah to understand when her daughter insisted on wearing leather in the California heat. It was safe to say Emery came home a sweaty mess almost every day and crying most of the time too. The superhero phase was the longest and Micah was glad when she *refused* to wear spandex. She'd also settled into her *Lord of the Rings* phase where she spoke like Legolas while dressed like Aragorn and it was a whole complicated mess.

For the last six months, she'd been obsessed with punk rock from the 2000's—"these classics are epic bangers, Mom, how did this not change your life?"—and Micah was having daily flashbacks. But she was glad that Emery was obsessed with finding her passion instead of aiming to become popular or getting into trouble. In so many ways, Emery took after her and she was glad for it. Because all Geoffrey brought to the table were good looks and the sad ability to talk about only five things—money, cars, golf, Cancun, and cigars.

What Emery did get from her father made Micah grateful, because growing up Brown, fat and sassy hadn't done her any favors in the world. At fourteen, she stood at five feet six inches with an athlete's body, blonde hair and beautiful brown eyes. Micah sometimes wondered if they'd switched babies in the hospital, because there was no way she had given birth to this kid.

Not to even mention how often people thought she was the nanny when Emery was growing up. *Ah, casual racism, how I love you.*

"Black one, stick to the darker tones with your outfit," Micah said.

"Can you help?"

Nodding, she tapped into years of helping her ex with his tie and looped it around Emery's neck. Making sure not to strangle her daughter, she pushed the knot up and then stepped back. "Perfection."

Emery shoved the second tie into her bag as she said,

"You remember that we're going to Big Waves after school, right?"

Right, Hank Scott's music store.

A month ago, Emery had come home with her best friend and both of them proceeded to talk at her about how Hank's music store was under new management and they were offering lessons. Growing up in Sirena Beach, the store had been a staple and when Emery first showed interest in music, she would drop her daughter off with *Uncle Hank*—no relation, just the friendliest old man their hometown had to offer —to get a solid musical education.

When Hank died four years ago, something shifted in her daughter. Having grown up with the older gentleman, Emery was attached to him. He functioned like a pseudo grandfather, one who celebrated all of her quirks. She was hesitant about visiting the store after that and more importantly, struggled to spend Christmas at Santa's Village. For as long as Emery had been alive, Hank had been Santa every year. After he passed, the newspaper announced a new Santa would be taking over and Emery couldn't come to terms with it.

The fact that she was ready to go back to the store now was a huge deal and Micah wasn't going to question it.

"I remember." She filled their water bottles before handing one to Emery. "Do you want me to pick you up?"

"Nope. Nico wants to go as well, so we'll ride our bikes over."

"You have all your questions ready?"

"*Mom.* Please don't bring that up when you get there. I don't want Mr. Kelley to think I'm some kind of dweeb."

"Is that the new owner?" Even as she asked the question, her mind wandered to the *Mr. Kelley* she did know. The very same one who had delivered the most number of orgasms she'd had in a single night. The man who was a beast behind the drums, but soft and gentle in bed. She'd had more chemistry with Fletcher Kelley in one night than she'd had with her ex in the three years they were married. A part of Micah wondered if her marriage had failed because she held onto those memories of Fletcher.

"Don't be weird, okay? Benson said Mr. Kelley is like super cool for an *old dude* and I don't need you being…*you*."

"Watch it, kid." Micah frowned, but her tone was all humor. "I'm still plenty cool."

Emery groaned, head tipped back. "I'm already regretting this."

"I'll be on my best behavior and I won't embarrass you in front of the super cool dude or Nico."

At the mention of her best friend—and person she was convinced her daughter had a crush on—Emery blushed. "Nico knows you're weird, they expect nothing less from you."

"So I can't embarrass you in front of *Mr. Kelley*."

"God, you're going to be insufferable." Emery grabbed her lunch and stomped to the front door. Micah chuckled and packed up her bag for work, knowing that any minute now, she would stop and turn around. The stomping ceased and she looked up to find her daughter smiling wide. "I love you, Mom."

"I love you, too, kid. You're the best thing I've ever done in my life."

"Damn right I am."

She blew her daughter a kiss and smiled to herself as Emery grabbed her sticker covered helmet and walked out the front door. When silence enveloped the house, her mind wandered to Fletcher again. Which was silly, because even though she'd listened to The Rescuers for years after their one night stand, she hadn't really thought about the man himself too much. He was a part of her history, but that's all he could ever be. A checklist on her life list—have the most epic one night stand with a famous person.

And that's all he can ever be.

Six hours into her work day, with all thoughts of her former lovers and partners erased from her mind, Micah opened her office door to let her eleven year old client in. His mother offered her a small wave from where she was seated in one of the reception chairs and Micah smiled in response before closing the door behind Dexter.

"Good afternoon, Dexter, how are you?"

He smiled and then inhaled deeply, steeling himself before he released his breath and said, "I'm g-g-good." Dexter nodded and she did the same, gesturing to the other chair. He sat down, fidgeting until he was comfortable. "I visited my grandparents last week."

"They have horses, right? Did you go for a ride?"

He nodded excitedly, flashing Micah his teeth and when she laughed, he pointed at the gap in the front. "I fell off the p-p-po-pony—" Micah nodded at the soft sound that accompanied the word before Dexter continued, "She left me there!"

"Did she take your tooth with her?"

He giggled. "She did! So, no money from my fairy godmother."

"We can't have that!" She grinned and held out the bowl of candy she kept for her younger patients. Dexter's smile widened, flashing his missing tooth, and he took a few minutes to decide which candy he wanted. Once he was settled back in his chair, Micah reached for the picture book from her stack of children's books. "You up for some reading today or do you want to tell me more about your visit?"

He hesitated and took the book from her, flipping it open

to the first page. The table beside where they were seated was stacked high with books for different age groups. So no matter which client came in, she had something for everyone to read. Because of Dexter's stutter, she always had him read easier books. He had already graduated into books with bigger words that had more consonants and syllables, but the progress was slow.

"We're not in a rush, okay?" she said, reminding him that there was no time limit to how fast or slow he needed to improve. "You read at your pace. Take the time to sound out the words in your head, repeat them as many times as you need to."

Dexter nodded firmly, gripping the open book. "I can do it."

"Do you remember how many pages you read last time?"

"Four. Today I will re-re—" He huffed in frustration and tried again, "—I will read five p-pa-pages."

"Great. Whenever you're ready."

Cautiously, Dexter started reading the book about the unicorn and the mouse. His finger traced the words as he said them out loud. She was glad that even though he'd read the first four pages many times already, he didn't assume that he was ready for the more advanced pages.

Watching, listening and guiding Dexter made her think about her own struggles with her speech when she was a young girl. Her parents moved to the States from South India when Micah was five and she already had a stutter, struggling to get what she wanted to say out in a timely manner. Combine that with her still learning how to speak English properly—she'd been raised in a house with grandparents who only ever spoke in Malayalam—and Micah was made fun of, bullied and mistreated in the neighborhood and then at school.

Like a lot of South Indian parents, Micah's didn't believe

that you needed to get tested for speech disorders, so she suffered silently. Her mother would always say 'you'll get over it' or 'try and focus on your words before you speak' like it was *that* simple. It was her English teacher in the fourth grade that finally encouraged her parents to see a speech therapist.

Years of sessions, reading slowly, being taught how to sound out words in her head and then out loud helped her learn the best way to overcome her stutter. It didn't go away completely, but she'd finally learned how to ease herself into it. By the time she was in high school, Micah had become the student body president and could give speeches without problem. But there were always kids who remembered what she was like in middle school and had no qualms being assholes about it.

She continued meeting with her speech therapist all the way through college, where she studied Audiology and Speech Language Pathology. The decision wasn't made lightly, no matter what her parents said, and she worked her ass off to graduate. She was applying to schools for her Masters program when she found out she was pregnant, so Micah put that on hold and spent the three years she was married raising Emery. Once the divorce was finalized and she was able to find people to help out with Emery, she went back to school and followed through with her clinical hours. It was a lot of work and hours she spent away from her daughter, but Micah did everything she could to be a present mother. By the time she got her certification, she was ready to sleep for an entire year. But she got so lucky when she met with Haven Williams, founder of the Haven Clinic which was outside the town limits of Sirena Beach.

The clinic housed therapists that provided different services and often one client saw multiple people in the clinic. But the whole place was started by and run by queer women, making it an extremely safe place for queer folk to come by without the fear of being judged. Within twenty minutes of meeting Haven, Micah was hired. It took her a few years to build a reputation and a client list, but now she was well known for her skills, no matter the age of the person visiting her.

"The mouse p-p-poi-pointed—" Dexter huffed and looked up, she nodded for him to continue. "The mouse pointed at the rainbow and the unicorn sm-sm-smiled."

When he slammed the book shut, she leaned back in her chair and waited for Dexter to go through the emotions he was feeling. She remembered how frustrating it had been to struggle through books she usually had no trouble with. While she was fluent most of the time, there were situations where she still stuttered. Micah was working towards showing her younger clients that it was absolutely normal to have moments like that.

"Dexter, tell me why the book made you angry."

He set the book in his lap, refusing to meet her eyes. "They were…easy words. I str-str-struggled."

"Words might seem easy the first and second time, but they can sometimes get difficult later. The important thing to acknowledge is that you got them all."

"I finished five pages!"

She held a hand up and grinned when Dexter gave her a high-five. He was still quite young, but Dexter was determined and that was enough. She could help him if he was interested in being helped, beyond that it was impossible to even consider guiding someone in the right direction. After escorting him out to his mother and a quick update on how the session had gone, Micah grabbed herself a large mug of freshly brewed coffee and returned to her office to new texts in the group she had with her best friends—Sadie and Tatum.

SADIE

Remind me again why I thought one night stands this close to 40 were a good idea?

Especially with younger men.

This stud blew my back out and I fucking thanked him for it.

TATUM

Does this mean you're going to let him ride you again?

SADIE

Possibly. Depends on if he can keep it casual. Because I saw 'love' in his eyes last night.

MICAH

How do you see love in someone's eyes?

SADIE

When their eyes sparkle as their balls deep inside you, it's love.

TATUM

Micah doesn't know what that's like, she's been celibate for a millennia.

MICAH

Try raising a kid on your own and you'll be celibate too.

I encountered cobwebs during a self care session the other week.

TATUM

You should definitely get that checked out.

SADIE

Or you can borrow my stud for one hot ride.

MICAH

No more one night stands for me, thanks.

TATUM

I'm sorry, NO MORE one night stands?

SADIE

OH MY GOD THE ROCKSTAR

TATUM

The one from when we were kids?

MICAH

We were 22!

SADIE

Jesus, you were walking funny for days after that.

TATUM

Oh shit, that's right. You said he was the best you ever had.

SADIE

And you said that AFTER you filed for divorce from Geoff.

MICAH

Sometimes I forget that you've known me all my life and know everything about me.

TATUM

Even the things we don't want to know.

SADIE

I like knowing everything, Mick. But hey, we're due a girl's night out.

Nonna will be happy to keep Emery for the night.

MICAH

You know she'll say HELL YES to spending an evening with Nonna.

Sometimes I think she loves your grandmother more than me.

But then she says she loves me before leaving for school and I know I'm good.

TATUM

Fuck that's cute. Your kid is the best.

SADIE

She's my favorite young person.

MICAH

She's pretty great.

But yes to girl's night out. I want to know what it's like to be flirted with.

TATUM

And what it feels like to get your back blown out by some young stud.

SADIE

Worth the money I'm spending on this midday massage, I'll tell you that much.

fletcher

Put on your big boy panties, Kelley.

Now, 2024 | Sirena Beach, California

NOBODY TOLD him that when he became a business owner, his latent anxiety would suddenly reappear in full force. It didn't matter that Fletcher had been running Big Waves for the last four years—part-time the first three years and full-time the last year—he still woke up every morning panicking about the little things. Did he do inventory the night before? Had he placed the orders for new equipment? Now, he had another thing added to his list of anxiety inducing headaches—music lessons.

No matter what he did—painkillers, every bottle of water in his fridge and yoga—nothing helped with the throbbing behind his eyes. He *had* fallen asleep at some point, but it hadn't been enough. If anything, it made him feel worse.

After a freezing cold shower to wake him up and a large cup of coffee—half of which he spilled on himself—he had driven the twenty minutes to work, only to park and walk up to the front and find that his bag and pockets were empty of keys. So he made the trip back home, grabbed his keys and then opened up an hour later than usual. Walking through the store, he thought back to how he ended up saddled with all these responsibilities, whether he wanted them or not.

When the band decided to finally take a break—"we're not calling it a retirement, just a much needed sabbatical"— Fletcher had been floundering. Music and The Rescuers were his whole world. His relationship with his family was strained, his ex-wife had moved on and he needed to go somewhere to deal with all these big changes. Almost like he'd heard Fletcher's pleas his father's brother, Uncle Hank, called.

"I heard you got old and decided to retire."

"Takes one old man to know one," Fletcher fired back with a laugh.

"Come on down and visit this old man, kid. It's been years."

"I guess I could. Not like I have anything else going on."

"Sirena Beach awaits," Hank said before hanging up.

Either his uncle knew what those words would mean to him or he was being clueless as always, Fletcher took it as a sign. Only someone who'd written a song about a mermaid— a *sirena*—would know that that's where he was meant to be. So he packed up his things and went to California.

Growing up in small town Iowa, visiting Uncle Hank was an annual treat. Unlike his siblings, Hank had always liked living along the coast with access to beaches and the surf. He'd heard his father refer to Hank as a hippie countless times, but those were all the reasons why he loved his uncle. Besides being fun and open to almost anything, he lived a lawless kind of life. The only thing he looked forward to every summer was seeing Hank. When Fletcher got famous and toured the country, Hank would come to as many shows as possible. They'd hang out after the set, Hank would regale the boys with stories of his misspent youth and his soul would be instantly recharged.

Hank launched Big Waves Music in the early seventies, the first of its kind music store and recording studio. Tons of small local bands cut their albums in the basic studio in the back, and Hank had become something of a legend. As he moved from city to city, Big Waves Music moved with him, until he finally settled in a small beach town when Fletcher was in the middle of making it big.

So when he got to Sirena Beach, nothing seemed amiss with his uncle. Hank's first task? Take over running Big Waves.

"Get all your musician friends to visit, make a big scene, bring people back to this kind of life."

"Which musician friends should I call?"

"Paul McCartney is a good friend, right? How about Paul Simon?"

While he didn't call any of his friends, he did help Hank repaint the store and put up new signage and organized things that brought customers back to the store. That took them the better part of the year and when Christmas rolled around, Hank asked for one more thing.

"Look kid, I'm too old to play Santa anymore. So I told that Mars fella you'd take over."

"You did what now?"

Hank patted him on the back with a jovial laugh. "You're the only person I know that likes Christmas as much as I do. So you're suiting up."

"You're fucking joking."

"Santa doesn't cuss. You better work on that."

Then he became Santa. It was unpleasant that first year, wobbling around in Hank's old suit, being careful not to trip over his boots and learning how to modify his voice so as not to scare the kids away. It took some practicing and lots of coaching from Hank, but he finally got the hang of it. Just in time for his uncle to drop a third and final doozy on him.

Hank was dying.

He'd apparently battled cancer for years, ignoring it at first and then seeking treatment until it was pointless to keep going. He'd lost the love of his life years ago and he'd held on for Fletcher, or so he said.

Now, everything that had once been in Hank's name was being transferred to Fletcher—the house that he'd fully paid off years ago and Big Waves Music. Oh, he also introduced Fletcher to his lawyer, hoping that the two of them would hit it off and get married. Unfortunately for Hank, Fletcher and Erin settled for being great friends, because the chemistry and sparks Hank hoped for? Non-existent.

If he was being honest, there was only one woman in the world he'd had sparks with instantly. And she was long gone from his life.

Music was the only consistent thing, which was why taking over the music store felt right. What he didn't account for was how it wouldn't be as exciting as when Hank was running the place. All the old musicians had passed on and those that came into the store were usually there to get directions to somewhere else. He had kept only one of Hank's original staff members—because the others were pretty useless and knew nothing about anything—and some days he felt like he was struggling to keep them busy.

So he decided to give music lessons.

Which was a joke since Fletcher was a self-taught drummer and had picked up the other instruments from watching his friends rehearse and perform every night. But if he offered music lessons, then maybe it would bring in more people. Or at least that's what Erin said. Even if they didn't purchase instruments—the store wasn't bankrupt, just empty

—there would be something for Fletcher and Benson to do on a daily basis.

Soon after Halloween, Benson presented a poster advertising the music lessons which he plastered everywhere. In the week following there was an influx of messages and phone calls enquiring who was taking the lessons and how much they cost. Despite having been with an internationally acclaimed and award-winning band, most people didn't know the name Fletcher Kelley. He'd never been one to flaunt his fame either, so it took some wrangling before they updated the poster with mention of The Rescuers, using words like 'award-winning' and 'legendary', and suddenly everyone was interested.

His first session was with two teenagers who, according to Benson, had sent in messages on Instagram that looked like 'excited keyboard smashing'. He understood about two things in that whole conversation. Even with all of the assurances that he'd do great and it would be a total breeze, Fletcher's anxiety was telling him otherwise. Which was so convenient, since he hadn't had a panic attack or the urge to curl in on himself in years.

FLETCHER

Why did I let you convince me this was a good idea?

My sweat has sweat.

ERIN

....

That is disgusting and information I didn't need.

Grunting at his phone, Fletcher took off the green and yellow plaid shirt he was wearing and fanned himself. Like that would chase away the worry. He'd never interacted with kids outside of meet and greets when touring with The Rescuers. He'd never taught someone else how to play an instrument. Regardless of what people thought when they looked at him, he was a permanently stressed walrus.

FLETCHER

I'm sure there was a better and less stressful way for me to get more people through those doors.

ERIN

You shot down all my other ideas.

FLETCHER

They were pretty terrible, E.

ERIN

Inviting people to host themed parties is a great way to bring them in.

FLETCHER

Then I have to clean up after they leave.

ERIN

You can't have everything, buddy.

Fletcher rolled his eyes and replied with the middle finger emoji before tucking his phone away. Erin had been a godsend the last few years after Hank died. As his lawyer, Erin knew how Hank ran the business, all of his partnerships and friendships. So she helped him connect with those people and keep Hank's spirit alive in Sirena Beach the best he could. Even though she lived in San Diego, she drove to see him pretty often so they could go through the books and make sure everything was on the up and up. They might not have been a romantic match, like Hank wanted, but they forged a bond neither of them expected.

ERIN

> You're going to do great, Fletcher. Breathe through it, don't overthink what you're doing.

> Besides, today is just about getting to know the kids.

> You're a world famous, award-winning musician. They're just kids.

FLETCHER

> Not sure that's more comforting or terrifying, but thanks.

> Keep your junior associates on hand in case these kids say shit to me that makes zero sense.

ERIN

> Pull on your big boy panties, Kelley.

FLETCHER

> Fuck you very much, Decker.

Hours later, well into the work day, he heard the bell above the front door ring. Shockingly it wasn't the first time the bell rang, but it was the first time Benson called out for him. Fletcher had spent his day doing research on how to teach people to read music and give lessons, none of it seemed to ease his nerves. Benson had handled the first few customers, but clearly it was time for him to face the kids that were eager to learn music from him. Slipping on his glasses, he untied his long dark hair from the bun he'd kept it in all day and then walked to the front where excited chatter greeted him.

Two kids decked in punk rock fashion were talking animatedly to Benson, who was nodding along. Maybe his friends-slash-employee knew what those words were, but Fletcher tensed at the thought of not understanding a damn thing. Blowing out a slow breath, he raised a hand in an awkward wave when the teenagers turned to him, their eyes wide.

"Oh my god. You really *are* Fletcher Kelley. I was so sure the poster was using your name to get more attention," the Avril Lavigne look-alike said, before a deep blush spread across her cheeks. "Sorry, that was too much fangirling."

Benson chuckled and Fletcher shook his head. "You seem kinda young to know who I am, fangirling or not."

"Well, I *was* raised on your music."

"Your folks have good taste," he said with a chuckle, then turned to the other punk rocker and smiled. "Welcome to Big Waves."

"We've been here before, when Uncle Hank used to run the place. But thanks?"

Okay, we're not doing a good job with conversing today.

"Right, well…" he trailed off, looking to Benson for help, but his friend shrugged.

The kids looked at each other and burst into laughter. The blonde one turned to him, her blush deepening. "*Sorry.* Mom says I need to tone back the sassiness. I'm Emery, she/her. This is Nico, they/them."

"I'm uh…Fletcher, he/him?" He glanced at Benson who gave him a subtle nod. "That's Benson, also he/him."

"Nice to officially meet both of you. So," Emery said, rubbing her hands together like some kind of evil mastermind. "How does this work?"

Fantastic question, kid. Fantastic fucking question.

"How about you two browse through the store and see what instruments get your attention, then we can figure out how to go from there," Benson suggested and the kids nodded, practically bouncing as they moved through racks of instruments. Fletcher shoved his hands into his pockets and followed a few steps behind, smiling as they stopped at strings, then winds and moved back and forth a few times. Growing up, he'd been drawn to music too and it took him a while before he realized that drums were always going to be his focus. It might take Emery and Nico a while too, but for these lessons, they needed to start somewhere.

When Emery turned to him with a wide grin, he was hit with a memory of a curvy brunette smiling at him the same way. He blinked to clear the thoughts and focused on the kid. "I've always been interested in the drums, because I watched a lot of your live shows and think you're like so badass."

"Thanks," he mumbled, adjusting his glasses for something to do. "I should warn you that I taught myself the drums, so my teaching methods might be different from what you'd get elsewhere."

She shrugged, that familiar smile still lighting up her face. "Given I have zero training outside of using my pillows as drums, I think we'll be fine."

"I got my start with pillows too."

"I know. That's what my mom told me," she said and then bounced off to find Nico and Benson. He chuckled and watched her go, his mind filling up with more memories of that night sixteen years ago. It wasn't meant to be more than one night, not when Mick pulled out her 'list' and rattled off all the things she wanted to do in this lifetime. Still, waking up the next morning to an empty bed and a clean hotel room had been disappointing. Fletcher had wanted a few more hours with her, a few more days even. She'd left behind her underwear, a stretchy hair tie and leather bracelets that he held onto for a bit.

When the bell above the door chimed again, he snapped out of his thoughts as Emery raced past him. Nico followed with an amused smile as they said, "Emery's mom wanted to meet you and make sure you're not some kind of serial killer or whatever. She's cool, a little neurotic, but she's a good mom."

Before he could respond, he heard Emery whining. "You're not going to embarrass me, right?"

"What do you take me for, huh?" a husky voice said and goosebumps exploded across his arms. *First, I see her smile. Now I hear her voice. What the fuck?* "So have you decided what you're going to learn?"

"The drums, duh."

"Of course," Emery's mother said, a warm laugh filtering through the whole store. "All right, so where's this Mr. Kelley you're so excited about?"

Fletcher straightened his clothes and glasses, then walked to the front of the store ready to introduce himself. Benson was already there, shaking Emery's mom's hand when he stepped around the corner. Then the woman turned to face him and his heart stopped.

My mermaid.

His memories didn't do justice to the woman standing in front of him. She'd always been deliciously curvy, soft in all the right places. While her hair was much shorter now, the curls were still thick and dark. The nose ring that had once been slightly bent out of shape was now thicker and her eyes were so much brighter. He couldn't help look her over—a wide necked long sleeved black top hugged her chest and arms, paired with a green skirt that had an uneven hem that ended at her calves and white sneakers.

Fuck, she's still the best thing I've ever laid eyes on.

"Mick."

Her eyes widened slightly and she swallowed, gaze roving all over his body. "Fletch."

Fuck, that nickname still gets me.

"You know Fletcher Kelley?" Emery squealed, snapping

him out of the filthy thoughts his brain was about to embark on.

"Yeah, we…uh…met…"

"We met sixteen years ago when I was on tour," he quickly added, unable to look away from the woman in front of him.

"Wow, you two are *old*." Emery laughed, the sound following her as she walked away.

Fletcher didn't care if she stayed or if they had an audience, because all he could focus on was Mick. Now it made sense why Emery's smile had seemed so familiar, she looked so much like her mother. Then another thought entered his mind, panic squeezing his heart so tight.

"Is she mine?"

"What?" Mick's eyes got even wider.

"Emery, is she mine?"

"That's the first thing you say to me after all these years. Really?"

He pinched his eyes shut and shook his head. Memories of that night assaulting his brain—stripping each other naked, sex in the shower, sex on the couch, their hands wandering and gripping, foil wrappers strewn across the floor.

"We ran out of condoms that night," he whispered.

She nodded, that familiar blush creeping up her neck. "Took the morning after pill on my way home the next day."

Fuck. The fist around his chest loosened and he let out a shaky breath. He'd never really been interested in kids or thought of himself as father material. But if Mick had been pregnant with his child, Fletcher would have wanted to know. At the same time, the twinge that she wasn't his surprised him.

"I would have told you if she was yours. You know that, right?"

"I know. Fuck, I'm sorry, that was...I shouldn't have assumed." He rubbed his forehead with a sigh before looking at her again. "You look good, Mick."

"Actually, it's *Micah*," she countered, watching him curiously. "What are you doing here, Fletch?"

Micah. "I live here."

"Since when?"

He smiled at the tone, all fire and moxie, like that night. "Been in and out of town since Hank died. Officially a resident since about April," he explained.

"Wild that I haven't run into you before."

"I'm more of a hermit these days."

She laughed, the sound taking him by surprise. The last time he'd heard her laugh, he had her pinned to the bed, his fingers digging into her sides as he got her to apologize for making fun of his age.

"Fletcher?"

"Sorry...seeing you again is startling. In a good way, obviously." He'd thought about this woman constantly for two years after their night together, he'd written a song for her, won awards for it and people called him Romeo for years after. Then he'd let all thoughts of Micah fade away when he met and married Alice a few years later.

"I tend to have that effect on people," she joked and tucked a few curls behind her ear, drawing his attention to the black ink on her arm. "It's good to see you, too, Fletch."

"Even if you did sneak out of bed and clean the entire room."

Another laugh burst out of her. "I had places to go, things to do..."

"I promise to take good care of your kid."

She chuckled and shook her head. "I'm more concerned about *you*. That kid is all me, and I'm guessing you remember that I was *a lot* to handle."

"Rude," he mumbled, not needing any help in remembering how good it had been to *handle* her that night. "I think I handled you fine."

"You did." Her expression softened, brown eyes locked on his and he watched as her tongue swiped out to wet her bottom lip.

A phone ringing snapped them into attention. He rubbed the back of his neck, embarrassed to be caught thinking of her *that way*. Especially since his fingers tingled to trace every dip and bump of her body.

"I have to go, but I guess I'll see you around?"

"Absolutely."

"Bye, Fletch."

"Mick," he said softly with a slight tip of his head. She chuckled and walked out of the store, a crisp floral scent lingering in her wake. He stood at the door and watched as she climbed into her car, his heart thudding at the memory of the last thing they said to each other.

"I'm gonna miss you, Mick."

"The night's not over, Fletch. Don't say goodbye yet."

micah

Micah's hot for teacher.

"WAIT, START AGAIN," Sadie said as she returned to the couch with a new bottle of wine. "He's Em's music teacher?"

"Micah's hot for teacher," Tatum offered and then launched into the Van Halen song with gusto.

Micah rolled her eyes as her friends joined forces, their collective volume rising. The song itself was one of her least favorite tracks by the band, hearing her friends *butcher* it only made the experience worse. Instead, she focused on refilling their wine glasses and waited until they were done performing like lunatics.

"Got that out of your system?"

Tatum nodded, grinning broadly, while Sadie bounced around, still humming. "I've got tons more questions, especially now that our munchkin is in bed."

"Ask away," Micah grumbled. She should have been far more prepared for this interrogation when she walked through Tatum's front door and heard Emery announce that she'd met 'the Fletcher Kelley'.

The original plan had been to fly up to San Francisco for Thanksgiving weekend. But when her parents got tickets on a last minute cruise, Micah decided to spend it with her best friends. Emery was thrilled to not leave Sirena Beach, especially since Nico wasn't going anywhere for the break. Plus, she loved Micah's best friends too. They'd each brought two dishes, but it was the most random selection of food to ever grace a Thanksgiving meal. Even though Emery's announcement had both her friends itching to ask a million questions, Micah was impressed that they kept it simple. In fact, outside of vague questions about work, Sadie and Tatum put their entire focus on Emery.

And Micah was glad for it.

She loved her friends, they'd known each other since they were twelve, and had stuck together through marriages, divorces and then some. But once they got started on something, they would not let it go.

Sadie Harlow was the risk-taking, hair color changing, living life on the edge friend. As a fashion photographer, she traveled the world and met some of the most beautiful people. She took life by the balls at every opportunity, following her passions and heart, instead of focusing on making 'good choices'. Micah and Tatum were convinced that half of the fashion industry had their hearts broken by Sadie and her love 'em and leave 'em mentality. That evening, Sadie's long hair was bright pink and split into two thick braids that fell down her back. Even though she had access to all the makeup people in the industry, Sadie never wore anything; the most she swiped on was gloss.

Tatum Faulks was the more focused and serious of the three, as well as an indie music producer. Tatum shook off her famous family name to set up her own record label and then took on local musicians and helped them produce their albums. Curvy and sassy, Tatum had wavy dark brown hair that always magically had beach waves. She also rarely wore makeup, but when she took the time, Tatum's beautiful golden eyes were always highlighted as were her plump lips. Most of the light she had when they were teenagers was gone, thanks to the work of her ex-husband who destroyed Tatum bit by bit over the course of their marriage.

Heartbreak had rocked all three of them a few times over the past few years, but there was very little in the world that could destroy the friendship they'd built as kids.

"Okay, so he lives here now?"

"Yup. Seemed to know Hank well enough that the old man gave him his music store."

Tatum pursed her lips in thought. "Sirena's not that big that you'd never see each other."

"He said he's only been here permanently for a few months," Micah said and then shrugged. "And something about how he's a hermit these days?"

Sadie groaned loudly. "I'm glad we're doing this, but that reminds me that we haven't had a Slutty Saturday in a long time."

"Focus, slut. We've got bigger things to sort through," Tatum snapped, poking Sadie in the thigh with her foot. Turning back to Micah, she nodded. "Go on, we're listening."

Micah took a big gulp of her wine, needing a few minutes to gather her thoughts before telling them how Fletcher looked when he thought Emery was his. In some weird way, Micah wished he *was* the father, because Emery's life would have been so different. *Better.* At the same time, maybe their magical one night would not have translated into a magical forever.

"He asked if Em was his," she finally said, twirling her glass for something to do. Silence stretched around her and Micah lifted her head to find her friends staring at her. "She's not!"

Tatum and Sadie exchanged a glance before nodding. "Why would he ask that?"

"By the end of the night, we didn't have any condoms, so we fucked without."

"Whoa," Sadie mumbled, eyes wide.

"It was already the best sex of my life, and somehow it was even better bare?" Micah sighed and took another sip of her wine. "But the next morning, I got the pill and erased any chance of me being pregnant. Not because I didn't want that with him, because I did. I was completely obsessed with him for days after that, remember? If I was pregnant with his kid, it would have brought us back together. But I was twenty-two and not ready to be a mom."

Her friends were still staring at her, wine glasses untouched. She rolled her eyes and nudged them both gently. "I thought I was in love with him, but falling in love because the sex was good? Ridiculous."

"You never told us that."

"That I might have been in love with Fletcher? Come on. I practically followed them on tour for three weeks *because* I was borderline obsessed with him."

"But like a fan. Everyone was obsessed with The Rescuers back then," Tatum added, then pointed at herself. "I wanted to climb Jack Rush like a fucking tree and might have if we weren't so late to meet everyone else for drinks."

Micah smiled at the memory. Sadie and Tatum had joined her for the first night of their East Coast tour—before Micah hitched rides with anyone who had room in their cars. They'd been so close to the stage that when Jack, the lead singer of The Rescuers, dropped to his knees to belt out the chorus for their biggest hit, Tatum had handed him her bra. That was also the first night she caught Fletcher watching her.

"So…does seeing him again bring back any of those feelings?"

"No. Maybe. I don't know." Micah finished her wine and got up to refill her glass. "He's so hot, though. Like, he was this grungy, awkward drummer back then. Now?" She whistled and shook her head.

Micah had never thought much of men with long hair, but he made it look so fucking good. His once shaggy hair now fell to his shoulders, with silver streaked through perfectly. There was even gray at the temples and peppered through his well-groomed beard. It framed his mouth and jaw so beautifully, it took everything in Micah not to stare at his pink lips for too long. He was also no longer lanky; Fletcher stood tall with his shoulders pushed back, drawing her attention to his broad form. Even under his clothes—a dark gray T-shirt paired with a plaid shirt and jeans—she could tell that he had some muscles. The thing that really rocked her were the black framed glasses he'd been wearing that day. *Killed* her.

"Ooookaaaaaaay," Sadie said, dragging out the vowels with a wicked grin. "Maybe you two need to fuck and see what happens. Sometimes the best kind of magic comes from when you say 'fuck it' and remind yourselves of what you once had."

"Nope."

"Why not?"

"I'm not dating these days." Tatum snorted and Sadie guffawed, making Micah frown as she glanced at her friends. "What?"

"Nobody said anything about dating. I said *fucking*. If the sex made you feel like you were in love with him, made you walk funny for days and was good enough that you skipped condoms…do it again," Sadie told her, earning an approving hum from Tatum.

"What if fucking him makes me fall in love with him again?"

"Well, that's something to deal with *if* it happens," Tatum said.

Micah nodded slowly, weighing the pros and cons of

getting involved with Fletcher again. On the one hand, she'd have sex for the first time in years. On the other hand, she could fall in love with him. And her friends were right, it didn't have to be anything more than sex. Part of the reason why she didn't date was because she didn't want to introduce people to Emery and then have them vanish one day. Plus, dating was so exhausting. Her last tryst had been with a woman named Veronica, who said that she was only interested in continuing the date if Micah was looking for a serious relationship. She barely had the time for herself most days, so a serious relationship?

Then again, for the right person...Micah might make an adjustment.

Two days later, on Saturday, she sat in her office waiting on a new client. The clinic was closed for the break, but when the request had come in before Thanksgiving, she couldn't refuse the person. Not that she knew anything beyond the basics—woman in her early eighties with learning difficulties. While most of her clients were under the age of eighteen and had speech troubles, Micah had been taking on a few with other learning problems. A lot of the time, the two things went hand in hand. It wasn't so much about *reading* as it was about reading *aloud* in many cases. Like her, if you had a stutter, reading out loud or presenting in front of people sometimes made the stutter worse. Most people put it down to nerves and stage fright, but more often than not, it was so much deeper than that.

At the knock on her office door, she pulled it open to find her childhood neighbor waiting on the other side. When her parents were still in Sirena Beach, they'd lived next door to Mrs. Hershey, a widow who was both opinionated and hilarious. Micah had been scared of her as a kid—telling her older brother about the witch that lived next door who ate small children—but looking at the woman now, she seemed pretty harmless.

"Are you sure you're qualified to help me?" Mrs. Hershey asked as she waddled into the office, nose up in the air.

Micah closed the door and gestured to the diplomas she'd hung up on the wall. "More than. Graduated at the top of my class, got all my certifications." She didn't like flaunting her achievements, but the other doctors at the clinic told her that it would go a long way if she had some *proof* visible for everyone to see.

"But you're so young."

"I'm thirty-eight, Mrs. Hershey."

The old woman's eyes widened behind her thick glasses and a hand landed on her chest. "Not possible. I still remember you running into the backyard to do number two because that's what Basil did."

Basil had been Mrs. Hershey's cranky, one eyed dog who hated everyone. Micah, on the other hand, *loved* Basil and smothered him with so much love and affection. She caught him pooping in their backyard while her parents were out and decided that if Basil could do it, so could she. Mrs. Hershey had come out at the moment when Micah rushed to the spot where Basil had done his job a few days ago, dropped her underwear and pooped like it was the most normal thing in the world. Safe to say, Mrs. Hershey gave her parents an earful and then pointed her already mangled fingers at little Micah and told her to behave like a young lady before vanishing into her house.

No wonder Micah thought she was a witch who ate small children.

"That was at least thirty years ago," Micah told her with a laugh, then waited for the older woman to sit down before doing the same. "What brings you by, Mrs. Hershey?"

Patting down her coif, Mrs. Hershey hesitated and then pushed back her hunched shoulders. "I don't know if your mother ever told you this, but I never learned how to read and write. I understand that it's late in life, but there's a book club that I'm a part of and they're starting to pick books that don't have audiobooks. And I don't want to miss out." She then lowered her voice and flashed, what could only be called, a salacious smile. "We're reading those new age historical romances with mentions of *cocks* and *pussies*. It is quite the experience having a young stud mumble those words into my ear. Alas, the ladies want to *read* a book and apparently I have to do the same."

Micah stared at her in shock, but mostly amusement. She loved that Mrs. Hershey was in a book club that read sexy romance novels with open door sex—oh, she was in a club or two of her own—but it was only slightly disturbing to see that smile accompanied by those words.

Clearing her throat, she shifted in her chair and tilted her head. "Is that why Mom used to do all your grocery shopping?"

"Your parents were very generous with their time and understanding of my plight. I was raised in a home where my father believed my only purpose was to cook, clean and procreate. So education wasn't important."

Micah hated how that generation believed women served such ridiculous purposes, like they were there for one thing and one thing only. It took away the importance of who and what a woman was and could do.

"Do you also want to learn how to write or are we only focusing on reading?"

Mrs. Hershey shook her head. "Only reading for now. I'm hoping they'll pick more that are available as audiobooks again. Here," she rummaged around in her bag and pulled out a paperback that featured a shirtless man in half of a Santa outfit, abs fully on display, "this is what we're reading."

"How about we start with something a little simpler?"

The older woman didn't look impressed. "Does it have a sexy half naked man on the cover?"

"Unfortunately not," she said, fighting back her smile. "Do you have some time today?"

"I suppose so." She sighed dramatically and then set her bag on a chair before giving Micah her full attention. "What are we doing?"

"We'll go through the alphabet and some really easy words and see what your base level is, then work from there."

"I don't have a lot of time before this book club, I better be ready by then."

Chuckling, Micah reached for the children's book with big words and pictures. "We'll have you reading that book in no time."

"We're out of milk," Emery announced from the couch as Micah cleaned up after dinner. "And probably cereal, too."

Her session with Mrs. Hershey ran a little longer than expected, so when she got home, Emery had made dinner. But also very kindly left the kitchen an absolute mess. No matter how much she tried, teaching her daughter to clean up after herself was a difficult task. They'd eaten together on the couch, watching an old episode of *Cheers*. Then while Emery switched to her phone, Micah had gone to clean up. It was their deal from the minute her daughter had the ability to carry heavy things—one person cooked and the other person cleaned. The difference was that Micah cleaned up as she cooked, so all Emery ever had to do was put the leftovers away and load the dishwasher.

When Emery cooked, Micah had to power wash the kitchen.

"Are you still snacking at midnight?"

"I'm a growing teenager!"

She rolled her eyes and wiped down the counters. "We're switching to fruits for midnight snacks. Put it on the list."

She heard Emery groan and she smiled, setting her shopping list on the table before heading up to her bedroom to change. Switching into paint-stained denim overalls and an old T-shirt, she dragged a hand through her hair and returned to find Emery hunched over the list.

"What are healthy fruits?"

"All of them?"

"Ammachi said some have too much sugar and those are not good."

Of course her mother would tell her daughter this after spending years trying to control Micah's diet. Tugging on her sneakers, she snapped her fingers. "Put down what you like or come with me."

"Late night shopping? That's so lame." Emery quickly scribbled something on the list and handed it to her. She'd always enjoyed late night shopping, because nobody else was around and she could wander the aisles without being jostled. The Mermaid Mart was the only one that stayed open until 2 a.m. and had everything she needed. She'd become friends with all the staff and cashiers over the years, so if she couldn't find something on the shelves, they snuck it for her from the back.

She'd been slacking off with her shopping, because Emery was out of the house most of the day and dinner was the only meal they ate together, so it wasn't a big deal. But it was clear that she needed to pay more attention to the crap her daughter might be eating. She started with the veggies, then tossed in fruits that Emery had picked and also grabbed a few snacks that she could hide in the back of the cabinets. With meat the last thing on her list, she turned into the bread section and froze at the sight before her.

Man bun and glasses in place, pencil sticking out of his mouth and a slight frown crinkling his forehead, Fletcher Kelley was examining the shelf of bread. His light blue printed shirt had pink flamingos riding surfboards and was paired with dark shorts. All of his tattoos were now on display and she wanted to trace each one slowly. If anyone was to wonder why she'd been obsessed with him, that sight alone would have been a good answer. Swallowing hard, she started to back away, but of course the cart chose that moment to squeak loudly and drew his attention.

His frown vanished and eyes softened, making her knees wobble. *Goddammit body, you fucking traitor.* He pulled the pencil out of his mouth and tucked it behind his ear as he turned fully to look at her.

"Hey Mick."

That nickname.

Lifting a hand in an awkward wave, she steeled herself. "Hey Fletch." *And that nickname.* "Never seen anyone look so confused by bread before."

"Didn't realize that there were so many different types and colors. I just need bread."

The frustrated look on his face made her laugh and she abandoned her cart to join him. "Okay, this is way more than I'm used to as well."

"Right? Bread is bread, why does it have to be so complicated?"

"Well, it depends on what you want the bread for." She smiled when he shrugged, his forehead wrinkling again. "PB

& Js or a grilled cheese or breakfast sandwich or something a little more fancy?"

"Let's go with grilled cheese."

She reached for the white bread that Emery favored and handed it to him. "That's Emery's favorite, she says it adds a little something to the grilled cheese."

"What's your favorite?"

She shrugged, eyes fixed on the shelf even though she knew he was looking at her. "I like bread, it doesn't matter really."

"So, what are you buying tonight?"

Grabbing another loaf of the white bread, she waved that and a loaf of brown bread and smiled at him. "Both, we like mixing it up in our house sometimes."

He nodded, but kept his eyes on her. Micah blushed and turned to toss the bread into her cart. Her heart was racing, palms were sweating…the beginning of that damn Eminem song "Lose Yourself" filtered through her head.

"You okay?"

Blowing out a breath, she glanced at Fletcher with a forced smile. "Yeah, been a long day. You good?"

"Now that I have the perfect bread for a grilled cheese, yeah."

"You'll have to thank Emery for that choice."

He smiled and she saw the wrinkles around his eyes, the lines around his mouth and she wished that she'd been able to see him age so beautifully. *What are you doing? None of that, Micah Elisabeth George!* Shaking off the thought, she started to move around Fletcher when he said her name. Not Mick, he called her *Micah*, the way the consonants sounded in his deep voice sent shivers up her spine.

"Yeah?" she whispered.

"We're friends, right?"

"Are we?" She looked back at him as he dragged a hand through his now untied hair.

"I'd like us to be, yeah."

Nodding, she turned to face him fully. "Okay, we're friends."

"Great," he said the word softly, eyes locked on hers. "Do friends get coffee together?"

"It's 10 p.m., Fletch." She was paying such close attention that she saw the way he reacted to the nickname—chest heaved and fingers flexed.

"Did you know you're the only person to call me that?"

"Even now?"

He nodded, taking one step towards her and Micah bit her bottom lip at the dark look in his eyes. "Always seemed to correct people if they called me *Fletch*."

Oh fuck it, give yourself to him right here in this aisle.

"So, coffee," she forced out, the words breathy and almost squeaky. She had to curl her toes inside her sneakers to stop from swaying in Fletcher's direction.

"Maybe another time. When it's not so late."

"Okay." If she didn't rein it in, she was in serious danger of wanting to hump him every time she saw him. "Good night, Fletcher."

"'Night, Mick."

She flashed him her best smile and turned around, casually hurrying out of sight before she sucked in a deep breath and closed her eyes.

fletcher

Fletcher Claus is back in town!

IN THE FOUR days since he'd seen Micah at the grocery store, Fletcher hadn't thought of anything but the gorgeous brunette. The wildest part was that no other woman had ever taken up this much space in his brain. Not Alice when they were married for eight years and definitely not the woman he'd had a long-term fuck buddy situationship with. Micah had captivated his waking and sleeping moments for two years after they met and now in four short days, she'd infiltrated his mind again.

He wasn't surprised, not really. She'd hooked him long before they'd spoken sixteen years ago and now with all that sass and beauty still firmly in place, she was even more irresistible.

Then there was the whole 'single mom' thing that threw him for a loop. He couldn't believe that he'd flat out asked her if Emery was his, because her reaction had disappointed him. Which was strange considering until that moment, he'd never thought about being a father. He'd kept that to himself when he'd flown out to Los Angeles to spend Thanksgiving with his friends.

Sitting around a table with Jack, Soren, their flavors of week, Brandy and her partner; Fletcher told them all about reconnecting with the woman that inspired "Mermaid". Then he'd spent the whole evening answering every question, which was a lot more than he expected.

"I remember she was hot, is she still hot?"

"Smoking hot. Beautiful too."

"And she's a *mom*? That's also hot."

"Okay, that's enough of thinking about her."

"Does she know you wrote a song about her?"

That made him pause. His eyes drifted to the tattoo on the inside of his left forearm, the one he got when the song went platinum and was nominated for a bunch of awards. The cerulean mermaid tail was the last piece of art he'd added to his body, for good reason.

"I don't think so. She didn't mention it," he said, sipping on his whiskey. "I also don't want to assume that she listened to our music after that night."

Brandy tossed a napkin at him, flashing a smug smile. "I'm pretty sure she's not the only one who left a mark that night."

He chuckled, running a hand through his hair as he looked around at his friends. They'd all seen the nail marks on him the next day and listened patiently as he talked about her for weeks after. Jack and Soren had helped him polish up the song, and they'd worked tirelessly for a week with Fletcher as he turned his lyrics into something beautiful. In the studio, the producers asked them multiple times if they thought releasing a rock ballad was in their best interest. It was so completely out of their repertoire, but his friends had been certain.

None of them could have predicted that it would go on to be their biggest hit, win them two Grammys and stay on the Billboard Top 100 Chart for an entire year.

Clearing his throat, Fletcher raised his glass to his friends. "I'm glad we could spend at least one holiday together this year."

"Is it sad that we only see each other once a year?" Soren asked, topping off everyone's drinks.

"The last time I suggested meeting for birthdays and other big holidays, a certain *someone* laughed at me," Brandy countered, narrowing her eyes at Soren.

"That's way too many times to see each other. We took a sabbatical for a good reason."

Fletcher snorted. "Let's stick to once a year and then go from there."

"Fourth of July next year?" Jack asked, extracting himself from the arms of his young girlfriend, and arched an eyebrow at the group.

A round of confirmation went up and Fletcher thanked his lucky stars that everything was solid between them. Two years after the sabbatical, Brandy went through her transition surgery and all of them gathered to help her through recovery. In the years since, they'd met a few times even though the intention was to meet more often. But with all the changes in their lives, it became impossible. The fact that they were consciously planning for a future together comforted Fletcher. Micah coming back into his life was another sign that the future was looking brighter.

"Fletcher Claus is back in town!"

He groaned at the excited cheer as he walked into the office for the town's event planner, Jensen Mars.

"Four years and we're still not making that a thing."

"Why not? It's perfect. You're Fletcher and you're Santa Claus. Fletcher Claus," Jensen explained, like it was not completely obvious already. "Besides, it's what everyone here calls you anyway."

"Unbelievable," Fletcher muttered and settled into the chair in front of Jensen's very messy desk. After Thanksgiving with the band, Fletcher returned to Sirena Beach and his duty as Santa for the holiday season. Every year since Uncle Hank had volunteered him for the job, he had been visiting Jensen in his office to discuss plans for Santa's Village. It was a tiring job and coupled with running the store, he was usually run off his feet by the time Christmas actually rolled around. And still, he did it. Mostly to honor Hank, but also because there was a certain kind of joy to be found when kids looked at you like you hung the fucking moon.

At first they put him in Uncle Hank's incredibly uncomfortable suit with a fake belly and everything. Then he protested—he would play Santa, but without the wildly offensive outfit. So they got the kids of the town to pick and choose what kind of Santa they wanted to see that year. His second year, he'd been Dino Santa and wore a slightly less uncomfortable T-Rex suit with a Santa hat on top. Halfway through that Christmas, Fletcher had insisted on Santa being able to wander around the Village instead of staying seated the whole time. So he traded the Dino suit for pajamas with dinosaurs wearing Santa hats and the kids loved it. Last year the kids had voted for elves, instead of Santa, so Fletcher had dressed up like Buddy from *Elf*. It had been okay, except for the constant wedgie he got from wearing those damn tights.

Being at the whim of the town's kids was a little daunting, but Fletcher liked that everyone got so involved in the celebration.

"What disastrous look are we going for this year?"

Jensen rolled his eyes and set a mason jar filled with colorful strips of paper on his desk. "The folks of Sirena

Beach have spoken and this year you will be…" he picked up a pink strip, unrolled it and laughed, "Rockstar Santa."

"Hilarious," Fletcher grumbled playfully, his mind already thinking of fun ways to bring that outfit to life. Hank's tailor had been disappointed by the T-Rex suit and the Buddy costume, so maybe the old lady would be happy to stitch something worthy of a rockstar for him that year.

"Come on, this is totally up your street. Besides, it also means you don't have to put too much effort into your clothes."

Fletcher had to admit that was definitely appealing. He could wear his standard uniform of darks and flannel, adding a Santa hat or something else to the mix every now and then. It was only for three weeks, walking around Santa's Village and interacting with people. He could totally do it in his sleep.

"I have full control over my outfit this year, right?"

"Well…" Jensen trailed off and gestured vaguely towards the mayor's office. "She has final say, really. But I trust you."

Shaking his head, Fletcher pushed to his feet. Pictures from the Christmases past hung up around Jensen's office. He was damn proud of his work and Fletcher could see why. There were some from the years Hank had been Santa, always in that god-awful suit. There were pictures from other events hosted around town and Fletcher was surprised that not even once had he run into Micah and Emery.

"Quick question," Fletcher said, turning back to Jensen. "You know Micah?"

"George? At Haven?"

Fletcher frowned. "Those are words I don't understand."

"Micah George, works at Haven Clinic. Yeah, I know her. Why?"

"I'm giving her kid music lessons."

Jensen nodded slowly, like he didn't believe a damn thing

Fletcher was saying. "Right. And it has nothing to do with the fact that she's drop dead gorgeous."

"Absolutely nothing to do with that."

"I'm going to get the truth out of you eventually, you might as well spill now."

Fletcher huffed out a laugh and turned to the photo wall again, his eyes finally snagging on a picture of Micah and Emery during a Pride March. Both of them had colorful flags painted on their cheeks, and their faces were split into wide grins. How could he ever walk away now? When the sight of Micah in an old photograph made his heart race.

"We have some history, and I didn't expect to see her here."

"Ah, another gentleman left heartbroken by our resident badass."

Fletcher's head snapped to Jensen so quick, he felt the twinge in his neck. "What?"

"I'm kidding. She's got her kid and her best friends, and that's it. But your reaction says way more than your silly comment about history."

"Asshole," he said under his breath and with one more glance at the photograph, he headed to the exit.

"I'll see you in a few days, *Fletcher Claus*."

"Not if I see you first, Mr. Mars," Fletcher responded with the creepiest smile he could muster up. At Jensen's wide-eyed stare, Fletcher cackled and walked out of the office.

"You weren't kidding, you're a *terrible* teacher," Emery said with a look of disdain he was sure she'd obviously perfected over the years. Her Avril Lavigne outfit had been traded for something more akin to a small beach town—bright pink shorts and a black cropped T-shirt that read 'die beach, die!'—but her hair and personality were still intact.

Still so much like Mick, it's unsettling.

"Blaming the teacher because you can't understand simple instructions is childish."

"I am a child!"

Fletcher stood up from behind the drum kit and twirled the sticks in his hands. "You're a teenager."

"Teenagers are children."

"Actually," Nico started, from where they were hunched over a bass guitar, tiny hands struggling to touch all the frets Fletcher had showed them earlier. "Teenagers are not children, we might still be called *adolescents*, but not children."

Emery shot her friend a glare and then turned to Fletcher with a huff. "Okay, fine, I don't understand what you're telling me to do."

Fletcher held the sticks out to Emery with a small smile and nodded at the stool. "You remember what I did, right? You need to repeat those movements, without actually hitting the drums."

She sat down, adjusted the stool, released a heavy sigh and looked up at him. "Snare, pedal, tom, snare, pedal, hi-hat?"

"Sure, let's see how those movements feel to you."

Emery rolled her shoulders back and without hitting anything, swung her arms around and then made a face. "Maybe I should start with the tom and work my way right to left instead," she said, not even glancing at him as she followed her own instructions. Smiling when she seemed to settle into the movements a little better, he nodded for her to keep going.

Even though she'd been drumming on her pillows, she was absolutely messy behind a kit. She jumped and swerved and swung around without a care for herself or anyone else.

The first few sessions, Benson had to grab them earplugs to block out the *noise* she was creating. Since then, he'd been teaching her to read sheet music and get a better under-standing of what it meant to be a drummer.

But despite being a menace behind the kit, she was really eager to learn and listened to his instructions carefully. Like her mother, she challenged him at every turn, making sure to keep him on his toes. And she also worked well as Nico's cheerleader since they were having a much harder time picking up the bass. Neither of them gave up, though, always asking questions and making sure Fletcher and Benson were being honest with their progress.

Since they didn't have a timeline, Fletcher knew that he could show the two of them the best way to enjoy their instruments. It would take longer than he expected.

"Emery, your Mom called to say that she's going to be late tonight," Benson said as he walked into the back. "She wanted to know if one of us could drop them off."

Fletcher nodded. "I can do it."

"Thanks, man." Benson patted him on the back and headed for the offices. His wife had left him and their four year-old daughter recently, and Fletcher knew that Benson was struggling to find the balance.

Turning to the teenagers, Fletcher clapped his hands to get their attention. "Do you two want more time or are you ready to head home?"

Nico sighed and set the bass aside. "I'm good to go home. I need to rethink my choice of instrument."

Emery scowled at her best friend and then turned to him. "I guess I can go home."

"Love the excitement," he deadpanned. "All right, why don't you both *wrap* up and meet me out front."

Muttering and whining followed, but they didn't protest. Fletcher put everything away and left himself a note to spend some time teaching Emery how to properly read music. She had the determination and the excitement, but she was lacking in talent and patience. It was incredible how much Fletcher saw of Micah in the kid from the frustrated pout to the sass that poured off her constantly. He turned off the lights, ushered Benson out and found Emery and Nico giggling at something on their phones. He escorted them out, turned off the lights and locked the store before leading the way to his truck.

Nico gave him their address and the two of them sat in the back talking about things he could barely understand. After dropping Nico off, and waiting till they were inside their house, Emery climbed into the front seat and directed him. Pulling up in front of a beautiful white house with a dark blue roof, Fletcher's brain finally registered that he now knew where Micah lived. He'd tried to keep her out of his head for most of the day, but seeing her house changed all of that.

Emery undid her seatbelt and started to get out of the truck before turning to him. "You're coming in, right?"

"I am?"

Rolling her eyes, she hopped out and nodded before slamming the door shut. He looked back at the house and considered his options—he could drive away or he could stay until Micah came back home. Truth was, Emery didn't look upset by the fact that her mother was going to be late and she clearly didn't need him babysitting her. But he felt like he needed to make sure that the kid was safe. Especially when she let herself into the house and left the front door open.

Yes, let's use that as a reason to go inside.

He huffed at his inner voice and turned off the truck. He locked it as he climbed out and carefully walked into the house, like something might jump out at him. Closing the door behind him, he toed off his sneakers and set them along with the other shoes organized neatly on a short shelf.

"Downstairs!" Emery called out and Fletcher descended the stairs as his eyes drank in the details of the house. There was a long hallway with doors leading off at that level, but he couldn't see into any of the rooms. Instead, he focused on what came into sight as he hit the lower level—a spacious living-dining-kitchen area with big windows that opened onto a small patio. With the colors of the setting sun, the room was painted in shades of gold and pink, changing the essence of the space.

"What do you wanna eat?"

He turned at Emery's voice and stared at the large kitchen that swallowed the teenager whole. Standing in front of an industrial size refrigerator, Emery had her lips pursed and one hand on her hip.

"Pasta?"

"I'm not allowed to make pasta anymore," Emery said with a pout and closed the fridge. "Too messy."

"How about *I* make the pasta and you assist?"

"What does assisting entail?"

Fletcher smirked and started opening cabinets to find what he was looking for. "Cleaning up as we go, making sure that we're not messy."

"Ugggggggh, that's the worst part."

Once he'd found the pasta and cheese, he set them on the counter and then grabbed a few tomatoes, set them aside as well. "True, but the best part is getting to eat what we make. What meat does your mom keep in the house?"

Emery mumbled something under her breath, but after some rummaging in the freezer, pulled out a bag. "Mom bought that for tacos, but I guess we can use it for pasta."

"Perfect."

He looked at everything laid out and then handed out instructions to Emery, smiling when she only protested a few times. He wasn't an expert at cooking, but Fletcher enjoyed the process. While on tour, he'd gotten so sick of eating fast food and the same shit every night that he picked up a cooking habit. Whatever he could whip together on the tour bus would be devoured by the guys, then during his time off, he attended cooking classes and made friends with chefs. Cooking could be tedious and a lot of work went into it. But for him, that was actually pretty therapeutic.

Despite her whining, cooking with Emery turned out to be so much more fun that he expected. Like with teaching her the drums, she asked questions and followed his instructions properly. They cleaned as they went, mostly because Fletcher didn't want to leave Micah's gorgeous kitchen an absolute mess when he was done. But also because it was a good habit to pick up.

micah

This was a setup.

LETTING HERSELF INTO THE HOUSE, Micah groaned as she dropped her things on the bench by the front door. With one hand on the wall, she peeled off her pumps and let them fall where they may. Stepping onto the shag carpet, she released a sigh of relief and curled her toes into the soft surface. She thought that working a job that allowed her to sit for hours wouldn't be so tiring, but apparently there was a limit to how long you could sit without feeling pain. That coupled with the stress of the sessions was a lot for any one person to handle. But she'd survived another long day of one-on-one sessions with her adolescent clients and then an hour of reading with Mrs. Hershey.

She carefully ran a hand through her curly hair and inhaled deeply, mostly to center herself, when the scents of tomato sauce and meat greeted her. Then sounds came into focus—Emery's laughter alongside a much deeper male voice. When she'd bought the house, Micah had liked that there were two entrances—one at the upper level from the street and the one she came through with a driveway. Given that she used the main entrance most of the time, she wouldn't have known that they had a guest.

Frowning, she grabbed her phone, pushed her feet into her fluffy narwhal slippers and hurried to the kitchen, only to freeze at the sight of the broad shouldered form with a high ponytail. Emery's head was tipped back as she laughed, her blonde ponytail bouncing with the movement. Swallowing hard, she took a step back and out of sight as she attempted to process the fact that *Fletcher Kelley* was in her kitchen and cooking up a storm.

He probably thinks you're a terrible mother, letting your kid cook for herself while you work.

Forcing away the thought, she shook her head. No. Fletcher wasn't going to react like Geoffrey, or like her parents did when she first got this job. He would be understanding. Or so she hoped. She held onto enough guilt when she worked long hours, she didn't need anybody else making her feel like shit as well. Her job *was* demanding and on some days, it felt harder than others. And because she knew how difficult speech impediments could be if not treated properly, she worked twice as hard on a daily basis. Micah never wanted kids to struggle and suffer the way she did. She never wanted them to be bullied like she had been.

After the divorce, when Micah went back to school and then worked her clinical hours, her parents had a lot to say. She understood that they were looking at it from the point of view of a two parent home, where one was there for the kids and the other earned money. But she was a single parent and had to provide everything for Emery, even if Geoffrey was paying child support and alimony. They'd guilted her for a while, always in some subtle way or the other. They made her feel like a terrible mother for not being there with Emery all the time.

But even when she was studying and earning her hours,

Micah made sure that she was there when Emery woke up every morning and before she went to bed at night. In the last few years, her schedule had gotten better. But there were always going to be nights like this one. This was partly why Micah didn't date, because how could she justify staying out late every night when her daughter was home alone. Even if Mrs. Cannon—their neighbor and Emery's favorite babysitter—was okay keeping her until late at night, she didn't like bothering the widow. She was already so good to the George women, taking advantage of her further was unfair.

Now even Fletcher was supervising her teenager while Micah worked to help other kids and an older woman learn how to read. It was *a lot*.

"You're a fantastic mother, nobody can take that away from you," she whispered to herself and smoothed her hands down the front of her pink dress. Pushing her shoulders back, she repeated the words and then returned to the kitchen.

"Welcome home!" Emery greeted her with a broad grin and all of Micah's worries faded away instantly. Her daughter was the light of her life, the best thing she'd ever done and her entire soul.

Before she could respond, Emery was hugging her. Her daughter *never* initiated hugs and certainly not when there was company. But Micah wouldn't question it, instead, she hugged her daughter back and kissed the side of her head as she released her.

"Sorry, I commandeered your kitchen and put your kid to work," Fletcher said, his hair still up in a ponytail and foggy glasses edging to the tip of his nose. He used the back of his hand to push the glasses up and smiled, making her knees wobble.

Fucking glasses.

"You're forgiven, because that smells good." She moved around the counter, needing something to do so she wouldn't stare at his exposed arms. The tattoos were calling to her, she wanted to explore and understand them. But that meant getting close and Micah knew that if she got anywhere near him, she'd do exactly what her best friends suggested—fuck Fletcher.

Maybe I'll lick him first. Sniff him too.

"Fletch made pasta sauce from scratch and it tastes amazing," Emery said, excitement still lingering in her voice. *Is he letting everyone call him* Fletch *now?*

"It's almost ready, if you're hungry," he added.

Micah nodded and worked to calm her fucking heart down. "Yup, sure."

Emery grinned and bounced, rushing around to set the table. Micah forced her feet to move and she pulled out two stemless wine glasses from a cabinet—she was too jittery and accident prone for stemmed ones that evening—and a bottle of red wine she knew would go well with the pasta and handed it to Emery. She was trying not to stare at the man in her kitchen, but also trying not to have palpitations about the man being in her kitchen.

"Hope it's okay that I'm using these dishes," Fletcher said, his voice breaking through the noise in her head. "Emery said that you'd be fine with it."

Micah glanced at the bowl in front of Fletcher and nodded. That was her usual pasta bowl, the difference was she filled it to the top and ate right out of it when she was alone. He never needed to know that.

"I told you she'd be fine with it." Emery bounced back into the kitchen—this bouncing thing needed to stop or be explained, or both—and took the big bowl of pasta once it was filled. When she was gone, Fletcher pulled a salad bowl out of the fridge with freshly chopped vegetables and Micah's eyes widened.

"You found all that in *my* kitchen?"

"Your neighbor gave me the lettuce, apparently she's been trying to get Emery to eat more greens?"

She laughed at the mention of Mrs. Cannon and nodded. "Ever since we moved here, she's been trying to sneak the greenest veggies into Emery's food. She fell for it initially, but now my kid is too smart to be tricked into it."

"I was like that as a teenager. Greens were too gross for my refined palate of chicken nuggets and French fries."

Chuckling, Micah followed Fletcher to the table and frowned when she saw that it was only set for two. Emery was already loading up her plate with pasta, smiling sheepishly when Micah cleared her throat.

"Nico's free tonight, so we're going to storm the castle together," her daughter explained, looking at her with puppy dog eyes. "Besides, I don't want to be a third wheel."

"Third…what?" Fletcher looked between them and Micah rolled her eyes at his genuine confusion.

She shouldn't have been surprised that Emery was meddling, because after that first meeting at Big Waves, she'd been not so subtly asking questions about their history. She didn't think it was important for Emery to know anything, because there was *nothing* to know. Except, her daughter was smarter than she gave her credit for. Micah wondered how she tricked Fletcher into this, because her plan had been flawless. Shaking her head as Emery batted her gorgeous long lashes, Micah sighed. It didn't matter anyway, she was going to have to eventually be alone with Fletcher, so in the comfort of her own home while she was wearing fluffy slippers seemed like as good a time as any.

"Have fun!" Emery called out, vanishing out of sight in less than ten seconds.

Fletcher watched her go, then turned to Micah with a puzzled expression. "This was a setup."

"Took you this long to figure it out," she replied with a

chuckle and settled at the table. At least Emery hadn't lit candles or lowered the light in the room, because that would have been too much.

"I can go if this is…"

Shaking her head, she stretched one leg to push the other chair out. "It's not whatever you're going to say. And you *did* cook dinner, might as well eat it."

He hesitated before sitting down and she smiled, because even confused and stiff, he was really something to look at. To most people, Fletcher might not be handsome, but every angle of his face was appealing to her. When he started to serve her, Micah tore her eyes away from his face and poured out the wine. Their gazes met once or twice as he filled their plates, but then both of them focused on their food. The sauce, freshly made and perfectly seasoned made Micah moan, eyes slipping shut as she took her time chewing and swallowing the food.

When she opened them, Fletcher was staring at her with a pleased smile. He'd taken off his glasses and untied his hair, tucking it behind his ears. *Why is* that *so fucking hot, though?*

"Good, huh?"

She nodded, focusing on scooping up more food so she wouldn't stare at his face. "Where did you learn how to cook like this?"

He twirled the spaghetti around his fork as he spoke. "I've been really lucky to meet tons of great people while on tour. There was this chef in New York who said he'd feed me for free if I could get his buddies into a sold out show. I asked him for cooking lessons instead."

"Incredible," she mumbled and shoved another forkful of pasta into her mouth, resisting the urge to moan again. Her tastebuds caught every flavor and she felt lightheaded with the pleasure of eating amazing food.

She wasn't a bad cook and could follow a recipe, but

Micah didn't have skills like this. She used sauce from a bottle or a can, her pasta wasn't always this soft and well-seasoned. And she definitely didn't put this much effort into something so simple.

"What kind of work do you do that keeps you out so late?"

The question caught her off guard, especially since she was so busy enjoying her dinner, so she set down her fork and leaned back to look at Fletcher. He was busy stuffing his face, but when his eyes met hers, he froze. While she knew he was only *asking*, Micah was instantly on the defensive.

"Is that judgment in your tone or curiosity?"

"Why am I judging you?"

"For not being at home when my kid is here."

He frowned, setting his fork down and leaning back as well. "Did someone make you feel that way?"

"Answer the question, Fletch."

"First of all, this is *your* family and I have no room to make judgments or have opinions on what you should be doing. Secondly, your kid? She's practically an adult and from everything I've seen of Emery, you raised an independent and pretty badass kid."

Micah nodded slowly, watching him as she tried to process his words. Not what she expected him to say, but she appreciated that that's how he was handling the whole situation. Reaching for her wine, she let that distract her for a moment. Except, he was still watching her like he wanted answers.

"Who made you feel that way, Mick?"

"My ex was a bit of an asshole," she said, stilted laughter spilling from her. "Our relationship was a mess and he used that to his advantage."

Through his beard, she saw Fletcher's jaw flex and added it to her little mental library of things she liked about this man. He looked like he had something disparaging to say about Geoffrey, but her ex wasn't worth his time.

"I work as a speech therapist," she started, rolling spaghetti around her fork as she spoke. "Some sessions run long because my clients need extra time to complete their exercises. However, I've started working with an elderly woman who is part of a book club and they…" she trailed off and scrunched up her nose, realizing that she almost told Fletcher all of the details about Mrs. Hershey.

"Doctor patient confidentiality, I get it," he said, smiling across the table at her.

"I sometimes tell Emery or my best friends about my clients, I forgot who I was talking to for a moment."

"We're friends, right? Maybe not *best* friends, but friends."

Micah set her glass down and leaned forward. "Is that what you want us to be?"

"Don't…" He blew out a frustrated breath and laughed. "It's weird to say that being around you is hard, because we don't really know each other anymore. But it is hard."

"I don't think it should be *hard* to be around your friends, right?"

"I should have known you'd still be trouble after all these years."

"Somethings will never change." She licked her lips, biting down on the bottom one when his eyes lowered at the action.

"Eat your dinner, Mick."

"Bossy." Laughing softly, she twirled the spaghetti around her fork and put the food in her mouth, eyes fixed on his face. He'd been so polite that night in this hotel room, *please* and *may I* and *can we*. Something about the way he commanded her right then made her wonder if he'd sound like that in bed now. Even as the thought entered her mind, Micah tried to wish it away. There was no point in having those kinds of thoughts about Fletcher. She couldn't afford to let herself think that way.

Instead she focused on simpler stuff. "So what's it like being a former rockstar? And what do you do with all your time?"

He watched her for a long moment and then blinked. "I uh...I live off my hard earned money, run Hank's store and now I apparently teach unruly teenagers to play instruments."

"Why did you retire?"

"It's a *long* sabbatical," he corrected and then smirked when he added, "Have you been keeping tabs on me, Mick?"

Even though he knew what her official name was, Micah was glad that he still called her *Mick*. She snorted and took a sip of her wine. "When your favorite band decides that they're taking a break after almost fifteen years of making music, you want to know what happened."

"*Favorite* band, really?"

"Did you think that I followed you guys on tour for shits and giggles?"

"I thought it was because you wanted to get railed by a rockstar."

She smiled against the rim of her wine glass. "I *did* get railed by a rockstar. But also because I was a fan."

"I walked into that." He shook his head, but smiled as he settled back in his chair. "All jokes aside, Brandy wanted to start a family and being on the road didn't make sense for that. Jack was finally clean and touring was a lot of temptation. And Soren wanted to travel without having a strict schedule."

"And you?"

He shrugged and dragged a hand through his hair with a heavy sigh. "I could have continued making music, but it didn't make sense to do it without the band."

"So you retired and moved to Sirena Beach, of all the places in the world. Why not go home?"

"My family and I have nothing to do with each other," he started, eyes dropping to the food. "Uncle Hank has always been *family*, so when he called, I showed up."

"*Uncle* Hank?"

"Dad's brother, they never got along."

In her minimal research about him, she had never uncovered anything about his past or his family life. She didn't know if he'd been married and had kids since they last saw each other. And given that he wasn't sharing much with her right then, she was extra curious.

"What?" he asked, eyebrows dipping.

"What?" she echoed.

"You had this weird look on your face."

"That's my face, Fletch."

"*Mick*."

She blew out a breath that fluttered her lips. "If we're going to be friends, we should be a little more open and honest with each other, no?"

"Does that include telling me about the sperm donor for that rebellious teenager?"

"Really?" When he nodded, she sighed dramatically. "I met him a year after I was railed by a rockstar. He was punk rock, charming and selectively funny. The sex was eh." She made a see-saw action with her hand and continued, "But he did knock me up and then thought that the right thing to do was to marry me. Apparently his Catholic guilt *insisted* that he make an honest woman out of me or whatever bullshit he spewed. So we got married, I had Em and then we lived in not so perfect harmony for a few years until I filed for divorce and kicked him out."

"Why?"

"Because I wanted someone who *wanted* to be with me

and vice versa. I didn't want to be in this sham of a marriage for my kid. Besides, Geoffrey didn't really bond with Emery or care about her enough, so when I filed for divorce, he didn't fight me for custody."

Fletcher's mouth turned down. "He's missing out on an incredible kid."

"His loss. A few years after the divorce, Emery and I had a fight and she ran to find him, thinking he would help her. He stared at her in confusion and called me to come get 'your kid'." Micah had been so angry that day, she almost wrung Geoffrey's neck when Emery ran into her arms, crying. It was one thing to not want the kid, but to say it in front of her? "So there you have it. My biggest mistake gave me the greatest gift and I'd do it all over again if it meant I got to raise Emery."

"You're amazing."

She lifted her chin and dusted off her shoulder. "I know."

Then got to her feet, gathering their plates and carrying them to the kitchen. She heard Fletcher come up beside her and without any discussion, they worked to put away the leftovers, wash the dishes and wipe down the kitchen. Every so often, he'd make a wiseass remark about her cleaning technique and then show her how he'd do it instead. When Emery came down, pillow marks on her face and hair a mess, Fletcher took that as his cue to leave.

"Thanks for a fun evening, ladies," he said, backing out of the kitchen with a silly smile.

Emery yawned and waved. "See you tomorrow, Fletch."

"I'll walk you out," Micah said, smoothing down her dress and heading to the front door, but found Fletcher standing at the stairs. "What are you doing?"

"Emery brought me in this way."

"Of course she did." She waved for him to go up as she grabbed her keys and then followed him up the stairs—at a respectable distance, but still ogled his ass—and opened the door as he pulled on his sneakers.

Fletcher stepped outside and paused as she stepped outside with him. He turned, putting them closer than she realized. "Go out with me."

"As friends?"

"Fuck no," he said, rubbing a hand over his jaw. "I have never wanted to be friends with you."

"Jeez, Fletch, don't hold back."

He rolled his eyes and took another step towards her, bringing him close enough for her to inhale his cinnamon and leather scent mixed with pasta sauce. "You know what I mean. Go out with me."

"Okay, fine. My god, you don't have to *beg*."

"If I remember correctly, you liked it when I begged."

I really fucking did. Smirking, she said, "I'm free on Friday."

"I'll be here at one. Dress comfortably."

"Naked or minimal clothing?"

Fletcher shot her a glare and shook his head, walking to his truck. She smiled as she drank in his strong legs and dark hair, the confident stride that got him from her front door to his vehicle. He glanced back at her once more before hopping into his truck and driving away. Slumping back against the door, she chuckled. *A date, with a rockstar. Who would have thought.*

fletcher

It was one hell of a love song.

"I'VE LIVED in Sirena Beach my whole life and I didn't know this even existed," Micah said as she hopped out of his truck. Fletcher smiled as he came around the front to take in the building in front of them. Except for a large hand-painted sign that read *Shepley Cellars Tasting Room*, there was no sign of what the place could be. Big windows were framed by weathered walls with vines clinging to them for life.

"In your defense, I think they *just* opened this one."

She hummed, drawing his gaze to her face. He was still pinching himself about being on a *date* with 'the one that got away'. Ever since Thanksgiving, his friends had been referring to her that way. He had assigned that term to Micah when they were recording "Mermaid", but he'd never held onto the hope that he'd see her again. If he was being honest, he knew that even though he wished they had another shot, he'd accepted that it was a one time thing. He met Alice, they got married and he effectively pushed Micah into the back of his mind.

Until now.

He had replayed Micah's flirty words on a loop. He had

been so good at trying not to think of their night together, but the minute she brought up begging and being naked, that was all his brain could focus on. And it wasn't even Micah of sixteen years ago that lay naked and spread out in his bed, it was the Micah of now with those curves and short curls and tattoos that took his breath away.

"How did you find this place?" she asked, interrupting the inappropriate thoughts of her brown skin against his white sheets.

He mentally kicked himself and pulled open the glass double doors. "The owner is an old friend."

"Of course they are," she mumbled and brushed past him, a small smile tugging at her lips. Chuckling, he stepped into the reception area and let his eyes adjust to the darker room, while she wandered out of sight.

When he'd insisted they go on a date, he had no idea where he was taking her. He'd never gone out of his way to plan things with Alice when they were married, because his ex-wife didn't enjoy the luxury that his name and fame brought them. She preferred quiet nights at home, avoiding the band as much as possible and any time he was recognized in public, she walked in the opposite direction.

He didn't consider himself the most romantic person, but Fletcher liked the idea of doing something more than the standard dinner and a movie that everyone suggested.

On his way home after dinner at the George house, he made a few calls and tried to find something that would appeal to Micah. Thing was, he didn't know all that much about her to begin with. He knew that she liked food—evidenced by the way she inhaled room service years ago and how easily she finished the pasta earlier that week—and she had good taste in wine too. Based off that, Fletcher got in touch with an old friend.

When The Rescuers had been at the height of their career,

they were lucky enough to make friends with some pretty famous people. Kevin Shepley had been one of them. He came from a large family of vintners who owned one of San Diego's biggest vineyards—Shepley Cellars. Kevin had hosted a listening party for one of The Rescuers' albums and he and Fletcher had become instant friends. While he had no intention of driving them to the vineyard itself, Fletcher hoped that his friend would have a recommendation or two.

Not only did Kevin tell him about the Tasting Room, he told Fletcher that someone would be there to take care of them during their visit. Even though Kevin insisted their afternoon was on the house, Fletcher was going to make sure he paid for the experience. Outside of spending money on the store, feeding and clothing himself, the fortune he'd amassed as a drummer for one of the most popular bands of the 21st century was sitting in his bank account and growing moldy. Treating the woman of his dreams to a delicious day at a winery was a good way to spend his money.

If she knew exactly how many people he'd met along the way who owned businesses like this, she would either stick around forever or run a mile. This was one of the reasons why he didn't date, because it was hard to decipher if the women he was going out with wanted him because he was *Fletcher Kelley*, or because he was Fletch. With Micah, he didn't have to worry. She didn't treat him like Drummer of the Year, six years running. Even with their history, she behaved like he was just another dude.

As he looked around the space trying to figure out where Micah had gone, a woman in a pantsuit and a severe hairstyle that stretched her face approached him.

"Mr. Kelley?" At Fletcher's nod, she smiled and continued, "I'm Marguerite, welcome to Shepley Cellars. Mr. Shepley asked me to let you know that everything on the menu is available to you. We have a small group wine tasting starting in fifteen minutes, if you'd like to join that or you can order the wine flights instead and make yourself comfortable anywhere in the courtyard."

"Nice to meet you, Marguerite. Did Mr. Shepley also tell you to refuse my card if I handed it to you?" Fletcher asked, pulling his credit card out of his wallet.

The woman blushed, but laughed. "He did warn me that you would attempt to make a payment, but please don't. Mr. Shepley said that you're an old friend and he's honored that you're here."

"I'll have to find other ways to make my payment."

"We have a donation box, if that would be suitable. A large percentage of our daily earnings go to helping families all over the state. I won't tell Mr. Shepley if that's what you choose to do."

"Thank you." He chuckled and slid his wallet back into his pocket.

"You're most welcome. If you need any assistance, ask for me. I hope you enjoy your visit."

"I appreciate it, Marguerite, thank you." Marguerite smiled and pulled open another set of glass doors, letting loud music and chatter engulf him.

He nodded at her and stepped through the doors, his eyes adjusting to the brightness outside. The courtyard was larger than he expected, with long strings of lights hanging from large trees. A heavily decorated Christmas tree filled one corner of the space, with tables of different sizes and heights dotted the rest of the area. Three counters were dressed up as bars in different sections, with a relatively big stage set up as well. There were already lots of people milling about, glasses in every hand. Waitstaff moved through the crowds with trays laden with more wine glasses. He had to admit that bringing Micah here had been a good idea, even if he had no idea where she'd gone.

It took him a few seconds to spot her, the bright orange of her dress a beacon in the sea of darker clothes. She was standing in front of a wall covered in an intricate and colorful mural. Even with her back to him, he could imagine the wide eyed look on her face as she admired the art. When he picked her up earlier in the day, Fletcher hadn't allowed himself to check her out, because he knew that once he cataloged what she was wearing, it's all he would be thinking about. Now, as he wove through the crowd, he drank her in. The sleeveless orange dress had ruffles over the shoulders, was cinched beneath her breasts and fell above her knees. Her well toned legs were bare and ended with her feet tucked into a pair of well-worn white sneakers. Her curly hair fluttered in the wind, drawing his attention to the tattoo in the middle of her back exposed by the wide neck of her dress. He'd already documented the smattering of tattoos along both arms, but this one shocked him—a purple mermaid tail bursting out of the waves.

There's no way she knows the song is about her, right?

He intended to tell her, but Fletcher hadn't decided when. Besides, she was from *Sirena* Beach, so the tattoo could be in honor of her hometown as well. Coming up beside her, he gently nudged her and saw her lips curve into a smile.

"I met this artist a few years ago at a Pride Parade and they were talking about how their art is inspired by the thoughts in their mind," she told him. "Can you imagine having such colorful and vivid thoughts that you have to create something out of it?"

"Yeah, I can." *And I did.*

"Well, you *are* a creative soul, so that doesn't surprise me." She turned halfway to look at him and he smiled.

"This is beautiful, though. I don't know if my *creations* would have this kind of effect."

"You clearly don't understand the impact your music has on people, Fletch."

"You wanna tell me about it, Mick?"

She grinned and turned back to the wall as she moved down a few feet. He dragged his eyes up and down her body before forcing himself to look away. His mind had already started playing a melody and his fingers itched to write down the words; because Micah George was inspiring another song.

"So, what's the plan?" she asked, adjusting her bag over her shoulder as she examined another piece of the mural.

He moved with her, staying a few steps behind. "There's a group tasting, if you want to do that. Or we can enjoy the courtyard, the wine flights, eat all the food and relax."

"I love that wine flights are a thing now." She stopped in front of a painting of a curvy woman that was naked, except for the flowers in her hands and around her feet. "The group tasting sounds too crowded for my taste."

He smiled, stopping right behind her so he could attempt to see that piece of art through her eyes. "What do you see, Mick?"

"Myself," she said softly, leaning back against him and Fletcher rested his chin on top of her head as they stared at the woman. "I see someone who has finally found a way to be comfortable in her skin, to love herself, to cut herself some slack and simply live."

"Have you not been *living*?"

Micah shook her head and straightened up, turning to face him with a contemplative smile. "After my divorce, I struggled with everything. The balance of raising Emery and finding myself. I was so young when I got pregnant and married, and sure, I had the whole wild college life and did all the things that people at that age do. But I..." She sighed and lifted a hand to tuck her hair away, drawing his attention to the semi-colon inked into the inside of her wrist. "I feel like I didn't pause to understand myself."

In a way, Fletcher understood that. He'd been going through the motions for years and even in his own marriage, he'd been along for the ride and never really *present*. It wasn't because of any one thing or person, Fletcher and Alice didn't seem to fit beyond that first year of being together. They stuck it out for reasons he could no longer remember, never really being in love, but not letting go either.

"What does living look like to you now?"

She lifted her head and their eyes locked as she smiled. "Letting my daughter be herself, guiding her along the way when she needs it. Working a job I love, even when it takes a lot out of me. Spending time with my best friends, wearing the clothes I like, singing along to every trashy song on the radio…going out with a man from my past."

He chuckled at the last point and shook his head. "I feel like the man from your past should have a better title."

"What would he like to be called?"

Yours, he whispered to himself. But before he could say something a little more subtle, a soft voice said his name. Fletcher turned to the young waitstaff who was blushing as they smiled at them.

"Sorry to interrupt, Mr. Kelley. We've got a table open for you."

"Thank you so much," Micah told them and wrapped her hand around his arm. "Come on, Mr. Kelley, we've got wine flights to enjoy."

Harriet, their waitress, showed them to a table, handed them a menu and rattled off all the specials. Fletcher wasn't listening, he was watching Micah as she nodded along and asked a million questions. The moment they shared at the mural played on a loop in his head. Her ex hadn't seen the incredible woman in front of him and he'd made a mess of his relationship with that brilliant kid. If Micah and Emery were his —even at a time when he didn't want a family—Fletcher would have bent over backwards to make it work. He would have gone to the ends of the earth to ensure the two of them were loved with every fibre of his being.

"That sound okay with you?" she asked, bringing him back to the present.

"Yes?" He grimaced, because he didn't know a damn thing they were talking about.

She laughed and looked up at Harriet. "I think we'll take the surprise flight and go from there."

"And the standard cheese board?"

Micah nodded, her smile lighting up her face. Once Harriet was gone, her attention turned back to him. "You okay, Fletch?"

"Thinking about how lucky you and Emery are to have each other."

"Are you still thinking about what I said?"

"Always."

She stared at him for a long moment and he winced internally, because he might have been too honest. It was true, though. While he might not have thought about her all the time, she had burrowed under his skin and stayed there for the last sixteen years.

"Is your mermaid ink in honor of Sirena Beach?"

Fletcher smiled, turned his arm over and pushed up the folded sleeve of his shirt. Finding her mermaid underwear in his hotel room that night was the first time Fletcher had any interest in mermaids. Then the song happened and Uncle Hank's invitation to visit followed, now he was staring at *the one* that started it all.

"Would seem that way, right? I actually got it after our song went platinum," he told her, eyes fixed on the cerulean tail.

"You wrote the song, didn't you?"

He hesitated, because never once did he think that he'd be looking the object of the song in the eyes and telling her that it was about her. But maybe this was the opportunity to *tell* her the truth. Instead, he cleared his throat and nodded. "Yup. Didn't think it would make it onto the album or that it would do as well as it did."

"It was one hell of a love song, Fletch."

"Wasn't really a love song." *Liar, liar, pants on fire.* "Merely a dedication of sorts."

"She's a lucky woman, whoever she is," she said, giving him a 'if you say so' look.

"What about your mermaid tattoo?" He leaned back in his chair, pulling his arms off the table and watched as pink spread across her face.

"A double whammy tribute—" she rubbed her lips together, eyes darting everywhere but his face "—for my hometown and your song."

His heart clenched at the realization that Micah had done it for the same reasons he had. Except, she didn't know all the details. But before he could say anything, Harriet returned with a tray of wine glasses. She set the drinks on the table and explained each one, but Fletcher was still unable to listen. His mind spun with all the ways he could tell Micah that she was *the mermaid.* The one that called him out to sea, seduced him and changed his life. He might not have pined for her all these years, but every now and then, his soul craved her company. Especially when the song played on the radio.

"What do you wanna try first?" Micah asked once Harriet was gone, turning the tray sideways so both of them could see all the glasses.

"The rainbow sparkles. What did she call it?"

"My Little Rosé."

The name made them both smile and he picked up the small glass to sniff. It was a brighter pink than most rosé he'd drunk, but it was the glitter that really threw him. Micah arched an eyebrow at his hesitation and after toasting her, he took a quick sip. He'd been prepared for something else, so was pleasantly surprised when the wine went down smooth.

"Surprisingly not offensive," he mumbled and handed it to her to try.

Nodding at his assessment, she reached for the next one— a white that was almost colorless—and pursed her lips at the glass and sipped, her nose scrunching up as she held it out to him. "That's tarty."

"It *is* called Tartonnay," he teased, reading off the small name cards he didn't see before. He took a sip of the wine and grimaced as a shudder worked its way through his body. It was good, but maybe a little too much for his palate. "Damn, okay."

She laughed and nudged at the tray. Fletcher reached for the dark red one and peered at the card. "Dark of Noir. Seems like the most unimaginative name." But he took a sip and was relieved that the Pinot erased the tarty Chardonnay off his tastebuds.

Micah seemed to think the same thing about the Pinot, because she set it beside the rosé and reached for the final glass of white. "It only says Blanc, so maybe it's not anything too fancy?"

"Or maybe it's really boring," he countered with all of the skepticism he could muster.

She laughed and sniffed the wine, eyes widening slightly before she took a sip. Holding glass away, Micah whistled. "Oh, it *is* fancy."

He narrowed his eyes and took the glass from her, sniffed

and shrugged before taking a big sip. The explosion of flavors was most unexpected and as the grapefruit, guava and hints of chocolate swirled around his mouth, his eyes slipped shut. When he opened them, he found Micah watching him with a playful smile, bottom lip tucked between her teeth.

"I think this is the winner," he said softly, not wanting to say something cheesy and ruin the moment.

micah

You ruined me too.

THE FACT that Micah thought she could be around Fletcher and not completely lose her mind was a joke. They'd barely done anything together that day and she was already wondering if he still kissed the same way, if the calluses on his hand would still scratch against her naked skin seductively. When they talked about the song, she wanted to ask who he dedicated it to. For so long, she'd forgotten about the mermaid tattoo on her back, so when Fletcher had pointed it out, she'd been startled. Jealousy had sparked through her at the thought that someone else had inspired him to write a song about being drawn into the deepest depths of the ocean to lose himself. Was it silly to wish that the song was about her? Probably. But anybody listening to the song would wish that he'd written it with them in mind.

She still remembered the first time she heard the song—six months pregnant and standing in line at the grocery store. They were playing a local radio station and the host was talking about how a new song by The Rescuers was holding the top spot on the charts. Micah hadn't listened to their music since her night with Fletcher, so she'd been caught off guard. What really stumped her was that when the song started, it was slower than their usual stuff and had a more acoustic sound to it. Then instead of Jack's smooth and silky vocals, a deep and scratchy sound came through the speakers. The memory of Fletcher singing softly in her ear that night, his wants and desires whispered as they fucked filled her mind. And it only got worse when she heard the lyrics.

> *Luring me away from the shore*
> *She's got me moving my oars*
> *Bringing me in closer with every smile*
> *I'd row for miles just to have her again*
> *Those hands in my hair,*
> *A mouth that stole my air.*
> *She's got me moving my oars,*
> *Luring me away from the shore*
> *She's got me hook, line and sinker*
> *Dragging me into her depths*
> *The brightest star, a siren*
> *My mermaid.*

Everywhere she went for a year after that—bringing Emery home from the hospital, visiting her doctor for a standard check-up, doing another grocery run—Fletcher's voice followed her. When Emery was a year old, Micah made the decision to get the tattoo. Because of Geoffrey, she decided to get it on her back where he wouldn't see it. After all, it was a tattoo she got in honor of a man that blew her mind and nobody else needed to know anything about it.

Picking at the cheese board, she stared at Fletcher's empty chair while he visited the restroom. She couldn't quite believe that of all the towns in the world, hers was where Fletcher Kelley ended up. Besides, she wasn't the first person to fall for a rockstar and definitely not the first to have the best sex of her life with one either. The difference was that she had a second chance and she wanted to make the most of it.

Movement in her periphery drew her attention to Fletcher's tall form. Dressed in dark jeans and T-shirt with a black and white plaid shirt over it, he fit right in with the rest of the people. His shoulder-length hair and salt and pepper beard was what made him stand out. A small smile tugged at her lips as she tried to connect the rockstar from the past with the silver fox walking towards her. He'd grown up really well. His eyes met hers and he arched an eyebrow, clearly confused by her smile and Micah shook her head.

If she let herself enjoy this, she was going to fall head over heels for Fletcher all over again.

"You okay?" he asked as he pulled out his chair and sat down.

"Thinking about how good it is to be here with you."

The wrinkles on his forehead smoothened out and his lips spread into a smile, making her heart trip over itself. Nobody would call Fletcher 'classically handsome', but he was the kind of attractive that would make you look twice.

Harriet returned with fresh glasses and a bottle of the fancy Blanc, poured some out for the two of them and made herself scarce. The chatter around them had been pretty steady since they arrived and she hadn't even paid attention to the other guests. But as she sipped on the wine, watching Fletcher do the same, every sound and color came into focus.

"So," he started, setting his glass down to lean forward. "You know all about me taking over for Hank at the store. What about you, why speech therapy?"

She swirled her wine, crossing one leg over the other as she relaxed in her chair. There wasn't anyone new in her life that wanted to know why she picked the career she did, because everyone already knew enough about her. So talking about it felt weird.

"I grew up with a stutter that only got the attention of a teacher once I was in high school. Do you know how many kids are told that they'll 'outgrow' their stutters?" she asked, throwing finger quotes around 'outgrow', because it was what her parents did. "You don't really outgrow it, you become really conscious and scared and nervous around people who speak without any problems.

"I was bullied a lot for not being able to express myself confidently. Kids are really mean when they want to be and I wanted to help others like myself as much as possible. Not all speech therapists have had impediments or difficulties, so they might not really know what it's like. But my therapist did and she helped me so much. I wanted to do the same thing."

He nodded, his eyes fixed on her face. "Do you remember stuttering the night we met? You tripped over a few words and you looked so mad about it."

"I remember." She'd been embarrassed to be stuttering in front of him then, but ignored it. They'd fucked a few times by then, mouths having explored each other already. And then she had trouble with the simplest words. "I'm surprised *you* remember."

"I remember a lot more than you realize, Mick."

She bit down on her bottom lip, heart racing as she stared at Fletcher. It wasn't only the words he used, it was the *way* he said it. His tone was firm, focus unwavering and he put emphasis on the nickname she gave him years ago instead of her full name. She had so many questions, so much she needed to know and understand. Micah wondered if they remembered the same things, if he sometimes dreamed about that night the way she did. Instead, she released her lip with a soft sigh, drawing his gaze to her mouth.

"Did you ever really imagine that you would retire from music and do...*this*?" Micah asked, needing to quickly step away from the intense way his attention and words made her feel.

He hesitated, eyes narrowing briefly before he shook his head. "I honestly didn't think I'd retire. Truly believed I'd be playing music until the day I died. But I understood why the band needed time off, why they needed to take the break. Did I ever imagine moving to a small town to run my uncle's music store? No. But I'm *really* glad that I made the move."

"Me too," she told him honestly, not even bothering to hide her blush or smile. "Emery is glad too. She's in her rock phase of life and The Rescuers are her favorite band."

"Kid's got good taste. Speaking of phases, the first time I saw her she was decked out like Avril Lavigne, now she's rocking this punk rock Barbie vibe."

She laughed, surprised that he had caught onto what her daughter was doing. "I don't even know where she comes up with these things, but since she was eight, Emery has tried everything. There was a time she thought she was a Tolkien elf and learned the whole language."

"Fluently?"

She nodded, recalling the first time Emery had an entire conversation in Elvish. "I assume so. Once she commits to something, she goes all out."

"That's pretty impressive." He sipped on his wine and then added, "Gotta admit though, seeing that Avril Lavigne outfit was a flashback I didn't know I needed."

"Right? I was so surprised when she showed up dressed that way one morning. I'm not even sure what prompted her to listen to that music, but she claims they're all *bangers*."

He laughed, wrinkles forming at the corner of his eyes and Micah hid her smile with her glass. Talking about her daughter was safe, because it took her away from those intense feelings she was trying to stuff down. Their conversation drifted into comfortable banter, discussing what it was like being a single mother and why she'd stayed in Sirena Beach when she could go anywhere else—"I lived in big cities and they're too much for my quiet soul." Most of her dates wanted answers to superficial questions like favorite movie or book, celebrity they most looked like, restaurant that was overrated. Fletcher had always found a way to get her to talk about the things that she thought to herself about regularly, never cared to voice them before.

The sound of someone tapping against a microphone drew their attention to the stage where four men in brightly colored shirts were setting up with their instruments. She had noticed the stage, but Micah didn't realize that she would be treated to a live show as well.

"Hello Sirena Beach, we're The Beach Quays. Hope you've drunk enough wine to get on the dance floor. We've got some originals, tons of covers and maybe even room for some special requests if you're lucky. Now, empty those glasses and get ready to boogie!"

She grinned as the band launched into a cover of "Dance, Dance, Dance" by The Beach Boys. Fletcher was watching her as she shimmied in her seat and when she got to her feet, he shook his head. She held both hands out to him, swaying and wiggling in place, all while she smiled at him. A few people had already made their way onto the dance floor and she knew that if she could get this man on his feet, they'd have the best time ever.

"Dance with me, Fletch," she pleaded, still grinning at him. And after what felt like forever, he put his hands in hers and she tugged him to his feet.

Joining the rest of the people on the makeshift dance floor, he wrapped one arm around her waist and held their other hands against his chest as they moved to the music. The band went through different genres, tempos and ranges and through it all, he held her as they danced. He twirled her out and back in, his hands always landing on her hips every time she was right against him. She wound her arms around his neck, head tipped back to stare into his eyes as the band performed "Songbird" by Fleetwood Mac. She mouthed the lyrics along with them, smiling when she realized Fletcher was doing the same thing. When the song ended, his forehead dropped to hers with a heavy sigh and before either of them could make a move, the lead singer was speaking again.

"I don't know how many of you know this," he started and Micah looked up in time to find the whole band staring at them. "The reason I became a musician is because of a band called The Rescuers and I'm losing my shit because standing right in front of me is one of the greatest drummers to ever exist in the world."

Fletcher blushed, but Micah saw the smile tugging at his lips. She knew that he was the most private member of the band and that being called out like this was not exactly the most exciting thing for him.

"I apologize for putting you on the spot, Mr. Kelley, but it would be my absolute honor if you could perform one song with us today?"

"He would love to," Micah said, drawing Fletcher's unimpressed glare. "Come on, Fletch, just one song. Do it for me."

He sighed heavily, like it was such a task to get up on that stage and sing with a band that admired him. Pressing a kiss to the side of her head, Fletcher squeezed her hip and to loud cheering, he climbed onto the stage as an acoustic guitar was handed to him.

"For the record," he said, speaking directly into the microphone, eyes drifting to hers. "I haven't performed in *years* and

I'm only doing this because my date won't let us go home otherwise."

The crowd laughed and she shrugged, arms crossed over her chest. His entire career with The Rescuers, Fletcher had sat behind the drums and while she knew that he could play every instrument known to man, she'd never seen him do it. Over the years, Micah had made it a point not to look up videos or any other kind of content in regards to him. Because she knew that once she laid eyes on him, she would completely lose herself and she didn't ever want to go down that road.

Fletcher cleared his throat as he strummed the guitar and then spoke again. "When I wrote this song sixteen years ago, I never imagined it would become so popular." His eyes found hers again and she pressed her lips together as the opening chords of "Mermaid" filtered through the speakers. "This was always for you, Mick."

Micah's eyes widened and her heart clenched as he started singing. In that moment, with her brain short-circuiting, she realized that he hadn't simply dedicated the song to her, the whole thing was *about* her. Tears pricked the back of her eyes and she pressed one hand to her chest, her heart beating so fast she was sure she was going to pass out any minute.

> *One night will never be enough*
> *Her curves so soft, her heart so tough*
> *With eyes that glitter in the dark*
> *Every inch of my skin sparked*
> *As she lures me away from the shore*
> *She's got me moving oars, faster.*
> *I'd row for miles, just to take her harder*
> *Those hands in my hair,*
> *A mouth that stole my air.*
> *She's got me moving my oars,*

Luring me away from the shore
She's got me hook, line and sinker
Dragging me into her depths
A siren, an angel, the brightest star
My mermaid.

When the rest of the band joined in on the second verse, taking Fletcher's attention off her, Micah stumbled backwards and away from the crowd. She blinked back tears and hurried to the restroom, Fletcher's gruff voice following her until she closed the door and leaned against it. Her heart threatened to beat its way out of her chest and her knees were not going to hold her steady if she didn't find somewhere to sit. Locking the door to one of the stalls, she covered the toilet and sat down, burying her face in her hands. She should have been happy to know that "Mermaid" was about her, but it was also startling to know that this man had felt so much for her then that he wrote an incredible song about her.

Once she'd gotten her breathing steady, she stepped out of the stall to look at herself in the mirror. The dull sounds of the song filtered into the restroom, but she focused on herself. The woman staring back at her in the mirror wasn't the same one Fletcher wrote the song about, she wasn't even the same woman that married Geoffrey. She'd changed so much since that night sixteen years ago, but at the same time that young girl still existed somewhere inside her. Wetting a paper towel, she dabbed it against her neck and chest, cooling down her warm skin.

Being with Fletcher already made her feel a certain way, but knowing how he *felt* was a whole other thing—discombobulating, exciting, and fun. He'd been so enamored with her sixteen years ago and Micah had been obsessed with him then. To be called backstage by a musician you admired and had a crush on was a really big deal. She'd put on this act of being a confident woman, sexually experienced and dominating in bed; truth was she had been none of those things. In Fletcher's presence, she'd put on her armor and she'd worn it recklessly.

Micah was *that* woman now. Geoffrey had never been interested in the kinkier parts of sex, not that Micah was experimenting that much. He was a missionary position, two pump chump. Some days, she wondered how she got knocked up when the sex was pretty average. Especially when she'd experienced mind-blowing sex with Fletcher, and then with other random partners in the years since. Though, it had been a long time since she'd indulged in a fun sex fueled night with someone. Between work, Emery, and trying to keep her head on straight, Micah barely had time for her best friends. So a one night stand that would disappoint? Not interested.

All right, that's enough lamenting. Get back out there and into the arms of that rockstar.

"*Former* rockstar," she muttered to herself. After one more quick look in the mirror, she opened the door to the restroom as a gaggle of young girls stumbled in. Stepping around them, she smoothed down her dress and headed back to the table.

Fletcher was standing there, frown marring his forehead and hands clenched at his sides, until he saw her. Then all of him relaxed. Her heart threatened to explode, tears pricking the back of her eyes.

"I was starting to get worried. Are you okay?" he asked, meeting her halfway. She wanted to throw herself into his arms, but she also knew that a conversation was way more important.

"You know, having a chat with myself."

"I'm sorry," Fletcher said to her, eyes dropping to his feet.

"I should have told you that in one night not only did you inspire a song, you also changed my life."

"Fletch..." she whispered, unsure if she wanted him to stop or keep going.

"I still haven't met a woman that could render me speechless and full of words at the same time. You ruined me and I am so fucking grateful for it."

Tears slipped down her cheeks and she pressed her lips together as she closed her eyes, processing everything he'd admitted. Her heart hadn't expected to feel so much all at once and she wanted to scream to rid herself of all these emotions.

"Fuck, Micah, I'm sorry." His voice was closer than before and she shook her head as she wiped at her cheeks. "I didn't mean to...*shit*."

Opening her eyes, she found herself staring into his distraught face. Lifting a hand, she cupped his cheek, feeling the roughness of his beard against her palm. His eyes flickered to hers and she saw distress in the brown pools.

"You ruined me too," she whispered and he blew out a breath, leaning forward to rest his forehead against hers.

fletcher

Sexy rockstar vortex.

IT HAD BEEN *years* since Fletcher had been recognized in such a public setting, years since he was asked to join a band on stage to perform a song. Years since he'd stared into Micah's eyes and sang anything at all. He was honored to be singing "Mermaid" while the inspiration behind the song stared up at him. What he didn't expect was for it to also be slightly unsettling. Especially when he saw the expression on her face change from adoration to shock. He hadn't lied as much as he'd omitted telling her all of the truth. When they talked about their respective mermaid tattoos, he should have said something. Instead, he climbed onto stage, confessed to her in front of everyone, and sang the damn song.

The band stole his attention when they came in on the chorus, their voices harmonizing with his perfectly, and he lost track of Micah. When he looked out at the crowd again, she was gone. In her place stood a young couple singing the song to each other. As the performance came to an end, the crowd cheered so loud it rattled in Fletcher's chest. Forcing a smile, he let his eyes do another sweep of the audience before mumbling a thanks into the microphone. He then turned to the band and thanked them for bringing him on. Handing the guitar over, he hopped off stage and peered around hoping that Micah was somewhere close by.

Then she appeared, head down and eyes still a little watery.

"Come on," he whispered, running a hand down her arm to link their fingers as he pulled back to look at her. Her eyes were fixed on their hands, but as he moved, she followed. She finally released his hand and walked towards a section of the mural they hadn't explored earlier. The artist had drawn two people facing each other, hair and clothes fluttering in the wind. The only contact between the two people were their hands, the tips of their fingers touching the other. Musical notes and brightly colored flowers were wrapped around them. If there was a piece of art that could describe him and Micah, it was probably that one.

When he came up behind her, Micah let out a shuddering breath and said, "I heard that song everywhere I went for years and never once connected it to me. I was jealous, you know? When I first heard it. That someone else made you feel deeply enough to write a song about them."

Only Micah would think that she wasn't worthy of a song, that she wasn't worthy of the best words the universe had to offer. His hands itched to touch her, to comfort her.

"You left your underwear in my hotel room when you snuck out in the morning."

"I didn't sneak out, I had to go home."

He smiled at her obstinate tone. "I woke up alone in my hotel bed. There was no note, only three things that you left behind," he told her, waiting until she looked at him. "Your mermaid underwear, a hair-tie and a couple of bracelets."

Micah's eyes widened and Fletcher nodded, then watched as her gaze slid down to his arms. "Where are they?"

"Developed an allergy six months in." He laughed at the memory of how much his wrists itched when he wore the beaded leather bracelets. "The hair-tie ripped pretty much after the third or fourth use."

"And my underwear?"

"With all my prized possessions." She made a face and looked up at him. "They were washed and then framed in a glass case."

"What?"

Fletcher snorted and shook his head. "I *did* wash them, but didn't frame them. You can have them back if you want."

She shook her head and for a long moment, didn't say anything. Her eyes were fixed on the ground and Fletcher sighed as he watched her. It was a lot. They'd just come back into each other's lives and now he was laying this on her. It was probably more than she ever imagined she would be subjected to.

"It sucked to leave you alone in that bed when I left," she admitted softly. "I had an amazing night, you know this. But you were famous and I was a twenty-two year-old college senior who was still trying to figure out where she fit into the world. I couldn't figure out if I was in love with you or harboring this ginormous crush, so I split.

"I thought about joining your tour the next year, but life got in the way." Micah sighed heavily, her head tilting to the side. "For a few years, I avoided everything to do with your music. Once I was divorced and Emery was old enough, I raised her on The Rescuers. Told her about the greatest drummer in the world. And now here you are, singing a song you wrote for me in front of strangers after filling me with so much wine and joy."

Her voice had taken on a wobbly tone and he didn't have to look at her to know that she was crying. He wrapped an arm around her shoulders and tugged her into his chest, sighing softly as he rested his chin on top of her head. Her arms slid around his waist and they held each other a long moment, everything else around them fading away. He knew the band had taken a break, but even the standard music or the people gathered behind them no longer existed.

"A part of me fell in love with you that night," Fletcher finally said, his hand loosely wrapped around the back of Micah's neck. "Every night we performed that song, I felt like you were standing in the crowd, staring up at me. Who knew that a rock ballad would get so much attention?" He felt Micah's shoulders bounce with a laugh and Fletcher pulled back to look at her. "You were…*are* my mermaid, Mick."

"Were you pining for me, Fletch?"

Every single day, sweetheart. "For a while." Because it would be a lie if he said that he'd waited for her all this time. He had thought about it, pushed the thoughts away and then buried them deep after he met Alice. "All these years, believing that you were doing all right, had found someone good to be by your side kept me going. To have you standing in front of me, looking even more beautiful than you did that night is rocking my world right now."

"It's an amazing song, Fletch. I mean…" she huffed softly and with a finger, traced the tattoo on the inside of his arm. "Maybe a part of me knew you'd written the song for me."

"Not *for* you, Mick. It's *about* you."

She blew a raspberry, tears filling her eyes again. Fletcher pressed his thumb to the spot behind her ear and gently tilted her head back so they could look at each other. When she closed her eyes, he chuckled. "Look at me, Mick. Please."

"No, you'll suck me back into your sexy rockstar vortex and I'll leave more underwear behind and then you'll write another song and I won't even kno—"

Fletcher cut her rambling off by covering her mouth with his. A startled sound came out of her and after a few seconds of hesitation, she kissed him back. He wound his other arm around her waist, pulling her flush against him. He felt her lips curl into a smile before her tongue swiped out to brush against his mouth. Parting his lips, he cradled the back of her head and flicked his tongue out at hers, moaning as they made contact. And then he was lost to the kiss, the hungry way Micah kissed him and the way her fingers gripped his hair. Honestly, he didn't even care that they were in public, because the minute he had her full attention, he'd been thinking of when he could kiss her. And now that he'd tasted her lips, known what it felt like to have her back in his life, he was never letting her go.

She pulled away first, his mouth chased hers and bumped against her nose, which made her laugh softly. He smiled at the sound and opened his eyes to look down at the woman who did have him hook, line and sinker.

"Sexy rockstar vortex, I knew it," she whispered.

Fletcher snorted. "Seductive mermaid call."

"Should print that on a t-shirt."

"Or just get it inked onto my skin."

"Sounds like a damn good idea." She traced the mermaid tail on his arm and leaned into him.

"Sorry for not asking before I kissed you," he whispered and she shook her head.

"Never apologize for kissing me like that. You've had some kissing practice."

"I'm not as nervous today as I was that night."

"You were not nervous." She scoffed.

"I'd spent a good part of a tour watching this beautiful woman sing along and mosh to songs I was performing, then managed to get her backstage, where she proceeded to announce she wanted to be railed by a rockstar. So when I got her into my hotel room that night, I was nervous as fuck, because I never did that. I was never the member of the band women wanted to be with and honestly, I was okay with that. But this woman…" He trailed off and found her watching him with wide eyes. "You made me so nervous that night, Mick. I wanted it to be the best night of our lives, so yeah, my kisses were a little sloppy, I might have tripped over my own feet while trying to take my clothes off. All because I *needed* to impress you."

"I was impressed, Fletch."

"Thank god," he said dramatically, laughing as she poked him in the chest. "Never thought I'd see you again, but I must admit that having you back in my life…you are back, right? In my life?"

Micah tilted her head and the brightest smile graced her lips. "I don't know, Fletch, what do you think?"

"Answer the question," he growled.

"How about *you* tell me what you think the answer is."

"Stubborn woman," he mumbled and she grinned, like she was proud of herself. "You *are* back in my life."

"Duh. *But,* there are some conditions."

He nodded, because he was expecting that. He couldn't imagine what it was like to date when you were a single parent and he was sure that she had laid down this law with every person she dated. *Nope, don't think about other people she's dated. That is none of my business.*

"How do you feel about getting out of here and finding somewhere to eat?" she asked. He held out a hand, smiling when she slid her fingers between his and squeezed.

"I'd go anywhere with you, Mick."

Thanks to Harriet's suggestion, they'd found a local hole in the wall that served all of the greasy food one could eat. The place didn't have a sign board or more than four tables and while that would usually concern him, Micah making a beeline for the last empty table was enough of a sign that it was where they were eating. A youngster with multiple piercings approached their table and rattled off the specials, then turned to Fletcher with wide eyes.

"You're Fletcher Kelley."

"Best drummer in the world," Micah supplied with a grin and the youngster nodded, flipping their order pad over and holding it out to him. "Would you also like a picture together?"

"Yes, please. I'm sorry, Mr. Kelley, could I get your autograph? I don't mean to lose my shit, but you're like…the coolest person to ever visit us."

Fletcher was glad his beard hid most of his blush, but he signed the pad and leaned in for a photograph. With shaky hands, they took down the order for food and hurried off, leaving Fletcher and Micah alone.

"Who would have thought a small town like Sirena Beach would be filled with your biggest fans?"

"Not me," he grumbled and leaned forward as Micah did, their arms bumping on the table. "It's surreal that people *know* who I am."

"You might have sat behind the drums for years, Fletch, but you're fucking famous for being so good at what you do. And also for being the most down to earth musician of your time."

Shaking his head, he dropped his eyes to their arms. When he was young, he wanted to be a famous musician. When he joined The Rescuers, he wanted to make music that he loved. Now in his forties, he simply wanted to exist and maybe even love the woman sitting across from him. It would never not blow his mind that people recognized him or claimed he inspired them to start playing the drums. And to have Micah look at him the way she did, it was icing on the cake that was his life.

Their drinks—bright pink lemonade for Micah and a ginger ale for him—were set on the corner of the small table and the youngster scurried off. Micah chuckled at his confused expression and he shook his head, not bothering to understand how that kid, who was definitely too young to have heard his music, knew who he was.

Pulling his glass towards him, he leaned back to look at Micah. "So, conditions."

"Right." She took a long pull of her drink, eyes screwing up briefly before she blinked them open to focus on him. "Emery is my priority. I haven't dated a lot because I don't want to introduce someone into her life and have them walk away like her father did. I know things with us might be different, but I don't want to assume that it's all going to be smooth sailing.

"She already knows that we've met before, that we have history, but I'd like for us not to put our relationship on display around her," Micah explained, twirling her straw and he nodded. "I want us to give this a shot, Fletch, but I don't want to give Emery hope yet."

"I get it, Mick. I won't make promises, but you are important to me and in that line, I don't want to hurt Emery either."

Micah nodded, her eyes searching his. "We can't sneak around my house, but anywhere else is fair game. No kissing or excessive touching when she's around. As far as Emery is concerned, we're friends."

He didn't like the idea of their relationship being a secret, but he could also see why she wanted to be careful. Clearly her ex had hurt her in ways that would take years to heal. Between marrying Micah out of obligation and abandoning his kid, Fletcher hated the man. While he had no guarantee of how long this relationship with Micah would last, he would show up for Emery every time she needed him.

"I can do that," he told her, flipping a hand over. When she put her hand in his, Fletcher smiled. "This means you'll have to spend more time at my house or you know, we can run away on the weekends."

"I definitely want to see how a former rockstar lives now."

"In a house that was once owned by his favorite uncle," he told her and she snorted loudly, playfully smacking his hand.

Their food arrived and after some more fumbling and mumbling, he learned that their waitstaff was named Pia and she had been raised on music by The Rescuers. That her father had once been a drummer and considered Fletcher the best of the best. After signing something else for her father, Pia thanked him and then ran away. The whole time, Micah sat there and watched him with a smug smile on her lips and Fletcher realized that she was right—he needed to accept that once upon a time he was good enough that people flew all over the world to see him and his band perform.

"Was there ever a Mrs. Kelley?"

Fletcher jerked back at the question and stared at her for a long moment. They'd talked actively about her ex but he'd never been interested in talking about Alice. He should have known that she'd ask.

"Uh, she never took my name, but for a bit."

Micah nodded, eating crinkle fries one at a time. "What was she like?"

"We don't need to do this, Mick."

"Of course we do. You know all about Geoffrey and what an asshole he was. Besides, we're now a couple and I want to know about *you*."

We're a couple, he thought to himself giddily and watched

her for a long moment. "Can't we talk about our favorite ice cream flavor and best movie ever made instead?"

"Fletch."

"*Fine,*" he groaned. "Alice and I met through some friends during a break. A lot like you, she didn't care that I was an award-winning musician or that I was going through a weird looking phase. We uh…it was good at first, then it got boring and we finally realized that maybe we were better off not married anymore."

"I'm sorry, Fletch."

He shrugged and looked up from the sandwich he'd ripped apart. "I wasn't as upset as I probably should have been. Last I heard, she got married to someone else, so I guess she moved on well enough too."

"Divorce, when you love your partner or not, is hard," she started and he used the break to eat his food. "I was glad to get away from Geoffrey, but it did hurt when everything fell apart. You're allowed to miss her."

"I don't," he said without hesitation. "I missed *you,* though."

"Really?" She smirked, eating another crinkle fry.

He chuckled, pushing his plate aside to rest his elbows on the table. "I wrote a fucking song about you, Mick. I think it's pretty clear that I missed you. A lot."

She leaned forward, still grinning as she stretched a hand out to him. "Is it wrong to feel powerful knowing all this information?"

"You're ridiculous," he told her with a shake of his head and slipped a hand into hers. "But everyone knows that you're the powerful one here."

"Damn right I am."

Once their drinks and food were gone, they shared a large slice of chocolate cake and then Fletcher drove her home. If Mrs. Cannon, her neighbor and Emery's babysitter, hadn't walked out of the house at the same time they reached the front door he would have kissed her stupid right there. But they'd made a deal and he was going to honor it. A quick wave, wink and blow of a kiss was all he got, but it was enough given how the rest of the day had been everything he'd hoped for and more.

micah

How slutty, Mick?

"HOW DOES THIS LOOK?"

Micah looked up from where she was sorting through a pile of bracelets to find Emery wearing a large rainbow fur coat and snorted. "Rainbow Brite called, she wants her monster back."

"Who?"

"Oh, my dear flower child. How have I not introduced you to the magic of *my* childhood?"

"Is that a no?"

"We live in California, Em, when exactly do you plan on wearing that?"

Emery shrugged, turning to look at herself in the mirror. "My first date?"

"Hell no."

"To the date or the coat?"

Micah released a heavy sigh. "Both."

"*Mom.*"

"Okay, fine. You can date, one day. But put that coat away."

Emery shot her a grin and then slid off the coat, hanging it off a hook near the large mirror. Micah shook her head, smiling as she spun slowly in place and took in the store. Ever since Emery was old enough to have opinions about her own clothes, the two of them would go thrifting. It was a monthly mother-daughter activity they took very seriously and it was one of her favorite days. They would start with a delicious breakfast at Emery's restaurant of choice, then Micah would pick the thrift store from a long list they'd compiled years ago and after shopping, they would go get ice cream. Sometimes it was planned in advance, other times it would happen when Emery didn't have school and Micah didn't have work. There was even one time, soon after Emery started her period, that Micah let her skip school and they went thrifting together.

That day, breakfast had been at Sugar Mama's where Emery ate her weight in cinnamon French toast which still had her very hyper. They were at *(Hit Me, Baby) One More Time*, one of Micah's favorite thrift stores in the area. Fondly known as One More Time, the store had clothes and all the fashion accessories one would need, as well as a second hand bookstore and an extensive vinyl collection. She'd found it by accident one day and knew that it was exactly the kind of place Emery would like. And when they finished shopping, Micah was dropping Emery off at the music store for drum lessons with Fletcher before meeting her girlfriends for drinks.

Thinking about Fletcher made her giddy.

They hadn't taken a single picture the day before, but she didn't need them. Her mind was already full of memories of their visit to the tasting room, the dancing, the singing, *the kiss*. She was still reeling from the knowledge that he had written a song about her. Now when she listened to it—she'd played it on loop while getting ready that morning—she could see how it was inspired by her. Everything from the dark hair to her curves and the way their bodies fit so perfectly together. He had taken one of her most intimate and cherished nights and turned it into a love song. She'd wondered if other women imagined that he was singing about them too and felt evil knowing that she was the only one that inspired him that way.

Pressing her lips together to hide her smile, she let one hand brush over the dresses in front of her. It had been a long time since someone had gotten her this excited about dating. After Geoffrey, there were a few hits and misses, some good nights and some terrible ones. She hadn't put a lot of stock into hook-ups and never expected more than what she was willing to give them too.

With Fletcher, she knew it would always be so much more. For a while, she'd jokingly refer to him as 'the one that got away', but she'd never tried to hold onto him after their night together. It just so happened that in one night, he'd wormed his way under her skin with his adorable charm and callused hands. To think she had a second chance with him— as her favorite rockstar and the man she dreamed about— made Micah giddy. Add to that the fact that he'd kissed the hell out of her the day before and she was still vibrating with excitement.

This feeling? Better than almost anything else she'd ever experienced.

"Okay, how about this one?"

Looking over her shoulder, she smiled at the T-shirt Emery held up—Rainbow Brite sat astride Starlite, while the rest of the Color Kids stood in the background. "Only if they have it in my size too."

Emery grinned and then got to rummaging, while Micah turned back to the dresses. Her whole life, she'd been told to hide her curves and not wear anything that would accentuate the wide shape of her body. So now that she could make her own clothing decisions, she always turned to dresses and skirts. She liked flaunting her legs and thick arms, she liked dresses that cinched at the waist and moved when she did. She even liked plunging necklines, because her breasts were great and it would be a shame to hide them away.

While Emery picked up random things, Micah's thrift purchases were always things she could wear to work or nights out with her girls. Which was why she had a bunch of dresses spread out across the table, scrutinizing each one and making sure that she *would* actually wear them one day. Her eyes landed on the red dress, liking that it was casual and could be worn for any occasion, but specifically perfect for Christmas. While she'd outgrown the excitement around the holiday as a jaded young adult, Micah held it together for Emery. Her daughter loved the holiday and waited with bated breath for December to roll around. They'd already pulled out all the decorations with the intention of getting everything up in the first week. Despite her dislike for the season, Micah was a good mother and that meant she would pull out all the stops for Emery.

Including buying a red dress to wear for their annual mother-daughter hot cocoa date.

Even though they'd skipped Santa's Village a few years— following Hank's death—Micah was hoping to convince Emery to go back that year. The year after Hank died, they'd spent it with Micah's parents and it had been most unpleasant; they stressed Emery out about her clothes, eating and lifestyle habits. It was a whole mess. Another time, they'd gone with Sadie and Tatum to Telluride for the holidays and it was a perfect escape. Emery had been ready to meet the new Santa the year before, but changed her mind at the last minute.

While she'd never push her daughter, Micah knew that encouraging her to do things she used to like was a step in the healing process. She'd was back at Big Waves for the first time in four years. Emery might be able to handle Santa's Village too.

"I like that one, Mama," Emery said from behind her and her heart clenched at the use of the term. "The color will look good on you too."

"Yeah?" She held the red dress against her torso, striking a pose for her daughter. Emery rolled her eyes, but gave Micah a thumbs up before moving on.

Closing her eyes to savor the moment, Micah smiled to herself. When Emery was little, she only called her *Mama* for a few years. Obviously being around other kids introduced her to the *Mom* term and she switched. Every now and then, Emery would still call her Mama and Micah's heart would explode with love for her daughter. She might be fourteen going on forty, but her little girl was the light of her life.

With Emery in her line of vision, Micah continued to examine the dresses she'd set aside. Four different colored outfits lay in front of her, including the red one Emery had already signed off on. The black dress was a little fancier than she was used to, but it would join her collection of LBDs, so it was a must have. Especially with the sheer bottom half and the deep neck that would accentuate her cleavage. The lavender dress was sleeveless and reminded her of the one she wore the day before with Fletcher. He hadn't really said anything about her clothes, but she saw the way he looked at her. That was enough. The final dress was one that Sadie would be proud of her for even considering—a full length black wrap dress with large flowers, made of soft material and hugged every inch of her body. It also had a slit that would flash her legs and that made it even better. Given that she so rarely found sexy dresses like that in her size, Micah didn't even think twice about adding it to her pile. She'd find an occasion to wear it one way or another.

Gathering the dresses into their shopping bag, Micah set it to the side and tried on a few earrings. She eyed the bracelets, remembering how Fletcher kept the ones she'd left in his hotel room even though he was allergic to it. If she asked him for it, Fletcher would give them back, but she liked the idea of him always having a piece of her. Adding a few pairs of earrings to her selection, Micah smiled when Emery hurried over and dumped her things in the bag as well.

This was the one time Micah didn't give her daughter a budget. While she wasn't living paycheck to paycheck, she also didn't want Emery to think they had lots of money to splurge and spend as they pleased. She got a monthly allowance that she was very good with and on their thrifting days, Micah let Emery go wild. Besides, before they cashed out, they would always double check their choices, so she knew that even though Emery was picking up the randomest of things, half of them would stay in the store when they left.

"I think I'm done," Emery said, peering into the bag and gasped as she pulled out the black dress. "Damn, Mom. This is *hot*."

"Thought I'd take a chance, you know?"

"You'll look amazing in this."

"Thanks, kid," Micah told her daughter, blushing slightly at the compliment. She'd never been good at saying 'thanks' when people said something nice.

Emery narrowed her eyes. "You're hot, Mom. It's weird when my friends say it, but you're crazy beautiful."

Hand over her heart, Micah smiled. "I love you, Em."

"I love you too. Now can we please stop with the teary eyes? It's getting weird."

She laughed and pulled Emery in for a hug, sighing happily when she hugged her back. Everyone told her that the older her daughter got, the less affectionate she'd become.

And Micah was preparing for it, which meant never taking all the hugs and moments like these for granted.

"All right, let's sort through our piles," Micah said, blinking back tears as she and Emery went through their selection. Despite putting most of it aside, they still walked out of the store with three shopping bags full of things.

TATUM

Location for tonight:

address for The Loose Lasso

SADIE

Why are we going somewhere new?

TATUM

Because we've been through the pool of datable people at our usual haunts. Mama needs variety.

MICAH

So you picked a country bar?

TATUM

People in tight jeans, Mick. And a mechanical bull. It writes itself.

MICAH

We're in California, Tate, there are no cowboys. We've got surfers galore.

SADIE

Ugh, surfers are so gross.

TATUM

I see the surfer that broke your back is no longer of interest.

SADIE

I don't want to talk about it.

TATUM

....

MICAH

So Slutty Saturday at The Loose Lasso?

TATUM

That's fucking perfect. I hope this place pans out, or the double alliteration and innuendo would be for nothing.

SADIE

See you sluts tonight. Yeehaw!

"Are you enjoying your music lessons?" Micah asked once she and Emery were seated on the low wall outside their favorite ice cream shop, Lickity Splits.

Emery made a noncommittal sound and shrugged. "I don't know if Fletcher is enjoying teaching me, though."

"What do you mean?"

"He's being really nice, but I'm pretty sure I suck."

Micah smiled around a spoon of chocolate caramel swirl, because it was clear that Fletcher would never actually say 'you suck', but do everything in his power to help Emery improve.

"Maybe you should ask him what he thinks of your progress today."

"What if he says I should quit?"

"He won't," Micah insisted. Fletcher was sometimes too nice for his own good and hurting someone else like that was not his style. "But you're having fun, right?"

She shrugged again, staring into her cup of dark chocolate

ice cream. "I guess. Fletcher and Benson are great, they're super encouraging, but maybe I'm wasting my time and your money."

"Em." Micah nudged her daughter so she lifted her head. "Don't worry about other people, this is about *you*. Life is too short to wonder what other people think. Besides, I'm happy to spend however much it takes for you to find something you're enjoying. So, let me ask you again: are you enjoying music lessons?"

"Yes. Fletcher's cool, he's patient and really nice even when I screw up. Plus, Nico's there," she added the last bit with a smile, blush spreading up her neck.

Micah laughed softly, eating more of her ice cream as she watched her daughter. Emery's crush on Nico started pretty early on in their friendship, but she hadn't done a damn thing about it. Micah got it, though. Admitting to your *best friend* you liked them could go the wrong way and that would ruin everything.

"Are you excited about drama club auditions next year?" Micah asked, switching subjects because she knew there was no way Emery would talk about her *crush*.

"Yes! Only if they choose a really good play. I'm so tired of *Romeo & Juliet* and *A Midsummer's Night Dream*. There are so many other great plays out there."

Micah smiled at her excitement. Drama club was the other new thing in her daughter's life—along with music lessons—and she was passionate about it.

"What would you pick?"

She brightened instantly and grinned. "*Peter and the Starcatcher* for sure. Even *Pygmalion* is a good one."

"I think you should make a list and share it with the club, get ahead of their selection process."

"Maybe. I don't want to step on any toes."

Micah leaned against Emery and kissed the side of her

head. "Step on toes, Em, especially when you believe you've got something better to offer."

Emery giggled and dropped her head to Micah's shoulder as they continued eating their ice cream in silence. She was so proud of her kid and while she wanted to take credit for the way Emery turned out, a lot of it was her own doing. Emery was driven and passionate, she knew what she liked and didn't like, she was opinionated and confident. Every day she got to watch her little girl grow up was another great day in Micah's books.

After tossing their empty cups in the trash, Micah drove them to Big Waves. The plan was for Emery to spend the evening with Nico while Micah went out with the girls. Since it was a weekend, there were no issues with sleepovers and Nico's parents adored Emery enough to never complain about her. Before she'd even put the car in park, Emery was out and rushing into the store. Micah checked her reflection, smoothing down her hair and dabbing on some tinted gloss before hopping out of the car. Walking into the store, she was greeted by Fletcher's broad back encased in a black T-shirt with the sleeves pushed up to his elbows.

"Hey stranger," she said, smiling when he turned around so fast he almost lost his balance. His face brightened as he grinned, adjusting his glasses and looked her over. She was dressed in faded jeans and a thin sweater that was two sizes too large, but felt so cozy and comfy against her skin. But by the way Fletcher was looking at her, it was like she was wearing nothing.

"Never get sick of seeing you, Mick."

"Maybe don't undress me with your eyes so blatantly next time."

He laughed and looked over his shoulder before moving towards her. She arched an eyebrow, ready to ask him what was going on, but his mouth was pressed against hers.

Gasping softly, she gripped the sides of his T-shirt, fingers curling into the soft material as she parted her lips to let his tongue in. A low moan fell from his lips as she licked into his mouth, their bodies pressing against each other like there were magnets in their pants.

She broke the kiss, her chin scraping against Fletcher's beard and forced herself away from him. She might have laid down the *conditions* when it came to their relationship, but Micah knew she was the one who was going to completely fuck this up. Fletcher licked his lips and she blew out a frustrated breath, taking another step back.

"I should apologize, but I'm not sorry." He smirked, pushing his glasses up. "Emery said you're busy tonight, something about Slutty Saturdays?"

She snorted out a laugh. "My weekly night out with the girls. We go for drinks and get a little slutty."

His eyebrows and mouth dipped slightly. "How slutty?"

"Are you jealous, Fletch?"

"How slutty, Mick?" he repeated, eyebrows practically touching.

Taking two small steps forward, she twisted her fingers into the front of his shirt and tugged gently. "I would usually get pretty slutty with the last person to buy me a drink. But, I recently met this guy and I kinda like him, so I might refrain from getting slutty."

"Lucky guy," he grumbled, eyes slipping shut as she patted his stomach.

"Nico's Mom will pick the kids up later, so you don't have to worry about her. Okay?"

He opened his eyes to search hers, nodding slowly. "Have fun with the girls."

"I intend to," she whispered and then pushed onto her toes, stealing a quick kiss before she backed away. He shook his head, a slight smile tugging at his lips and she laughed as she stepped out of the store.

"There are no cowboys or cowgirls, there aren't even cows," Sadie announced as she finished doing a 360-look around the bar.

"I don't even want to know what you'd do if there were cows," Tatum said with a snort.

"The cowboys would then show up to wrangle them, and me, home."

Micah snorted at Sadie's response, but her friend wasn't wrong. A little eye candy wouldn't hurt.

"Okay, I'm getting drinks. What are we in the mood for?" Micah took her friend's orders—white wine all around—and walked up to let the bartender know. She heard someone whistle, but refused to turn around, because they definitely didn't deserve even a minute of her attention. When she returned to the table, Sadie and Tatum were glaring at each other. Sliding their wines over, Micah waved her hands in front of her friends' faces. "What happened while I was gone?"

"How's Em?"

Micah arched an eyebrow. "Em's fine."

"How are her drum lessons going?"

"Seriously?"

"I didn't want us to talk about it, but Sadie insists that we do," Tatum said with a dramatic huff.

Sadie rolled her eyes and turned to Micah. "Have you fucked the hot rockstar yet?"

"Stop it. It's girl's night and we don't talk about them tonight."

"Tell us if you've fucked him again and I'll let it go."

"No, Sadie. We have not fucked. We've been on *one* date and you know I don't put out after one date."

Tatum frowned as she turned to her. "Even with *the one*?"

"You too?"

"I mean…you said he was *the one*," Tatum said, shrugging as she lifted her wine glass to her lips.

Micah closed her eyes, inhaled deeply and released it as she focused on her friends. "Okay, let's get this out of the way. I like Fletcher, a lot. We're taking it slow and figuring it out one day at a time." But then the melody for "Mermaid" popped into her head and Micah groaned. "Also, years ago, he wrote a song about me."

Tatum and Sadie slapped the table simultaneously, eyes wide as they stared at Micah. "Shut the fuck up, "Mermaid" was about you?" Nodding, Micah picked up her wine and took a long swig. Sadie cackled and shook her head. "You got a mermaid tattoo because of that song, not knowing that it was meant for you. Classic."

"Okay, that's enough. Moving on."

Tatum's grin was annoying, but Micah was glad her friends were happy for her. "Speaking of rockstars, I'm working with this really amazing all-female queer band. They've got *two* drummers and they're so fucking amazing."

"Are they hot too?"

Micah snorted and nudged Sadie. "No sleeping with Tatum's clients, we've talked about this."

"But hot queer women are my catnip," Sadie whined. It was true. She didn't label herself or her sexuality, Sadie liked people and the hotter the better. Lucky for her, people liked Sadie too.

Tatum shook her head, a fond smile on her lips. "They're recording their demo tomorrow, you two should come. Bring Em too, I think she'll really dig them."

"Stop trying to steal the title of favorite auntie, *Tatum*."

"I don't have to steal it when I have it, *Sadie*."

Micah looked between her friends and smiled. "Does it help if I say both of you are my favorites?"

"No, but thanks for your love." Sadie clinked her glass against Micah's and took a large gulp before getting to her feet. "Bottle?"

At their nods, Sadie strutted over to the bar, drawing the attention of every single person on the way. Micah reached over and gave Tatum's arm a gentle squeeze. "You good, Tate?"

"Yeah. I think?" Tatum sighed and brushed her hair back, fingers fiddling with an earring. "Ran into Ambrose the other day and it was awkward."

"As in Benji's brother?" Micah asked, referencing Tatum's asshole ex-husband.

Tatum nodded. "He's been in San Diego for a few years now, apparently. He apologized, Mick. Like tears in his eyes, fingers dragging through his hair in frustration apologized."

"Oh shit." Micah knocked back her wine and forced a smile on her face as Sadie came back. Tatum and Ambrose had the most intense fling—maybe it was even love—before she met and married Benji. If Ambrose was apologizing, and if he was back, that could only mean…

"Here's to Slutty Saturdays!" Sadie hooted, derailing Micah's thoughts as she filled their glasses. "And here's to the sluttiest and bestest friends a girl could ever hope for."

micah

Just be with me.

AFTER THE MENTION of Ambrose and the look in Tatum's eyes, Micah texted her friend the next morning and announced her plans to spend the afternoon interrogating her. Since it was a Sunday, Emery tagged along as Micah drove them down to Starlight Studios. When Tatum branched out and started her own business, offering independent musicians a space to record and produce their music, she'd set it up twenty minutes outside Sirena Beach town limits. Micah and Sadie had been there every step of the way as Tatum bought a piece of land close to the beach and built the studio up from the ground.

She parked her car beside Tatum's in the small parking lot and followed Emery into the studio, the sounds of chatter and soft music filtering through the space. Jada, the receptionist, greeted Micah and gestured towards the recording rooms in the back. Leaving her daughter to do whatever she pleased, Micah followed the music to where Tatum was hunched over the mixing board. Tapping her knuckles against the door frame, Micah smiled as her friend straightened up to look at her.

"Hey you, where's the kid?"

"Wandering around," Micah said, hooking a thumb over her shoulder. "You doing okay?"

Tatum sighed heavily and nodded, forcing a smile onto her face. "We don't have to talk about it, you know."

"Do *you* want to talk about it? Because if you don't, Em and I can hang around for a bit and leave you to it."

Before Tatum could respond, loud laughter filled the room. Micah turned to the six women and waved as they came to a halt. Tatum chuckled and draped an arm around Micah's shoulders. "Ladies, this is my best friend Micah. Mick, these are the ladies that make up Pretty Ugly."

They introduced themselves and gushed about Tatum, making her best friend blush and wave them off. Then after a quick discussion, the band filed into the studio and closed the door. Micah had been in there enough times to know how Tatum worked, so she sat on the couch in the back and waited. After discussing what to do, the songs they wanted to try out and record that afternoon, Tatum left the band to their own devices. She dropped onto the couch beside Micah and stretched with a loud sigh.

"You know what's crazy? I was really happy to see Brose again. My first thought hadn't been about Benji or the past. I wanted to hug him."

Micah watched her best friend, letting her set the pace for this conversation. When they were in high school, Tatum and Ambrose had been a couple. They'd been obsessed with each other, stupidly in love and everyone thought they'd end up together forever. Hell, Tatum had already planned a future with Ambrose. Except, they were ignoring the fact that Ambrose was part of a slowly emerging boyband. In a time when pop music reigned supreme and boybands were all the rage, Double Toned were starting to get famous. When the band released their second album with the support of a big name music label, everything changed. Ambrose dropped out of high school to go on tour and their relationship fell apart.

That's when Benji appeared. Older, charming and sexy as well, Benji was the perfect distraction for Tatum. At first, nobody knew that Benji and Ambrose were related. He charmed and seduced Tatum, they dated all through college and then got married. On their wedding day, Ambrose appeared and threw everything into chaos. Micah still remembered that day, watching as Tatum processed the truth of her new life. But she loved Benji enough to not think twice about that relationship.

Until he started to hurt her.

"He apologized, like everything Benji did was his fault. *Then* he apologized for not being there for me before and walking away the way he did," Tatum said, rushing through her words. "He kept insisting that if he could, he would have stayed. That he would have ignored everything their management told them and come back to me."

Micah blew out a slow breath, watching Tatum. Ambrose was the love of her life and she lost him to music. Sometimes, she wondered if Tatum went into the business because of Ambrose, with the hopes of one day crossing paths with him again and understanding why he left the way he did.

"What's he doing in town anyway?"

Tatum hesitated, worrying her bottom lip before she said, "He came to see me."

"Tate…"

"I know! Okay, I know. I get it. It's a bad fucking idea and I know that it can all go wrong. Mick, it's *Ambrose*. He's like my Fletcher."

"I wasn't madly in love with Fletcher back then," Micah protested. She'd been slightly in love with the drummer back then, but not the way Tatum and Ambrose had been about each other.

"He's gotten even hotter, if that's possible."

"He was always my favorite member of Double Toned for a reason." Tatum laughed, but the sound was tinged with sadness and Micah squeezed her friend's knee. "So, what are you going to do now?"

Tatum shrugged, slumping back against the couch and dragged her hands over her face. After a long moment, Tatum glanced at Micah with a pout. "He's gone to LA for a few weeks, something about writing songs and producing music for someone else. But he'll be back."

Micah nodded, still watching Tatum cautiously. "You want another chance."

"Yes," Tatum admitted softly, refusing to meet her eyes now. "I didn't settle for Benji after Ambrose left, I loved him in a different way. But my heart has always belonged to Ambrose. He was my first everything."

Micah could recall with clarity the day Tatum barged into her childhood bedroom to tell her all about losing her virginity. Everyone thought they'd go the distance, but fame had other plans. Fame took away all their opportunities and chances for something more.

"He better not hurt you again, or he'll have to answer to me this time," Micah told her friend and got a watery smile in response.

"I'm scared, Mick. I'm scared that I'll give so much of myself to him and he won't do the same for me."

"Take it slow this time, maybe?"

Tatum sighed, heavy and dramatic. "We've never done anything slow."

"Trust me, we all remember." Micah laughed, dragging a hand through her curls, fluffing it up as she shifted on the couch.

"Enough about me, how are things with you and the rockstar?"

"It hasn't changed since last night," Micah explained, letting her mind wander to the brief kiss they shared the day before. "We're taking it slow. I realized this morning that all we know about each other is what we're like in bed. And even that, what we *were* like in bed sixteen years ago. I don't want our new…whatever it is to be just that."

"Aw, you like him."

Micah rolled her eyes and scoffed. "He's beautiful, Tate. Plus…glasses, *tattoos* and fuck, he wrote me a song."

"An award-winning song too."

Shaking her head, Micah put a hand over her heart to calm the racing. She knew how lucky she was to have this second chance with Fletcher, but she wasn't going to let it be a repeat of their past. They were going to get to know each other this time, actually build a relationship and make something of it.

"Now we need to find someone musical from Sadie's past and all three of us can have a second shot with musicians," Micah teased, making Tatum burst into laughter that shook the couch. This then cracked Micah up and they were falling over each other as they laughed.

"What the…are you two high?" Emery's voice broke through their giggling and Micah gasped in air as she sat up to look at her daughter. Tatum pushed herself into a sitting position as well and Emery shook her head. "Are you okay?"

"You're my favorite kid, you know that?" Tatum asked, hands stretched out with a wide smile.

"I'm the only kid you know, Aunt Tate."

"That doesn't take away the fact that you're my favorite."

Emery rolled her eyes and turned away to stare into the recording booth. "Oh my god, that's Pretty Ugly!" she squealed, bouncing in place.

"Wait, you know them?" Tatum pushed to her feet and helped Micah up.

"I'm *obsessed* with them."

Tatum pressed a button on the console and said, "Ladies, if you've got a minute, I'd like to introduce you to someone."

"Aunt Tate...what...no..." Emery's eyes were wide as saucers and Micah couldn't help but laugh at the shock on her face. The band walked through the side door, still in good spirits and Emery looked like she was going to pass out. "Hi," she squeaked out and the band grinned at her.

"Emery, meet Pretty Ugly. Ladies, this is the offspring of the afore...introduced best friend. Apparently she's *obsessed* with you."

"*Aunt Tate*," Emery groaned and using her daughter's shocked state, she took a few photographs. Turning to the band, Emery waved awkwardly. "It's really nice to meet you all. I *am* obsessed and have been since I heard "Caught"."

One of the women clapped Emery on the shoulder and Micah saw her daughter sway, which only added to her amusement. *Like mother like daughter*. After all, Micah had raised Emery on this kind of music, to enjoy and appreciate the way musicians created their magic.

"Mom," Emery whisper-shouted and Micah arched an eyebrow. "Can you take a picture, please?"

"Sure, sweetheart." She waited as they arranged themselves around Emery and then took a picture. Her daughter looked so excited and teary at the same time, but it would be the kind of picture that Emery would hold onto forever.

"All right, ladies. Are we ready to lay down some music?" Tatum asked and after a quick round of 'nice to meet you' and 'see you later', the band went back into the booth. Emery watched them with one hand over her mouth and then turned to Micah to release a squeal.

"I'm going to tell Nico that I met Pretty Ugly!" And then she was off, phone in hand and fingers moving across the screen at a crazy speed.

"You raised her good, Mick," Tatum said from where she was prepping the mixing board and Micah smiled.

As her friend got down to work, Micah sent Emery the pictures she'd taken. Then returned to the couch, reminiscing about her own life and what it had been like when she was that age. She'd gone through her boyband phase with Tatum and Sadie, then she'd fallen in love with Fletcher for one whole year. As long as Emery didn't follow a rockstar around on tour and didn't fall in love with them, Micah would be fine.

Hours later, Jada pushed a trolley filled with coffee and snacks into the studio. Emery was sitting with Tatum at the console, giving her two cents and squealing as Pretty Ugly recorded their songs. Micah had watched for a bit and then fell asleep, waking up to the sound of Emery singing along with the band. She was grateful for friends like Tatum, people who took Emery in as their own. Grateful for the kindness of strangers like the women of Pretty Ugly, for not treating her daughter like some kind of rabid fan. Truth was, Micah didn't have to worry about Emery that much. She might be young, but her daughter was more than capable of surviving this crazy world.

"I'm looking for Em—Mick?"

Micah's head snapped up at the sound of the familiar voice and her eyes widened when she found Fletcher standing in the doorway to the studio.

"Hey. What are you doi—" Micah started, but was interrupted by Emery's squeals as she charged past her to grab Fletcher's hand and pull him into the room.

"I didn't think you'd actually show up!"

"You told me that I would be an idiot to not show up,"

Fletcher explained and then glanced at Micah, one eyebrow arched. "So, what am I doing here?"

"Holy shit, you're Fletcher Kelley."

Micah and Fletcher turned to the voice coming from inside the recording booth to find all six women staring at them.

"What is going on?" Fletcher asked, looking slightly startled.

Micah gestured to everyone as she introduced them. "This is Tatum, one of my best friends. Starlight Studios is hers and that's Pretty Ugly, apparently Emery's *obsessed* with them."

"It's good to finally meet you, Fletcher," Tatum said with a wide smile.

"Likewise," he responded, eyes drifting back to Micah. "Can we…can I talk to you for a minute?"

"Mr. Kelley," one of the women from Pretty Ugly said, stopping Micah from going anywhere with Fletcher. "We know this is a weird request, but would you be up for a quick jam session?"

Micah nodded, smiling as Fletcher looked between her, Emery and the band. After a long moment, he nodded and joined the band in the recording booth. Micah shot Emery a glare and her daughter blushed, before coming over to stand beside her.

"I was so excited and sent him the picture you took. I thought it would be fun to have him here. He's like super famous and whatever," Emery rambled, tripping over her words as she explained herself. "I'm sorry, Mama, I should have asked you first."

Kissing the side of Emery's head, Micah sighed. "It's okay, kiddo. But you'll definitely have to explain this to Fletcher later."

Emery nodded, eyes downcast as she leaned into Micah. "Maybe we can take him for ice cream?"

Micah chuckled and squeezed Emery's shoulder. All of a sudden, the entire room was filled with loud music, drawing Micah's attention to the booth. She found Fletcher behind one of the drum sets, smiling at the rest of the band as he twirled his sticks as his foot worked the pedal for the bass. Her heart lurched at the sight, eyes watching his every move. When Fletcher glanced over, his smile widening, she knew that without a doubt she was going to *allow* herself to fall stupidly in love with him.

Tatum recorded the whole jam session while Micah watched in awe as Fletcher seamlessly moved through every song Pretty Ugly threw at him. She'd always known that there was a good reason why he was named Drummer of the Year six years in a row, but watching it in real time again? That was a whole other experience. When they were done, Fletcher posed for some more photographs with the band, signed a bunch of things and walked out to a pouting Emery.

"I'm sorry, Fletch. I didn't mean to make this awkward."

"It's all good, kid. I had fun. Startling at first, but fun," he told Emery, giving her arm a squeeze. When he looked up at Micah, he smiled. "Are you ladies done for the day?"

"We could be," Micah told him, hands shoved into the pockets of her cotton shorts.

"Oooh, you up for some ice cream, Fletch?" Emery asked, beaming at both of them.

Fletcher shrugged, adjusting his denim jacket. "I could eat ice cream."

Micah smiled and shook her head slightly, glancing at Tatum. "Up for some ice cream, Tate?"

"We've still got some work to do, so you three have fun," Tatum said with a wink and not so subtly waved Micah off. They would talk about this Ambrose thing later, maybe with Sadie on her side too. While their third friend could get quite aggressive about relationships and the drama that went with it, Sadie sometimes brought clarity to every situation.

Grabbing her things, Micah followed an excited Emery and Fletcher out to the parking lot. Without even asking either of them questions about it, Emery climbed into Fletcher's truck and buckled herself in. Fletcher smirked and gave Micah's hand a gentle squeeze. She poked him in the side and then climbed into her car and led the way to Lickity Split.

At the ice cream shop, Fletcher bought them all ice cream and after a quick thanks, Emery was gone—something about seeing friends and going to spend time with them—leaving her and Fletcher alone.

"Is everyone in your life trying to set us up?" he asked, hand on her lower back as he guided her towards a table set up outside.

She chuckled, slipping into her seat. "Tatum was definitely trying, I don't think Em was doing anything on purpose. Was she?"

"Would it be so bad if she was?"

"I guess not..." she trailed off, eating some of the ice cream with a slight frown on her face.

"I'm okay with us taking our time, by the way," he said, drawing her attention to his beautiful face. "But I'm also glad I get to spend some time with you today."

"Me too. And you know what I was thinking...we don't know a whole lot about each other."

Fletcher arched an eyebrow and smiled. "What do you wanna know, Mick?"

"Strawberry ice cream, really?"

He glanced at his cup overflowing with pink ice cream and laughed. "Don't knock it 'til you try it."

"It's so pink, I'm afraid that if I eat it, I'll be pooping pink for days."

"What about you, huh? Chocolate and caramel, so predictable," he shot back with a laugh.

"Better predictable than disgusting."

"Whoa." He held up one hand, a fake gasp following. "I like this aggressive side of you."

She rolled her eyes and laughed, licking her spoon clean and enjoying the way his eyes narrowed at the action. She repeated it, slower this time and he growled. "So—" Micah licked the spoon again with a smirk "—you're into strawberries and what else?"

He hesitated, his eyes still locked on her mouth and after a long moment said, "Beer over whiskey, wine on some days."

"And you like to cook," she added.

"Especially if it's for someone else."

"What's your go-to dish?"

He finally turned his attention away from her mouth, eating his ice cream as he pondered her question. Fletcher squinted against the setting sun. "Pasta seems like a safe and solid bet. Can't really go too wrong if you've got all the right ingredients."

"Like what you made for us that night?"

Nodding slowly, his eyes darted everywhere before settling on his ice cream. "I have to admit, Mick, sitting here with you, talking about random shit is hard when you're so distracting."

"What would you rather we do, Fletch?"

He turned those beautiful eyes on her and Micah inhaled sharply at the way he stared. "Give me your free time," he whispered. "I'm about to be busy in the evenings, but I want us to spend some time together."

"Yeah? What are we going to do, Fletch?"

"Anything. Everything. Just be with me, Mick."

She nodded slowly, feeling his desire for her in every word. "Okay, Fletch, I'll be with you."

fletcher

You want it to be twirly?

FLETCHER HAD SETTLED into accepting that his Decembers would be quiet and uneventful. That he would work at the shop during the day and roam the Village every evening as Santa. Nothing in the world could have prepared him for the appearance of Micah George and her spitfire of a daughter. Now, he was making adjustments in his life and changing schedules. He was making *plans* so he could actually spend time with Micah. So far only Benson and his bandmates knew that something was happening, because he didn't want to jinx it. There were moments when Fletcher would open his text conversation with Erin to tell her, but then stop himself. What was he going to say? *The love of my life is back? I said I never wanted to get married again, but I lied? She's here, the woman of my dreams?* In all their years of being friends, he'd never talked about *anyone* that way before. She would be worried and probably hop on the next flight out to make sure he wasn't falling apart.

Instead, he was focusing on getting his outfit for *Rockstar Santa* put together.

Flora, according to Hank, was a Sirena Beach fixture.

Benson talked about her like she was a witch, that she'd been in town since the moment it came into existence. Fletcher thought everyone was losing their minds, until he met her. Formidable even though she was half his size, Flora could be all of the things rumors and stories said she was. But he was instantly drawn to her. She'd been Hank's tailor when he took on the role of Santa in town. And with the responsibility passed onto Fletcher, she was now *his* tailor.

Which wasn't the craziest thing he'd ever heard. During his time with The Rescuers, he had a tailor, an assistant, a manager, an agent and then a whole heap of other people who catered to his every whim and fancy. Unlike his band-mates, Fletcher didn't take his team for granted. In fact, they often had to beg him to give them work. He never under-stood the concept of having a battalion of people doing every-thing for him when he was capable of going down to the pharmacy to refill his meds.

But Flora? He wasn't going to trade her in for anything. In fact, when she wasn't putting together his Santa outfits, she was also stitching him new shirts. Flora made fun of his flannel wardrobe, but expertly crafted his clothes for him. Fletcher didn't have too many memories of his grandmothers, so he'd put Flora into that role whether she wanted it or not. Especially since she had opinions about everything in his life, including how he needed to date, get married and have a million children. In Flora's mind, Fletcher was young enough to be a father. Little did she know that he was pushing fifty and hadn't even considered parenthood until Emery George walked into his life.

"Quit daydreaming and tell me what we're doing," Flora said, tossing a ball of wool at him, making him drop his phone. "I've only got a few days to whip this up."

"Why are you so violent?"

"Because you're wasting my time mooning over whoever is on the other end of that *thing*."

Like most people her generation, Flora didn't trust smartphones. She still had a rotary phone hanging in her kitchen, one with a long cord that was so twisted up he was surprised she could hear anything through it. Fletcher had attempted to untangle it a few times, but realized it was pointless. Flora didn't mind the chaos, so he'd let her live in it.

"I'm Rockstar Santa this year," he told her, checking his phone for damage before opening up his gallery for the picture he'd saved. "I was thinking a long coat I can leave open."

Flora adjusted her glasses and peered at the screen, a naughty smirk playing on her lips. "That Kurt Russell always had a special something."

Fletcher made a face and took the phone back quickly. The picture of Kurt Russell from *The Christmas Chronicles* was a pretty good description of how he wanted his coat to look. Functional and sexy, because Fletcher was hoping Micah would like him in it.

"It doesn't need to be that fluffy, obviously. I'm planning to leave it open in front."

"Are you planning on going naked? I don't think this town needs to see all of you hanging out."

"Jesus, Flora," he groaned and rubbed his forehead, dropping into the chair beside her work station. "*Rockstar*, remember. Jeans and a T-shirt."

"Rockstars in my day walked around naked a lot. And moved their hips like they were humping the air. You doing any of that?"

Staring at her for a long moment, he tried to erase the visual Flora had put in his head. "I'm wearing clothes under the coat."

She rolled her eyes and waved him off. "How long are we thinking?"

"Shins?

"You want it to be twirly?"

"Uh…sure?"

She rolled her eyes and sketched it out. Fletcher smiled as he watched her mumble to herself, forehead crinkling as her pencil moved smoothly across the page. When she was done, Flora grabbed her tape measure and stood up.

"Up you go, *rockstar*," she said and directed him to stand in a spot that was free of furniture. He'd done this with her enough that he knew how it worked. Stretching his arms out and spreading his feet, Fletcher waited as Flora measured him. Once she was done, she waddled back to her chair and mumbled something again before setting her pencil down.

"I'll also need a new hat."

"What happened to the last one?"

"Gave it to a kid." Fletcher winced at the glare Flora shot him. "He said something about not getting any gifts that year and I felt bad."

"You and Hank…bleeding hearts," she grumbled. "I'll make you a few this time, don't go handing them out to kids with sob stories."

"I'll do my best, no promises."

Flora sighed, a heavy dramatic one that seemed to go on forever, before she was on her feet again. "Now be gone, so I can work on this masterpiece."

"You're the best, Flora."

"Don't sweet talk me, young man. I know your type."

He chuckled as he wrapped one arm around Flora and squeezed her shoulder gently. "What type is that?"

"Charming all the older ladies because you think we're into this wild untamed look."

"You said you liked my hair like this!"

"Would it kill you to comb it once in a while? And that beard...do something about it."

He pretended to look offended, but when Flora flashed him a playful smirk, he couldn't stop his laugh from bursting out.

"I'll keep that in mind when I come back."

"Two days," she reminded him, then nudged him. "Now go. Do whatever it is rockstars do when they're not harassing old ladies."

Fletcher laughed and dropped a kiss to the top of Flora's head before stepping away. He caught the edge of her mouth curling into a smile, but didn't say anything. With his phone in hand, he walked out of Flora's house, with the hopes of seeing Micah.

FLETCHER

I remember someone saying they'd be with me…

MICAH

That someone was clearly misguided.

Because she's booked back-to-back sessions and is hiding in the restroom to get a break.

FLETCHER

Well, that won't do.

Do you need a rescue?

MICAH

I wish. *sad face emoji*

I know you're busy this evening, and while I
haven't asked and am very curious, I might
have some time after dinner?

FLETCHER

I might be able to swing that.

MICAH

I promise that I'll get better at making time
for us.

His heart stuttered at Micah's use of the word *us*, because
that's what he was hoping they would be. An *us*, a *we*…
Micah and Fletcher, together. It was silly to get his hopes up
and wish for these things so early, but the way he felt about
her made him want all of that so badly.

FLETCHER

You've got an important job, Mick. Don't
apologize.

MICAH

And a very needy teenager.

FLETCHER

I happen to like said teenager, so don't shit
on her.

MICAH

Oh god, is this what it's going to be like?
The two of you ganging up on me?

FLETCHER

Probably.

And I like the sound of that, actually.

He liked the sound of that *a lot*. The more he weighed the
situation and where their relationship might be going, the
more Fletcher thought about being a sort of father to Emery.

Sure, all of that depended on whether or not the teenager wanted anything to do with him. But Fletcher liked to think that she did like him. Even just a little bit. He hoped that she would continue to feel the same way when they told her about their relationship. Or whatever he and Micah were doing.

FLETCHER

Question for you, if you're still hiding out.

MICAH

My client is late, actually. So shoot.

FLETCHER

What are we?

MICAH

Human beings.

FLETCHER

eye roll emoji

MICAH

A man and a woman?

FLETCHER

You're impossible.

MICAH

Nooooooo, I am Micah.

Pressing his lips together, he shook his head. He was sitting in the driver's seat of his truck outside Flora's house, texting and not giving a shit what people might have to say. He had a meeting with Jensen in a bit to discuss everything that was happening at Santa's Village. So Fletcher was giving himself a little while to relax before the next thing took all his brain space.

MICAH

To answer your question, we're figuring it out.

Right. That's all we are right now.

MICAH

Do you want us to be something else?

FLETCHER

We're figuring it out is a good place to be.

MICAH

Uh huh…what's going on?

FLETCHER

Nothing. Crossed my mind and I wanted to ask.

MICAH

side eye emoji

You'll tell me if something ELSE is on your mind?

FLETCHER

You'll be the first to know.

MICAH

Okay. *kissy face emoji*

My client just arrived, so I have to go.

FLETCHER

Go change the world, Mick.

MICAH

kissy face emoji *kissy face emoji* *kissy face emoji*

With his phone still open to their conversation and tucked into the cup holder in his truck—so he could see the emojis blowing kisses his way—Fletcher drove to meet with Jensen Mars about the next three weeks of his life. While they usually met at town hall, Jensen had insisted on meeting outdoors that day and Fletcher was glad for it.

The crew was already putting up Santa's Village when he pulled up beside Jensen's flashy sports car. Pocketing his phone, Fletcher took a minute to admire the design. While the concept stayed mostly the same—a candy lane decorated Main Street covered the entire space, with shop fronts on either side where local businesses could set up their wares and sell it during the three weeks Santa's Village was open— the decorations and designs changed slightly every year.

Jensen was in the middle of a huddle with men in hard-hats, shouting and pointing as he gave everyone directions. Fletcher stayed against his truck, watching everything unfold. He'd been doing this for four years and it still blew him away. The fact that people spent so much time and money on Christmas every year was quite unbelievable. And the fact that a small town like Sirena Beach had a Santa's Village that brought people from all over the state, and sometimes the country, was quite incredible. Fletcher had to admit that despite his hesitation about taking on the job and moving to the beach town, he liked how much they cared about the community.

Even though he'd grown up in a small town, he couldn't remember Christmas ever looking like this. And they had actual snow, none of the fake stuff that sometimes made him sneeze continuously. Christmas in the Kelley household had also never been a big deal. Fletcher had been to enough friends' homes where they had decorations covering every surface and he'd seen all the movies about the holiday to know *what* Christmas was supposed to be like. But to his family, it seemed frivolous and unnecessary.

His father would build the life size nativity set for the town every year, while Fletcher and his siblings watched in awe as everything came together so beautifully. That was the extent of Christmas spirit in their home. While they got gifts on Christmas morning, because there were four kids, they only got one each. And it was only when he was a teenager that Fletcher realized all the gifts were the same price. Whatever they got his eldest brother would be the benchmark and the rest would get gifts within the same price range. So often the gifts weren't even what the kids wanted, but Fletcher and his siblings knew better than to complain.

When The Rescuers was formed and they celebrated their first Christmas together, Fletcher was introduced to the magic of holiday cheer. Everything from the music to eggnog, mistletoe and a giant Christmas tree. Not to mention the thoughtful gifts and fun that came with the season. As their fame increased, they were invited to bigger Christmas parties where there were more gifts and large trees. One year, they were even in Rockefeller Center for the tree lighting. For Fletcher—a young man who had always craved the exciting Christmas—that night was one of the greatest in his life.

Once they were picked up by a record label, Fletcher actually convinced the producers and executives to let them record a few Christmas songs one year. Anything that would allow him to spread his cheer as much as possible. The EP didn't do as well as they hoped, but Fletcher didn't care. He'd been able to perform his favorite Christmas songs with his favorite people. And that was more than enough.

Fletcher might have protested and tried to refuse when Hank enlisted him for this job four years ago. But secretly, he was excited. The holidays were about family for everyone else, but for Fletcher it was about the joy that he felt. His chest always felt like it was going to expand and explode with how much he loved the time of year. Add the fact that little kids got so excited when they saw Santa and his elves, and Fletcher's life was made.

The only nuisance was the dumb outfits Jensen and the town made him wear, but Fletcher had decided that it was all part of the job and he would suffer for…art.

"Fletcher Claus!" Jensen called out, breaking him from his thoughts about Christmases past.

"I hate you," he grumbled and with his hands shoved into his pockets, he walked over to where Jensen was handing out the last few instructions to the crew.

"You ready for this?"

"Yes?"

Jensen laughed and clapped Fletcher on the back, both of them watching as the guys lifted one stretch of designed shop fronts upright. This was the other thing he liked about being Santa—he got to watch the Village come to life.

"How's your outfit coming along?"

"You know Flora. Gave me grief the whole time."

Jensen smirked. "But she's the best there is."

"Yeah. So…what's the plan this year?"

As much as he wanted to hang around and talk about Flora, Fletcher also wanted to get back to the shop in time for Emery and Nico's lesson. And then *hope* that he could see Micah when she wrapped up for the day. He'd allowed himself to get distracted by Christmas and holiday cheer, but Fletcher still itched to hold Micah. Nothing else, just hold her. Maybe kiss her. Play with her soft curls. Trace her tattoos and kiss her soft brown skin.

"…then you can probably do what you usually do," Jensen continued and Fletcher blinked when he realized he missed everything.

"Uh, one more time?"

"What?"

"Got distracted, could you say it all again?"

Jensen arched an eyebrow, a playful smile tugging at his lips. "Were you thinking about Micah George?"

"The plan, Mars. Lay it out for me."

"You can tell me, you know. I'm a really good wingman."

Sighing, Fletcher shook his head. "I don't need a wingman."

"Oh?"

"Can we just…" he started and saw the look on Jensen's face and decided to throw the man a bone. "I don't need a wingman, because I already have her."

"You…bagged the elusive Micah George?"

"Don't fucking say *bagged*, that's disgusting. I told you we have history and apparently some unfinished business," he explained and shot Jensen another look before waving a hand at him. "Now, back to the plan for this year."

Jensen stared at him for a long moment, still smiling like the Cheshire Cat as he said, "The mayor wants to do the grand opening in three days, cutting the ribbon and the whole shebang. She's got some special guests coming this year, so before everyone shows up, she wants to take them around. And Santa needs to be there too." Fletcher nodded, even if he didn't want to glad-hand rich people the mayor brought over every now and then. "So we'll do that a little earlier, then the opening ceremony with the kids' choir doing their usual song and dance. Then you and your elves can wander around as you please."

Fletcher sighed, already tired from how much work this would be. He enjoyed and loved it, no doubt. But it was exhausting.

"Our deal is still on, yeah?"

Jensen made a face, but nodded. "He'll be there on the first day too, so you two can work out your schedules."

The first two years, Fletcher had worked all seven days of the week and found that it was too much for him to handle. So he had an agreement with Jensen—Fletcher would work five days of the week and take two days off. It could be any five days, as long as he got time to rest and recover before the next week rolled around. Jensen and the mayor hadn't been happy about it, but Fletcher knew that he needed to put his foot down. Or they'd take him for granted. Sam, the replacement Santa, could be Fletcher's body double. Living in the town over, he was happy to take on the job for extra cash. And Fletcher was happy to have some time off.

"Great. I'll see you in three days." Fletcher not so gently punched Jensen in the arm. "Respect goes a long way, Mars. Don't talk about Micah, or *anyone*, that way."

"I know. I'm sorry," he said with a sigh.

Fletcher gave him one last look before heading back to his truck. His phone buzzed in his pocket and Fletcher pulled it out as he climbed behind the wheel.

MICAH

I'm sorry, Fletch. Raincheck?

I will make it up to you.

sad face emoji *kissy face emoji*

FLETCHER

Get home safe, Mick. And I'll hold you to that. *kissy face emoji*

fletcher

Be my love bug. I'll be your stallion.

DESPITE BOTH OF them agreeing to spend their free time together, it seemed pretty impossible. It wasn't just Micah who was busy, in prepping for his Santa duty, Fletcher had also stretched himself a little thin. Flora had finished his coat and hat, so he picked them up and dressed up for the mayor. She liked it, but wanted more *Christmas*, so Flora stitched faux wool at the ends of the sleeves and along the front, she even added big gold buttons to spruce it up a little more. Then made sure the mayor knew that was all she was willing to do. Nobody messed with Flora or questioned her work, so the mayor signed off on the outfit. Then her guests arrived a day early, while Santa's Village was still being set up, so Fletcher had to show up with his elves for the walk-through.

Texts and brief phone calls were all they managed for three days, but it was honestly more than enough. He was greedy, wanting to talk to Micah, eat with her, cook with her and just *be with her*. Maybe it was his age, maybe it was that he wanted more, but sex was the last thing on his mind. He liked kissing and touching and holding Micah, everything else could wait.

On his first day as Santa, Micah showed up at Big Waves during lunch. Armed with a beautiful smile, clothes suited for a corporate setting and a bag of food; she was the best sight of his day. They sat in his office, with the windows wide open, and ate their sandwiches while she told him all about her clients that morning. Despite being distracted by the way her mouth formed words and how good she looked, he actually registered most of what she was saying. As far as he could remember, she'd always been passionate about the things that meant something to her. Whether it was music or food, now her kid and her job, Micah was all in.

And he loved that about her.

The next morning, he showed up at the George house armed with coffee. Even though he was exhausted from the first night as Santa, he had decided he was going to do this. *Every moment, right?* He'd waited in his truck while Emery had climbed onto her bicycle and left for school. Only then did he ring the doorbell. Because as much as he wanted to throw the *conditions* out the window, he knew the rules were important to Micah.

"Oh god, what are you doing here?"

Fletcher laughed at the half-dressed state she was in—hair sticking up, she wore only a long T-shirt that stopped mid-thigh and sleep marks were still on her face.

"Brought you coffee," he said, eyes drinking her in with a wide smile. "And I was hoping to find out what you look like first thing in the morning."

She grunted and took a coffee from him, before turning around and walking away. Fletcher followed, eyes dropping to the stretch marks on the back of her thighs and up to the slight curve of her ass visible under the hem of her shirt. Forcing himself to focus, he instead took in the state of the house. Unlike the first time he'd been there, the place was a mess. In one corner, half a Christmas tree was set up. Boxes of decorations were strewn about, open with things spilling out. The dining table was covered in papers and the cushions that had once been on the couch were all over the floor.

"What happened here?"

"Christmas," she grunted again, dropping onto the couch as she took the first sip of her coffee.

"What's wrong with Christmas?"

"Nothing. Everything. I don't know."

He watched her for a moment, then lowered himself onto the coffee table in front of her. The idea that she wasn't a fan of the holidays hadn't even crossed his mind. He'd been so excited to show up on her front stoop one night dressed as Santa, but now that decision would have to be tabled. Outside of his family—and their reasons were still quite unknown—Fletcher didn't know anybody who didn't like Christmas. It was one of his favorite times of the year and he liked everything that came with it.

Then it made him wonder if she *hated* the holiday or didn't enjoy it. And if him being Santa would be a deal-breaker for this thing they were figuring out.

"Need some help?"

She blinked slowly and shook her head. "I'd rather we spend time together doing anything else. Besides, this is what Em and I do every year. It takes us weeks to get everything up and even longer to take everything down."

"If you need assistance, you know where to find me," he told her and Micah smiled, a soft and sleepy one that trans-formed her face. She scooted forward and climbed halfway into his lap, their lips meeting in a slow kiss. He hummed into the kiss, free arm sliding around her waist. "Morning."

"Thank you for bringing me coffee, Fletch. And seeing you first thing is a pretty good treat too."

He smiled and kissed her again. "All your free time, remember?"

"I seriously wish I had more free time." She huffed and dropped her head to his shoulder, fingers moving through his hair. "But I have a session near the shop tomorrow evening, if you're not busy."

"As long as it's before six, I'm yours."

He wondered if she'd get tired of him working every evening for the rest of the month.

She yawned and said, "I'll be there by four."

As promised, Micah was waiting outside Big Waves at 4 p.m. armed with a picnic basket that was bursting at the seams. She was wearing a beautiful smile—it lit up her entire face, brightening her eyes and drawing his attention to the smattering of freckles she'd developed living in a beach town.

The woman he'd seen in the crowd sixteen years ago had been breathtaking, it's why he'd singled her out and invited her back. The woman he was looking at in the parking lot of his music store was heart-stopping.

"Hey rockstar," she greeted him as he walked up to where she was leaning against his truck. "You ready for the best two hours of your life?"

"I already had the best two hours. More in fact. How are you going to top that?"

Her eyebrows dipped in confusion, but then she snorted out a laugh. "Aren't you the romantic."

"I wrote you a song, didn't I?"

"Indeed you did. An award-winning song too."

"For an award-winning woman," he added and leaned in to press a soft kiss to the corner of her mouth. "All right, where are you taking me?"

She held a hand out, blush rising up her neck and cheeks. "Come with me."

Fingers linked, palms pressed together, they headed down the boardwalk and towards the section of the beach where the concrete vanished into sand. As much as he loved living in Sirena Beach, Fletcher did not enjoy finding sand in all his clothes. So he was about to protest, when she directed them away from the beach itself and towards a set of picnic tables.

"Ta da!" She set the basket on the table and gestured towards the area with a wide grin. "I used to come here on hard days when I needed a distraction from life and all the chaos of it."

He nodded and sat down, their hands still linked. "Seems like a good place to be distracted."

She stepped between his spread legs and smiled, squeezing his hand. "This table has seen more than a few of my tears."

He had so many questions, but Micah released his hand to unpack the basket. Fletcher watched her, taking in the way her smile was authentic and her excitement palpable. There were obviously lots of dark parts of her life that she didn't like talking about, but he hoped that one day she would be open to sharing some of that with him.

"Okay, we've got smoothies and cookies for all the sugar rush," she started, ignoring his silent pleas to share everything about her past. "And we've got sandwiches if you want something a little more substantial."

He tugged Micah back towards him, gently pulling her into his lap, one arm snaking around her waist. "Cookies and smoothies, always."

"Man after my own heart." She grinned and kissed the side of his head, lifting off his lap briefly to grab the smoothies. Without asking him, because she already knew what he'd pick, she handed him the pink one and kept the purple one for herself.

He took a sip of his drink, the tarty goodness of the strawberry hitting him instantly. Smiling, he enjoyed the feel of her leaning against him and let his eyes wander over her exposed arms.

"Tell me about these tattoos."

"Which ones?"

"All of them."

She laughed and stretched her left arm out, twisting it slightly as she examined the random smattering of ink. "I saw this flower band at the shop when I went to get my mermaid tail and loved it so much. So a few years later, I got someone else to do it for me," she said as she pointed at the flowers that wrapped around her arm below the elbow. Smiling, she dragged her finger down to the one that read *Emery* in a messy font. "When she was six, Emery told me that I should get a tattoo of her. We settled on her name and handwriting instead."

"What about these two?" Fletcher traced the speech bubbles and then the safety pin.

"The speech bubbles are in honor of my job and working through my own stutter. Some days can be harder than others, but we push through. The pin is about solidarity, about standing by those who are marginalized and providing support no matter what."

Soon after Brandy went through her transition, she'd gotten a similar tattoo as well, but he'd never thought to ask. But now it made sense. Micah wanted to support those like herself who were often mistreated and pushed aside because they were *different*, the same way Brandy felt about the world today.

"The origami elephants are also for Emery. I've got a couple more on this arm too," she said, holding out her right arm to show him the cute little stick figures of a mother and daughter.

"You made a special kid, Mick."

She grinned, leaning against him as she nodded. "I take full credit for how fantastic she turned out, but she did get *some* of my ex's genetics and I'm sort of grateful for that."

"She's all you, baby," he added softly and then arched an eyebrow when she turned to him with the most adorable glower.

"Absolutely not."

"She's not all you?"

"*Baby.*" Micah shook her head and took a long sip of her smoothie. "Geoffrey used to call me that. Always sounded so condescending."

Fletcher couldn't even stop the growl that slipped out. "Maybe I can reclaim it."

"Maybe."

He hated that her asshole ex had ruined so many things. Sure *baby* was a little silly of a term of endearment, but it rolled off the tongue easily. Fletcher would call Micah whatever she wanted. Hell, she could stay *Mick* for the rest of eternity if she didn't want to be called anything else.

She pulled out her phone, typing furiously with one hand while Fletcher looked over her shoulder: *terms of endearment for your partner that are not baby.* "Okay, here we go... beau, flame, love bug, hunk, stallion, my man or my girl, bubba."

"I would like to be known as your stallion." She shook her head and he grinned, pressing a kiss to her shoulder. Dropping his voice to a whisper, he added, "Come on, *love bug*. We both know how much you like to ride me."

"Do we? I don't remember this."

He snorted and squeezed her hip. "Would you like a refresher?"

"These terms are terrible," she said, ignoring his question.

"Mick, be my love bug. And I'll be your stallion."

She turned to look at him, eyes fixed on his and then shook her head. "No."

"Then I guess you'll have to be *Mick* forever."

Instead of responding, she rolled her eyes and sucked on her smoothie loud enough for it to be grating. When he pinched her side gently, she squeaked and pushed her elbow against his chest.

"Resorting to violence now? You're better than that, love bug."

"You're unbelievable," she muttered, but he saw the corner of her lip curve up into a smile before she took a sip of her smoothie.

"I say that about you all the time." He smiled at her snort before she shifted on his lap to face him fully. "Love bug."

She rolled her eyes, but her smile was still evident. "We'll work on the nicknames later."

"What do you wanna work on now?"

"Us being here together."

He nodded and kissed her, smiling as Micah's arm wrapped around his neck. He never imagined that he'd find someone to feel this way about, to have conversations about nicknames and go on midday dates with. After his marriage fell apart, meeting women became something of a challenge. Fletcher was either too old for half the single women or he didn't fit into the 'handsome, sexy and charming' bracket they were all looking for. To cross paths with Micah again, to have her want him the way she did that one night many years ago, was pretty fucking special. And he wasn't going to fuck it up.

It didn't matter that he was forty-six, waking up every morning to texts from Micah made him feel like a teenager. Even during the work day, he'd catch himself smiling at texts or pictures on his phone. He'd never used his phone as much as he did now because of her. She was changing his life all over again and he was sure that she had no idea how much. He loved it. He loved *her*.

The thought caught him so off guard one afternoon while he was prepping for music lessons.

Sixteen years ago, when they had spent that night together, Fletcher had felt something akin to love tugging at his heart. He was convinced that was the reason why he was so disappointed when she was gone when he woke up. He'd written a song about her, for crying out loud. Nobody did that unless they loved someone or had their heart broken. He knew that it was too soon to fall in love, especially since they were only getting to know each other. But there had been a string that connected them for the last sixteen years that was now taut and stronger than ever before.

A string that kept drawing him back to her.

Thanks to Sam, his Santa double, taking the next two days, it was his first day off that week. Fletcher had texted Micah in the morning, asking her to meet him at Mermaid Mart when she finished work. The plan was simple—go grocery shopping, return to his house and make themselves dinner. He had never been the kind of guy to plan fancy dates or do anything extraordinary. And from everything he'd gleaned about Micah, she was the same way. He was also itching to get her alone and into his house. Whether the night ended with them in bed or not was besides the point, he wanted to be able to touch her and not have to worry about time limits or people catching them in the act.

Sneaking around wasn't as fun as it sounded when she suggested it the first time.

"Hey you."

He turned at the voice, pushing off the side of his truck when Micah appeared. "Damn, love bug," he muttered.

She was draped in a lavender dress with tiny white flowers, thick straps holding the whole thing up. The dress hugged her breasts and fell down to her knees, not flaunting the rest of the delicious body he had mapped years ago. Fletcher did a slow sweep of her, spending a little extra time staring at her chest before lifting his eyes to hers.

"Seriously?" she asked, one hand on her hip, smirking at him.

"You're a treat for the eyes." She rolled her eyes at him and Fletcher gently tugged her into his arms. "Missed you these last few days."

"Missed you too, Fletch," she whispered, wrapping her arms loosely around his neck.

"You ready for an adult date night?"

"Oh, what makes it *adult*?"

"You'll have to wait and find out." He chuckled and kissed the tip of her nose. Fletcher locked their hands together as he tugged her into the store, one hand reaching for a shopping cart.

"Tease," she grumbled and released his hand to walk ahead of him. "So, what are we making tonight?"

"Steak and potatoes. It's comfort food."

"And dessert?"

You, he thought to himself and smiled. "Whatever you're in the mood for."

With a lingering glance, she nodded and then walked off, leaving him alone with the cart. He chuckled as he walked to the meat section, grateful that he'd called ahead so they would have the cut he wanted ready for him. A quick conversation with the butcher later, Fletcher grabbed the potatoes and pushed the cart through the aisles until he found Micah staring into the display window of the bakery section.

"I feel like we deserve pie, but I can't decide which one we should get."

He came up behind her and peered into the selection. "Apple pie and ice cream is always a safe bet."

"They've also got rhubarb and strawberry," she said, leaning back against him.

"What about we go for something both of us like with the chocolate pie."

"Isn't that a little boring?"

He kissed the side of her head and smiled. "Nothing is boring when it's with you, love bug."

Micah huffed, but he caught the slight smile, before she told the lady behind the counter what they wanted. With everything paid for, they hopped into his truck and headed back to his place. Even though it was the first time she'd come to his house, Micah made herself comfortable by kicking off her shoes and wandering through the space.

"You know, a long time ago, Emery and I visited Hank here. I don't remember it looking this nice."

He followed her through the house, smiling as she touched bookshelves, fingers brushing over the photographs on the wall. To think that she'd been in the same place he'd spent so much time blew his mind. How was it that in the last sixteen years, Fletcher and Micah had never once crossed paths when she knew such a big part of his life?

"First order of business when I moved in was to fix up this place."

"Drummer of the year, incredible chef and talented handyman," she said, spinning around to smile at him as they stepped into the kitchen. "Is there anything you *can't* do?"

"Nope. I'm an all round awesome person."

Micah laughed and closed the gap between them, her hands cupping his face as she pulled his mouth to hers. "I'm honored to know this awesome person."

"Honored to be known by you, Mick," he whispered

against her mouth and kissed her again, free arm sliding around her waist to hold her close.

She hummed and pulled back, stepping out of his way as he unloaded their grocery purchases. Micah moved around him, taking a bowl to fill it up with water before dunking the potatoes in there. She pulled out all the drawers until she found the peeler and stole kisses along the way. Fletcher focused on slicing up the meat, his eyes following Micah every so often. There was something so fucking special about sharing this space with her and Fletcher wouldn't trade it for anything in the world.

"What's your least favorite food item?" he asked, glancing at Micah briefly.

She pursed her lips and dunked her hands in the potatoes. "I *hate*…and I mean *despise* oranges. And I have a teenager who is obsessed with everything citrus."

Fletcher snorted, nudging her gently. "So that's Christmas and oranges that you don't like, but endure for your kid."

"It's what parents do, right? Sacrifice shit for their kids."

"That's what I've been told, yeah," he said it softly, because it wasn't like he had good experience with positive parenting and good life choices. When he looked up, he found her watching him with a slight frown. "What's wrong?"

"Did you ever want kids?"

For years, the answer had always been a resounding *no*. But of late? Maybe. When he was young and starting out, the idea of a family sounded crazy. During his marriage to Alice, both of them knew it was a bad idea. Because he'd be on tour and in the studio a lot, which meant that Alice would have to stay home and raise the kids on her own. And she would resent him for it. Then there was the whole being raised by an average dad who didn't really love or care for them much that made Fletcher think he'd turn out the same way. While

Emery was a fully-grown teenager with a sparkling personality, the thought of being a *father* to her didn't scare him as much as he thought it would.

"I like kids, not sure I'd make a good dad."

"I said that about myself when I found out I was pregnant. I turned out pretty okay."

He smiled as she dusted off her shoulders. He could say it a million times, but Micah really was a great mother. Besides keeping her kid alive for fourteen years, Emery was a damn great kid too. He could feel Micah watching him, but he focused on slicing the meat and getting it prepped. When the weight of her gaze left him, Fletcher let his shoulders droop. He never wanted to bring his family drama into their relationship. That was a past life, one he no longer had anything to do with.

This...*this life* with Micah, it was the only one he wanted to focus on.

micah

I want you all the time.

DATING FLETCHER WAS SO MUCH MORE than she thought it would be. They didn't do anything extravagant, but every minute they spent together was great. After that night in his kitchen, she invited herself back and they cooked together again. Her whole adult life, Micah had cleaned the kitchen as she cooked. She didn't like having to clean up before eating and she always got so lazy *after* her meals, so cleaning while cooking was her safest bet. Which was why watching Fletcher in the kitchen was the best feeling. He cleaned as he cooked and by the time dinner was served, his kitchen looked like nothing had happened in there.

"Next time you cook in my kitchen, you should teach Emery how to clean up after herself," she told him, bringing things from the dining table to the kitchen.

He laughed, rinsing and loading everything into the dishwasher. Micah lifted herself onto the counter and grinned as she watched him, reminding herself that because the man wrote a song about her, cleaned up after cooking and looked good in glasses didn't mean that she could fall in love with him again.

Silly girl, you're already in love with him.

"I don't mean to be pushy, but speaking of Emery," Fletcher said, wiping his hands before standing in front of her. She spread her legs slightly and arched an eyebrow. "When do you think we can tell her about us?"

"Soon."

"Because while this is fun, I want to be able to hold you and touch you. All the time."

"Is that all?" she asked, dragging her fingers through his hair before untying the topknot he'd pulled it up in. Emery might not say anything, but she always watched Micah closely when she brought up Fletcher. And it took everything in her to not react at the mention of the man. He'd always made her feel something so intense, she didn't know how to not be that way around him.

He frowned, peering at her over the top of his glasses. "Should there be something else?"

"Nope." With his hair untied, Micah pressed the pads of her fingers against his scalp and smiled when he moaned softly. "We'll tell her soon, okay?"

"I get why you want to wait and I support it, but I'm a greedy bastard and I want you all the time."

She laughed and with one hand, pushed Fletcher's glasses up and then kissed the tip of his nose. She liked that he felt that way about her, because she felt it about him too. It wasn't even about the sexual attraction—though pulling away from Fletcher *would* start to drive her insane—she liked that whenever they were near each other, hands gravitated to the other and her lips tingled to feel his. She even missed the scrape of his beard against her chin and neck when they weren't around each other. She had gone sixteen years without having Fletcher kiss and touch her all the time, now it was all she wanted.

"What are your plans for the holidays?" she asked, voice

soft as his fingers brushed against the side of her throat, his thumb stroking down the length of her neck and up along her jaw. She shuddered, her body going slightly limp at the way he touched her.

"Don't have a whole lot planned, really. Why?"

Micah knew that Fletcher responded, but when his mouth joined the exploration, everything ceased to exist around her. He pressed soft kisses along her neck as the rest of his fingers settled on the other side of her jaw. She swayed into him and heard Fletcher laugh.

"Fletch…"

"Right here, sweetheart."

She whimpered and wrapped her fingers around the wrist that held her face, her other hand flat on his chest. Licking her lips, she arched into him as his mouth traveled down to her clavicle and he playfully nipped at the skin.

And then suddenly, his lips were gone.

"No…" she whined softly, fingers curling into the front of his shirt. "Come back."

He chuckled and Micah opened her eyes, his glasses were gone and his dark hair framed his gorgeous face perfectly. They stared at each other a long moment before he said, "Holiday plans."

"What about them?"

"You asked me, Mick."

She frowned and tried to think about their conversation, but all she could focus on was the way his beard felt against her skin. Licking her lips, she nodded. "Wanna spend it with us?"

"Yes." The answer came out before she'd even finished her question. With a shrug, he added, "I'm busy most of the week, but I'd love to spend Christmas and beyond with you."

"Aw," she said, lips turning down in the perfect imitation

of the sad emoji. "I'll find someone else to fill my empty time."

He gave her a flat look and she resisted the urge to smile, because while she could tell that he wasn't angry or irritated, possessiveness flashed through his eyes.

"That was kinda hot," she mumbled, her fingernails brushing through his beard.

"Which part—you fucking with me or…""

Micah snorted and leaned in to kiss him softly. "That look in your eyes."

"The caveman look?" He sighed against her mouth and then with the hand on her jaw, he pulled her in for a proper kiss. She tugged him closer as she slipped one hand into his hair, twisting the long strands around her fingers. "You're mine, Mick," he mumbled when he broke the kiss briefly, before diving back in, tongue sliding over hers.

She hummed and pulled on his hair, their lips parting as she used her other hand to trace his mouth. "*You're* mine, Fletch."

"Always been yours, love bug."

Damn that nickname is growing on me.

Their mouths crashed into another kiss, arms winding around each other as heads tilted and lips fitted against the other. She had kissed him countless times, but every single time was better than the previous one.

And this kiss? Incinerated her underwear.

"Let's take a br—break and come back to it later," she forced the words out slowly, tears pricking the back of her eyes as she faked a smile for her client. Two days after her amazing night with Fletcher and she was a mess.

Micah felt breathless and her heart was racing so hard she

thought she might pass out. Walking the client out of her office, she slowly thanked her for coming and then closed the door. With her back pressed to the wood, she slid down to the floor and finally let the tears spill out.

She was exhausted and on edge, result of a fight with her mother the day before. It had been a regular phone call at first, her parents laughing and talking with Emery. Then once her daughter had finished what she had to say, it was Micah's turn. She would have preferred it be a regular phone call, but her parents insisted on FaceTime. Which meant she had to endure her mother's expressions through the whole conversation. She wasn't happy with how much makeup Emery was wearing, she had thoughts about how Emery spoke and then all of that turned into how Micah was dressed. One thing led to another and Micah was raising her voice and getting angry for everything her mother was criticizing her about.

This was exactly why Micah didn't like spending too much time with them—they never had anything nice to say. And when they did, it was always laced with something else. Backhanded compliments were her mother's speciality.

While she was usually good at powering through her exhausted days, she'd barely slept. And there was the beginning of a headache starting behind her eyes. The last time she'd struggled through her sessions, Micah had rescheduled her clients and spent the day alone and quietly. Unfortunately she'd booked another full day and that meant that she needed to take each session one at a time.

She wasn't ashamed of her stutter, because it always helped her clients know that she wasn't helping them for fun. To Micah, the stutter was painful. It hurt her in ways she couldn't put into words. There was no *fix* for the stutter, but there were exercises and ways to learn how not to trip over words. Except, none of her usual tricks worked. It had been so long since it had happened, her tongue and mouth were not connecting with her brain to make everything come out right. And Micah fucking hated it.

It was also completely fucking up her mood, which was unfortunate because it was Fletcher's birthday and she'd helped the kids plan a surprise for him after their music lesson. Trust him to not tell her that it was his birthday that week, after she'd spent every single day with him. Whether it was coffee in the morning or a quick lunch together or a really late dinner; they had been together as much as possible.

She was *happy* and it had been a long time since she'd allowed herself to feel that way. After Geoffrey, raising Emery while studying, getting certified and everything with her job had taken up so much time. The happiness she felt watching Emery grow up was different to the happy Fletcher made her feel, both were equally important to her. But she missed this kind of joy running through her veins—the constant excitement about seeing someone you liked, knowing that by the end of the day you'd get to hug and kiss them.

Except, she didn't know how much of a happy person she would be that evening.

Using the fifteen minutes before her next session, Micah visited the restroom and reapplied her makeup. She worked through her exercises, sounding out words and repeating them when she had trouble. Blowing out a long breath, she formed the words without putting any sound into it and watched her mouth curve and stretch around the vowels, around the Rs and Ks. Once she was certain she could breathe through it, Micah returned to her office.

Four hours and two more meltdowns later, she changed out of her work clothes into something a little more dressy. While she'd never dressed for a man before, Micah wanted to wear something for Fletcher. Which included tight black high-waisted jeans that clung to every inch of her legs and a floral wrap top that flaunted her assets as well as a strip of her stomach. After all, it was his birthday and he'd kept the whole thing a secret. Which was partly why they were also keeping this a surprise, because he thought he could get away with it.

When Emery had crashed into the house earlier in the week announcing that it was Fletcher's birthday, Micah had gotten into action. Thanks to her best friends being creative and quick, she enlisted them to put together Fletcher's gift. Sadie sourced the mermaid costume from a previous photo-shoot and Tatum blocked out one of her studios, allowing them to do exactly what she needed. It might have been early in their relationship for a boudoir photoshoot, but Micah didn't care. She knew that Fletcher would appreciate it and honestly, that's all that mattered.

While she was still exhausted, she was focused on Fletcher and celebrating him. She picked up the cake on her way to Big Waves, along with a large envelope that contained her gift for him.

The bell above the door chimed when she pushed into the store and Micah took a deep breath. She looked up at the balloons tucked against the ceiling and the confetti that would drop onto Fletcher. Being there, surrounded by things that made the man she loved, Micah felt better. She smiled as Benson came around the corner and handed the cake to him. A few minutes later, Emery and Nico raced around the corner, bumping into each other and laughing as they steadied themselves.

"Damn, Ms. George," Nico said, holding up a thumb with a smile and released a whistle. Emery rolled her eyes and smacked her best friend, which made Micah chuckle. She *knew* that she looked good, but it was always comforting to have other people tell her the same thing.

"Thanks, Nico." Micah gave the teenager's shoulder a gentle squeeze as Fletcher appeared, eyebrows dipped in confusion until his eyes landed on her. She stuck a leg out and set a hand on her hip as Fletcher's throat bobbed with a hard swallow, the sound audible in the suddenly quiet shop. She could feel everyone watching them, but Micah was too focused on the way Fletcher stared at her. His hungry gaze dragged from head to toe and back, chest heaving as his hands clenched and unclenched at his sides. When his eyes lifted to hers, Micah's breath caught at the animalistic look present in the brown.

And all of a sudden, his gaze softened as he said, "You okay, Mick?"

Her chest ached at the question, because he could *see* that she wasn't okay. Nodding, she swallowed back the truth, pasting on a steady smile. But Fletcher's eyes narrowed, like he knew she was hiding something. They could talk about it later, she needed to celebrate him for a bit. Instead, she took him in—faded and well worn blue jeans hugged his thighs and a white T-shirt clung to his torso, putting all his tattoos on display. His hair was tied back in a topknot and his beard was showing more of the silver.

Seconds later, balloons fell down around them, shocking Fletcher. He jumped back slightly and watched her through the confetti with wide eyes before a laugh burst out of him. Emery, Nico and Benson started singing "Happy Birthday", but Fletcher was still looking at her. Micah's heart felt like it was going to explode with how much love lingered between them.

Then he was moving towards her, his hand sliding around the back of her head to pull her mouth to his. Micah stumbled slightly at the movement and her fingers found purchase in the belt loops of his jeans. Fletcher's mouth slid along hers before their lips parted to fit together. She gasped softly into the kiss as his fingers twisted through her hair and Micah pulled him close, their hips pressed together. In that moment, she didn't care that they had an audience and it definitely slipped her mind that her daughter didn't know about this relationship before that moment.

A throat cleared and Micah yanked away from Fletcher, sucking in large gulps of air as they stared at each other. His hand moved from her hair to cup her face, eyes searching hers and she shook her head. Words were at the tip of her tongue, but she didn't trust herself to speak without stumbling over them. Fletcher nodded, smiling softly before he pressed his mouth to her forehead for a lingering kiss.

"Oooookay, if you're both done…" Emery's voice broke through their little bubble and Micah huffed under her breath. She pulled away from Fletcher and smiled apologetically at her daughter, who was smiling so wide. "I knew you two were boning, but kudos on trying to keep it a secret."

"We're not…" Fletcher started, then shook his head. "How did you one, find out and two, pull this off?"

Emery and Nico flashed smug smiles then pointed at Benson. "He told us how you never celebrate your birthday anymore. And we thought what better way to do it than with your favorite people."

Smiling, Fletcher looked around at all of them and nodded. "Thank you."

Benson brought the cake over, Nico lit the candles and they sang for him again. Fletcher cut the cake and everybody had a slice. Micah participated quietly, aware that he was watching the whole time. Once everyone had moved onto different things, she pulled out the envelope with her gift and smiled as he walked over to her.

"What's wrong?"

"A hard day," she whispered, eyes dipping to the envelope.

Fletcher's hand brushed over her chin and he gently

tipped her head up. "Don't hide from me, Mick. You have nothing to be embarrassed about."

"I know." Micah blew out a shaky breath and then held the envelope out to him. "Don't open it here."

"What's this?"

"Happy birth—day, Fletch." She felt the word stick in her throat and sighed softly.

"You didn't need to get me anything, but thank you."

"I know you hate lots of attention, but the kids wanted to do this and I kinda did too. I like cel—ebrating you, Fletch."

"I like being celebrated by you, Mick." Their lips met for a soft kiss and she smiled against his mouth. "And I'm sure I'll be responsible for cleaning up this mess."

She laughed, patting his chest. "I'll help."

His arms slid around her waist and she sighed softly, pressing her face into his chest. Together, they swayed slightly and Micah couldn't help but smile at how comfortable and safe she felt in his arms. Every time she slipped into his embrace, Micah felt like she was exactly where she was meant to be. And to think she'd spent the last so many years without him.

"Do you wanna talk about your day?" he asked softly and Micah groaned into his chest.

"Later," she said.

"Does this happen often?"

"No."

"What do you do when it happens?"

She shrugged, her hands sliding up and down his back. "Take the day off, breathe through it."

"What would you like to do today?" he mumbled against the side of her head.

"Just be with you, Fletch. This is perfect."

"Okay, love bug."

And despite how much she protested the nickname, she

loved the way it sounded when he said it in that tone. When he said it with love and affection. Like she was truly his. Gripping the back of his shirt in both hands, Micah held onto him and let the familiar spicy scent of his cologne invade her senses, blocking out everything else.

"Why don't you wait in my office, I'll finish up this session and then we can talk?"

Nodding, she let Fletcher tip her head up so he could brush his mouth over hers. She sighed into the kiss and then released him. With his hand on her lower back, they walked to his office, where he settled her into a chair before heading out to where Emery and Nico were making an absolute racket. To have a man who cared, who was interested and patient with her wasn't a revelation, but it felt good. Forget Geoffrey, her own parents hadn't been this gentle with her stutter. She'd felt ashamed to be that person as a kid, not wanting to embarrass anyone with her inability to speak clearly. And here was this man who looked at her and *knew* something was off.

She zoned out at some point, Emery's thrashing and laughing petering out as she sat in his office, letting the peace settle into her bones. Because when Fletcher came back, it was quite in the store. Micah startled when he touched her shoulder and then smiled softly when he dropped into the chair in front of her. She leaned in, brushing her fingers through the gray hair at his temples, sliding down to trace his eyebrows and cheekbones. Micah swiped a finger over his nose and dragged her thumb over his mouth before she scratched at his beard with her short nails. The whole time, he watched her with a smile, his eyes soft and gentle.

"Do you want to talk about it?" Micah dropped her hands to her lap, blinking back the tears as she shook her head. "Would you like to sit here quietly instead?" he asked, leaning in slightly to take her hands in his. She shook her head again and he laughed, brushing light kisses over her cheeks. "What do you want to do, Mick?"

She shrugged and sighed heavily, watching her fingers twist between his. "This. Noth—ing else." Micah winced at the block, feeling the exhaustion weigh her down.

"I got you, sweetheart," Fletcher whispered and he gently pulled her into his lap. Micah wrapped one arm around him and buried her face in his neck. "Let the hard day work its way through, I've got you."

In his arms, she felt like she could conquer the world, save the dolphins and attain world peace. And that was enough.

fletcher

Maybe I have a thing for Santa.

IF HE'D BEEN okay with his quiet Christmases in the last few years, Fletcher no longer was. Because he was happy to have Micah in his arms every day and excited to teach Emery everything he knew about music. He hadn't expected how busy he would be. Certainly not as busy as he used to be during their tours. He had been on Santa duty for a week already and he wished that he had all the free time to be with Micah.

Keeping their relationship a secret hadn't lasted very long, not when he'd seen the sadness in her eyes the day she came into the store to celebrate his birthday. He'd wanted to hold and comfort her, kiss and remind her that no matter how terrible her stutter made her feel, it didn't take away all the hard work she'd done over the years. And fuck, he loved knowing that she leaned on him during an emotionally trying time.

The first time he'd heard her stutter, Fletcher hadn't known all that he did now. He didn't know that she spent her whole childhood tripping over words and being told that if she worked harder, it would go away. Seeing her so sad, pushing through the worry in her heart to celebrate him made Fletcher love her even more.

And I should have been better prepared for these feelings.

Which was why it was bothering him that he hadn't told her about his other job. Sure, she wasn't a fan of the holidays, but she didn't hate it. But he had certainly convinced himself that she would want nothing to do with someone who looked forward to Christmas every year. She'd invited him to spend the holiday with her and Emery, but Micah still only celebrated it because of her daughter. What if she had a negative reaction to his Santa role? What if that was a deal breaker? It was silly to sit in these assumptions when they hadn't talked about the holidays much.

Every morning, he said he'd tell her and then as the day progressed, he'd forget. It wasn't like he was keeping a life altering secret, Fletcher didn't want to lose the two important things in his life over something like this. Then again, not telling her might actually backfire on him. As usual, he let those thoughts and fears fade away as he stepped into his role.

He'd been wandering the Village for over two hours by the time he took his first break—hot cocoa and chocolate chip biscotti to keep up spirits—with his helper elves, Portia and Kyle. The kids had been working at the Village as long as he'd been Santa, but that was their first year working alongside him. In the week since they'd started their routine, Fletcher had also noticed that Kyle had a crush on Portia, who returned the sentiment but was too awkward to do anything about it. He was in the middle of watching them flirt awkwardly when his phone buzzed in his pocket.

ERIN

Who's the girl?

> **FLETCHER**
> What girl?

Looking around where they were seated at the fountain—he'd taken off his Santa coat and tied up his hair so nobody would approach him during his break—Fletcher frowned and then focused on his phone as another text came from Erin.

> **ERIN**
> Oh, sorry. Who's the woman?

> **FLETCHER**
> Still confused, E.

Of course he now knew who she was talking about, but Fletcher had no idea *how* Erin knew about Micah. His best friend was a badass lawyer and clearly a super sleuth, because within seconds of his previous text a photograph appeared on his phone.

> **ERIN**
> The woman in this picture of you taken by some tabloid slime ball.

Fletcher swore under his breath, but zoomed in on the picture—they looked happy. They were coming out of the Mermaid Mart after shopping for yet another cooking session together. Micah was laughing and Fletcher had one arm wrapped around her, while the other hand held onto their shopping cart.

Fuck, she's beautiful. Takes my breath away.

> **FLETCHER**
> Her.
> The one I thought got away.

ERIN

Now your rejection of me makes sense.

FLETCHER

eyeroll emoji I believe someone else did the rejecting.

ERIN

Only because you looked distracted.

How long has she been in town?

FLETCHER

She lives here, is from here.

ERIN

What's her name?

FLETCHER

Nope. Don't need you looking her up and finding all kinds of reasons why I should stay away.

ERIN

Whaaaaaat? I'd never do that.

FLETCHER

Sure, whatever you say.

My break's almost over, so I'm gonna go.

ERIN

I can't believe you still do this. Hank would be so impressed.

FLETCHER

That's why I keep doing it.

After staring at the picture for a few more minutes, Fletcher tossed his hot cocoa cup and napkins into the trash, then sent the picture to Micah. With a wide smile on his face, Fletcher grabbed Portia and Kyle so the three of them could head back out. The minute he slipped the coat back on, he was suddenly swarmed by tons of kids. Even if he thought it was high time parents stopped perpetuating the idea that Santa was real, he was really happy when kids were excited about Santa. It did mean he made a little more money for a few weeks in December and that was nothing to sniff at.

"Hi Santa," a soft voice said, interrupting his thoughts. "Can I get a picture?"

Fletcher looked down at the tiny ball of fluff grinning up at him and chuckled. "Absolutely." He squatted beside the kid and flashed his biggest smile as their parent took a picture. With that done, Fletcher waved at the kid and stood back up, all his bones and muscles protesting.

"Yo, rockstar. Lemme get in on a selfie." A teenager sidled up to him and threw an arm around his shoulders as they stuck a hand out with their phone. Fletcher grimaced as the picture was taken and then grunted once the kid was gone.

"I can be your personal security if you want, Mr. Kelley."

Fletcher turned to Kyle with a deadpan expression. "We talked about this, Kyle. It's either Fletcher or Santa, none of that *Mr. Kelley* bullshit."

"Does that mean I can be your personal security?" Kyle asked, almost like he missed the point of what was said.

Sighing heavily, he shook his head. "I'm good, Kyle. But thanks for the offer."

"I was thinking—" Portia bounced around to walk backwards in front of Fletcher "—maybe you could hold fort at the fountain for a few hours, that way everyone can come find you."

"That's not a bad idea."

"Then I can get my friends to help out with security too," Kyle added and Fletcher realized it was pointless trying to explain this to the kid.

"What do you two do before you're here for your shift?"

Even though they'd worked together all week, they hadn't actually had much time to talk like this. He wanted to get to know his elves, if only for the time they were together.

"I work at Stardust Diner through the week and Kyle helps out at his father's office," Portia supplied before coming to a stop as a bunch of kids came charging at them.

"During the school year too?" Fletcher asked as he squatted again, bringing himself to the level of the kids as they crowded around him for a picture.

"Yeah," Kyle said with a long-suffering sigh. "I mean, it's not fun. But my dad pays me, so I guess it's okay."

Fletcher nodded, smiling at the kids as he waved them off and to Kyle he said, "I have an opening at the music store, if that's more your thing."

"Seriously?"

"I know you have a crazy amount of information about music stored in that brain." Kyle looked like he was going to pass out, so Fletcher gripped his shoulder to steady him and smiled. "It's only a job offer, Kyle. Come by the store in the new year and we'll figure something out."

"Thanks, Mr. Kelley. I mean, Fletcher," Kyle fumbled and blushed, which made Portia giggle softly. Fletcher smiled and carried on with his walk, listening to his elves quietly chatter behind him.

Hours later, Fletcher was on his final break of the evening. He had another forty-five minutes of Santa duty before he could go home, and he was ready to collapse into bed. Hell, he'd get out of work early if it meant spending another evening with Micah. Now that Emery knew about their relationship, they didn't need to sneak around. But still, he didn't want to put them on the spot by showing up at their house randomly.

After his birthday, Emery hadn't brought up the relationship or said anything at all. And at first, that felt weird. But outside of a 'please don't hurt her' comment, the teenager had nothing else to say and Fletcher appreciated that.

Now, he and Micah could date for real. He could wander around Sirena Beach with her, see her hometown through her eyes. Enjoy the place the right way. Plus, if she wanted to, Emery could go along with them. The options were endless. Fletcher would be lying if he said the thing taking up most of his brain space was the knowledge that he could possibly get Micah into his bed soon too. It wasn't like she had flat out told him sex was off the table, he figured that while they were sorting through their relationship, sex would not be a priority. Which, to him, was totally fine.

But all the memories from the night they shared kept filling his brain and it was starting to become too much.

At the sound of buzzing, Fletcher swapped the paperback —a tattered historical romance he found in the locker room— for his phone and smiled at the text.

MICAH

Damn, I look good.

Where did you get this?

And why do you have this?

Before he could unlock his phone to reply, another two texts came through.

MICAH

Fletch?

sad face emoji I miss you.

FLETCHER

I miss you too, love bug.

> As for the picture, a friend sent it. Wanting to know who you are.

Smiling, Fletcher scrolled up to look at the picture again. With this thumb he stroked Micah's face and shook his head. No way was it possible that he'd won over this woman. He'd seen that unfiltered joy on her face every single day since their trip to the tasting room. The way he felt about her was scary, but it also felt right. He couldn't wait to tell her as much, to see her beautiful brown eyes widen in shock before they lit up with joy.

MICAH

> And what did you tell this friend?

FLETCHER

> That you're none of their business, you're mine.

MICAH

> Ooh, possessive. Weirdly sexy.

FLETCHER

> Is that a good thing? I can't tell.

MICAH

> I don't either. But you're mine, I'm yours. We can be possessive together, Fletch.

FLETCHER

> *kissy face emoji*

> What are you girls up to tonight?

MICAH

> Last minute Christmas shopping, maybe some hot cocoa.

> Think you might have some time for me later?

FLETCHER

I've always got time for you, love bug.

MICAH

I'll see tonight, then. *kissy face emoji*

I love you, he said to himself, shaking his head at how ridiculous he was being. Almost fifty and still giddy about texting with his *girlfriend*, making plans and sending emojis. The man that met Micah the first time never would have imagined he'd do this. Not because he was a badass rocker, but because romance and love and all that other stuff were so alien to him at the time. He might not have been bedding groupies every night, but he'd done his fair share of one night stands. And when you were famous, the number of people who wanted to climb into your bed were endless.

Then he saw Micah in the crowd at their show and everything fell into place.

Switching his phone to vibrate, he shoved the device into his pocket so he could go find his elves. Something told him Kyle and Portia were slowly building a relationship and he hoped that it lasted for a long time. They deserved it. Hell, right now, everyone deserved a good relationship. Like he did with Micah. The thought of seeing her that night, knowing that when he got home he'd get to be with her had him beyond excited. And for the first time since he'd become Santa, he couldn't wait for it to be over.

Fletcher went through the rest of his shift on autopilot. Despite the late hour, there were still so many kids hanging around, but meeting them blurred together. The only time he was alert and conversing was when he encountered some of Hank's old buddies. They insisted on shooting the shit and talking about the store, to find out if Fletcher had changed anything about the place. After Hank died, he hadn't invited any of his old friends back or given the producing music thing another thought. But clearly these old men thought that's what he should have done. Once they'd berated him— "we're messing with you, kid"—Fletcher was left alone with Portia and Kyle. His elves were also starting to fade and even though they had the same breaks, it was grueling work walking around and interacting with people for so many hours at a time.

So when Kyle suggested ending the night with a special hot cocoa—spiked with Baileys Irish Cream which was only served after 9 p.m.—Fletcher didn't protest. Kyle and Portia were standing by the photo booth waiting for their turn to get their pictures taken, while Fletcher stood to the side and sipped on his drink. He was so distracted by watching his elves being awkward with each other as they flirted that he missed the tiny humans charging at him. Saving his drink in the nick of time, Fletcher straightened up and smiled at the gang of kids beaming up at him.

"Mr. Santa, do you make wishes come true?" a little girl in a pink Santa outfit asked.

"That would be so cool, wouldn't it? However, I can pass the message along to the Fairies."

The kids gasped and giggled, which made Fletcher snort. He'd had similar conversations with kids over the years, so he had a script of some kind already in place. The little girl waved for him to bend, so Fletcher carefully squatted to her level and smiled as she whispered in his ear, "I wish for a unicorn, but I'll also accept a pony."

And then the rest of the kids started whispering their 'wishes', which he committed to memory with a smile on his face. Once they were all done, he straightened up and hid the wince at the crick in his back.

"I'll be sure to pass the message along," he told them and the kids cheered before running off. Fletcher scribbled the long list of requests into his notebook and pocketed it before heading to where his elves were bent over a strip of photos.

But before he could get their attention, a familiar voice filled the air.

"Oh my god, you're Santa Claus?"

Fletcher spun in place, eyes wide as he came face-to-face with Emery and Micah. The teenager was grinning as she bounced in place, while her mother looked as shocked as he was. Blowing out a slow breath, he shook his head and changed course to walk over to them. He could feel everyone around them watching, but Fletcher didn't care.

"Why didn't you say anything? This is like the coolest thing ever," Emery added, tugging at his Santa coat with unrestrained glee.

"Thanks," he told the teenager and then looked at Micah with a cautious smile. "Mick."

"Fletcher Claus," she said softly and he grunted, shaking his head.

"Don't say it too loud, it'll stick."

"How long have you been doing this?"

Fletcher pulled off his hat and tucked it into the pocket of his coat. "A few years. Hank enlisted me and I kept doing it in honor of him."

"Right." Micah nodded and Fletcher finally allowed himself to look her over when her attention was drawn to Emery. Her dress wasn't revealing or would even be considered sexy, but *God,* she looked good. With an open collar and buttons down the front, the dress hugged every curve. A matching belt wrapped around her waist and was tied in a bow, tucking in at the sides. The top three buttons were undone, flaunting all that brown skin. Her bare legs ended in her white Chucks.

"It looks good on you," she said softly and Fletcher blinked to focus on her. "Being Santa. The coat, the hat, the gray in your beard. You look happy."

If only you knew how happy I looked when you're around.

"Kids are weird, but fun when they're not crying or screaming for attention."

"Take the compliment, Fletch."

He laughed and bowed his head slightly. "What are you two doing here?"

"This is where Em decided she wanted to do last minute shopping and drink cocoa. Why didn't you tell me?"

Fletcher made a face at the question, because even though she didn't ask it accusingly, he felt that way. "Honestly? I don't know. Figured that since you didn't care for Christmas, this might be something of a deal-breaker."

"No way you thought that," she whispered, frowning slightly. "It's kinda hot, actually."

"Really?" He arched an eyebrow as Micah gripped the front of his coat and tugged him towards her.

"Maybe I have a thing for Santa and you helped unlock it."

Holy shit. Fletcher swallowed as he set his hands on her hips. She licked her lips and dragged her hands up over his chest and around his neck, smirking as her eyes met his. Her gaze moved up and a soft laugh fell from her lips. Fletcher followed her attention and found that they were standing below a sprig of mistletoe. He'd noticed it sprinkled all through the Village, but he never imagined he'd be standing there with Micah.

"It's the rule, right?"

"Absolutely," she mumbled as their lips met in a slow kiss. Micah's fingers tightened around the back of his neck and he deepened the kiss, his tongue sweeping into her mouth as he tipped her back slightly. She moaned and flicked her tongue against his, their bodies pressed together firmly as they held each other.

Someone started whistling "I Saw Mommy Kissing Santa Claus" and Fletcher leaned back to find Emery standing a few feet away, eyes averted from them. He chuckled at the frustrated look on Micah's face.

"I'm almost done with my shift, we're still on for tonight?"

She nodded, brushing his hair behind his ears. "Wouldn't miss it for the world, *Santa*."

A shiver of pleasure ran up his spine at the rasp in her voice on that last word and he stole another kiss before forcing himself out of her arms. With a playful tap against Emery's shoulder, Fletcher joined his elves to finish their shift for the evening.

Then he could lock himself away with Micah for the rest of the night.

micah

Worth the sixteen year wait.

IT WAS close to 11 p.m. by the time Micah pulled up in front of Fletcher's house. After Emery had done her necessary shopping and they'd indulged in hot cocoa, Micah had dropped her daughter off with Sadie's nonna. The plan was always for Emery to spend the night there, but now Micah was even more anxious to drop her off so she could see Fletcher again. It didn't help that Emery was still humming that silly Christmas song, enough that Nonna had a million questions the whole time Micah was attempting to leave.

Also, who knew she had a Santa kink?

Micah held Mrs. Hershey responsible.

She'd had a relatively light day at work, which she was grateful for after her stuttering days ago. However, she did have a session with Mrs. Hershey. After one week of reading picture books and helping her learn how to process certain words by the way they looked on the page, the older woman insisted they read her book club romance.

As luck would have it, the book that Mrs. Hershey's book club was reading featured a hero moonlighting as Santa and a heroine with a Santa kink. If you asked Micah, she would have told you that she'd never considered Santa to be a kink. But after spending an hour reading all of the deliciously sexy things the heroine did with Santa, she thought differently.

"Did you ever think that Santa could be so hot?" Mrs. Hershey asked, fanning herself with one hand while wiggling her eyebrows.

"He's not really Santa, is he? Just playing dress up."

"Oh sweetheart, where's your imagination? When he puts on the suit, he *is* Santa."

She rolled her eyes and tried to flip to a chapter or scene without sex, but Mrs. Hershey wasn't having it. "Reading sex is the easiest way to get me interested, stop skipping."

"You know you're gonna have to know what the rest of the story is about, right?"

Mrs. Hershey made a *psshhaa* sound and waved her off, wrinkled fingers turning the pages and tracing the words until she found what she was looking for. "Does that say pussy or pretty?"

"What do *you* think it says?" Micah asked, peering at the page before looking at the older woman.

"It could say pretty pussy for all I care."

"This is not helping with your reading, I hope you're aware."

"I'm living vicariously through Janet and her Santa fetish, nothing else matters."

She chuckled and finally took Mrs. Hershey through the scene—the word was indeed pussy and it brought the older woman much joy. But also because she got giddy over the sex scenes, they read two more that got Micah all hot and bothered before she walked Mrs. Hershey out to the cab waiting outside the clinic.

Then hours later, she'd seen Fletcher in his Santa suit and

her mind was filled with all the naughty things she'd like to do with him. If Emery wasn't with her, Micah might have said and done a lot more than kiss him under the mistletoe. For a brief moment, she was disappointed that he'd kept this from her. Sure, she wasn't a fan of the holidays and thought it, like all other holidays, was a capitalist mess. But she wouldn't have held it against Fletcher if he told her he liked Christmas or that he was Santa every year.

What if Emery had been ready to return to Santa's Village years ago? Would she have run into Fletcher then? Would they have what they did now? Micah wasn't a big believer in fate or destiny, but she know that they were meant to reconnect now. Now when both of them weren't expecting each other. When they felt like they were ready for something more.

However, Micah had to admit seeing Fletcher in that Santa coat had done something to her. It wasn't even the traditional outfit or something sexy, he'd managed to find a long coat that fit him like a glove. The combination of his regular clothes—dark jeans and a matching shirt—under the bright red coat with his Santa hat had been a visual she never thought she'd want to add to her spank bank. He looked so handsome, like he was *meant* to play that role. And the way he interacted with those kids, squatting to their level to talk and laugh with them, told her that he loved every minute of it.

The drive to his house took her about twenty minutes and the whole way, she wondered if he would still be wearing his Santa outfit. If he'd fuck her in it, because they *were* going to have sex. If he'd let her wear it while he did all those wonderful things to her body he once did. Or maybe he'd let her strip *him* naked and lick him from head to toe. *Okay, calm the fuck down.*

By the time she pulled into his driveway she was

completely horned up and breathing heavily. The front door to his house opened and the man himself stepped through, leaning against the doorway. Micah's chest heaved at the sight of him—long legs encased in black, full sleeved Henley that clung to his torso and strong arms crossed over his chest. He'd taken off his Santa coat, though, and she pouted for that. She loved him with every fibre of her being and she didn't even want to think about life without him now.

When Fletcher's head cocked to the side, she chuckled and got out of her car, smoothing down her dress. She grabbed her purse and locked up before walking up the driveway to his front door.

"Thought you were going to make a break for it."

"And miss out on kissing Santa again? Not a chance in hell."

He rolled his eyes, hooked his fingers into her belt and pulled her against him. Their lips crashed together and she moved as he did, stepping into the house, the slight chill vanishing the minute she heard the door close. She dropped her bag and set her hands on his chest, pushing him against the door as one of his hands cradled the back of her head and the other slid down to her ass, bringing their hips flush.

The kiss broke and Fletcher pressed soft kisses against her jaw, down her neck and she arched into him. Her fingers slid into his hair, holding him in place as he marked up her skin, his beard scraping against her.

"Fletch..." she whispered, rocking against him as he sucked on the sensitive spot behind her ear. Micah moaned, back arching as she tugged on his hair. But before she could say anything, a loud rumble echoed between them.

"Was that you?" he asked as he pulled back with wide eyes.

She nodded as her stomach released another obnoxious sound. "I haven't eaten anything since lunch."

"Jesus, Mick. That's *hours* ago."

"So feed me," she simpered and mentally patted herself on the back when he growled. Except, he released the grip he had on her ass and tugged her to the kitchen. In a move she didn't expect, he picked her up and set her on the counter before turning to his fridge to pull out multiple dishes. Micah rested her hands on the counter and swung her legs as she watched him plate the leftovers and stick it in his microwave.

When he turned to her, he frowned. "What?"

"I love you," she said simply, legs swinging and Fletcher went still.

"Mick…"

"I fucking love you, Fletch. I was a twenty-something in love with you that night. Now I'm a thirty-something who is still so stupidly in love with you."

He was frozen, eyes wide as his mouth flapped open and shut. She knew that she shocked him, so she laughed and hopped off the counter. When she stopped in front of him, Fletcher finally blinked and lifted both hands to cup her face.

"You love me."

Wrapping her hands around his wrists, Micah nodded with a grin. "So fucking much."

"Crazy," he mumbled and then his mouth was on hers again, kissing her slow and deep. His tongue swept into her mouth and they moaned in unison, teeth clattering as Micah tried to get closer. She'd never told anybody she loved them, not romantically anyway. Definitely not Geoffrey. When he proposed, she took the ring and put it on. When they got married, she struggled to maintain eye contact. The day they got divorced, she finally felt free.

She'd been in love with Fletcher for years, the feelings simmering beneath the surface as she went through the motions. The day they saw each other again, everything truly made sense. The reason why she couldn't give her heart to someone else and the calming sensation at staring into his eyes again.

The sound of the microwave beeping brought her back to the present and she broke the kiss with a gasp. He still looked shocked, almost like he couldn't believe what was happening. She rolled her eyes and tapped his nose before moving around him to retrieve her food—a very colorful and vibrant burrito bowl. Snagging a spoon on the way, she bumped her hip against his and tucked herself into his breakfast nook and dug into the food.

She was a few bites into her food when Fletcher dropped to his knees beside her, eyes unfocused. "I love you too."

"I know, Fletch." She grinned and set her bowl down, brushing hair out of his face.

"I blanked after you spoke and that kiss, goddamn woman. I could kiss you forever and never get enough."

She laughed and leaned in to peck his lips. "You *can* kiss me forever."

"Yeah?"

Humming in the affirmative, she returned to her food because her stomach was starting up its loud rumbling again. He sat in the chair across from the cushioned bench she was seated on and she could see that he was still processing what had happened.

"You love me," he repeated softly and then his face split into the most beautiful smile as he looked at her. "Worth the sixteen year wait."

"You're such a dork."

"I believe this makes me *your* dork, love bug."

She gently kicked him under the table. Fletcher finally leaned back in his chair and stretched his legs out. He looked so happy, so *content* and she was glad for it. They'd both had incredibly long days and yet, this quiet moment together was exactly what they needed. At the same time, because she needed the answer to one question, Micah broke the silence.

"Why didn't you tell me about your Santa gig?"

His shoulders tensed and she watched him fidget for a long moment before looking at her. "I love Christmas. Almost as much as you don't like it, maybe. I *was* going to tell you, but when I showed up that morning and heard your frustration with the holiday…"

"You really thought it would be a deal breaker?" she asked, one eyebrow arched.

"People have pretty wild and valid reasons for not liking certain things in relationships. I made a lot of assumptions, obviously."

She laughed at his wince. "You know what they say about assumptions. No wait…that doesn't work as well."

"I'm glad you find this hilarious," he deadpanned.

"Here all week." Micah stuck her tongue out and ate the rest of her dinner. "But for the record, I would love you in all your versions. The rockstar was always my favorite, but the *former* rockstar does things to me. And Santa? Holy shit, Fletch."

He shook his head, a light blush visible at the top of his beard. She scooped up the last of her food as she smiled to herself. Even at forty-seven, Fletcher Kelley could be a bashful awkward man and somehow that was so endearing.

When she finished, he was on his feet, taking her bowl and washing up. She watched him for a moment before she wandered through his kitchen, opening and closing cabinets and drawers. When she was there a few nights ago, she'd seen a box of fruit roll-ups and now she wanted to use them *wisely*. Retrieving it from the last drawer, Micah shook the contents into her hand and walked over to wrap one arm around his waist, her face pressed into his back.

"Are you tired?" she asked.

"Why?"

Micah playfully nipped at his back through his T-shirt and dragged her hand down to the front of his jeans to press her palm against his growing bulge. She'd felt it earlier when he'd kissed her and she already knew what he was packing. He grunted softly and rocked against her hand, making her smile.

"Turn around," she whispered, pulling her hand away and dropping to her knees. He turned and frowned down at her, but Micah pointed at his pants. "Take them off."

Despite looking like he wanted to protest, he undid his belt and zipper, then pushed his pants off. She leaned forward to kiss his dick through the cotton of his boxer-briefs and heard Fletcher growl.

Looking up at him, she smiled and said, "Actually, take it *all* off."

She loved that he didn't object. That he reached behind his head and ripped off his T-shirt, tossing it aside before pushing his underwear down. And then he was standing gloriously naked—minus the clothes around his ankles—in front of her and Micah sighed, a smile tugging at her lips. She wrapped a hand around the head of his cock and he hissed softly, so she dragged a hand down the full length of him, fingers twisting around his base. Another sound came out of him and she shifted on her knees, leaning forward to take the tip of him into her mouth. The bead of moisture slid onto her tongue as she licked him up. His eyes slipped shut and she opened up the fruit roll-up while taking him deeper into her mouth. His cock was heavy against her tongue and twitched as she sucked gently. Moaning when he hit the back of her throat, Micah set one hand on his thigh and carefully pulled back, sliding him out of her mouth.

And then she wrapped the roll-up around him, smiling when he startled and opened his eyes. "What the hell?"

"I saw this video—" she smoothed the roll-up around his dick with a smirk "—and the woman *insisted* that it was the best blowjob of her life."

"Huh. What is *that*, though?"

She giggled once she was done, leaving his tip exposed as she sat back to admire her handiwork. "A strawberry fruit roll-up."

He nodded, not entirely convinced, but she knew he was intrigued. She slid him into her mouth and the combination of his natural taste and the strawberry made her eyes roll back. She felt his hand on her jaw, his thumb brushing along her bottom lip as she took him deeper. Micah wrapped one hand around his base and stroked him as she sucked on his strawberry flavored cock. She forced her eyes open and found his head tipped back as her tongue worked him over. His grip on her face went slack as she took him deeper into her mouth, her eyes watering as she swallowed when his tip hit the back of her throat. A guttural sound came out of Fletcher and she silently congratulated herself on making that happen.

"Mick, fuck," he groaned and she sucked him harder, the flavors coating her mouth. She slipped her hand between his thighs and cupped his balls, getting the loudest moan in response. His fingers gripped her short hair and tugged gently, but Micah didn't let up. She watched him as she sucked and squeezed him, hand and mouth working in tandem to drive him absolutely wild.

His body jolted and his fingers tightened in her hair, so Micah popped him out of her mouth and Fletcher huffed. She removed the roll-up and licked him from tip to base, her eyes fixed on his face as he breathed heavily. And when he started to relax his hold in her hair, she took him back into her mouth and he gasped as he jerked forward and came, spilling down her throat. Micah moaned, head spinning as she sucked him up. Pulling off him slowly, she leaned back against the cabinets behind her and licked her lips as he caught his breath.

When his eyes finally opened, dark with desire, she shivered. With his chest still heaving, he held out his hands for her and pulled Micah to her feet. Both of them looked at his dick, covered in slightly pinkish red residue and she snorted out a laugh.

"It looks diseased."

"Tasted good, though," she countered and tossed the roll-up into the garbage. "Let's get you all cleaned up."

Fletcher opened his mouth to say something, but changed his mind. Instead, he pulled his underwear and pants up and led the way to his bedroom. Micah drank in the muscles in his back, the tattoos dotting his skin and smiled to herself. She scored this rockstar and he wanted *her* just as bad.

When he stepped into the bathroom, Micah took a minute to look around his bedroom. It was large, but decorated simply. Nobody would know that this was the bedroom of a former rockstar, because it was neat and tidy and not a single thing existed from his former life. The California King in the middle of the room took up most of the space and the sheets looked a little rumpled. There was a vintage desk against one wall, with a jacket hanging over the back of the chair. A laptop, a stack of notebooks and her envelope from his birthday rested on the table—it looked unopened.

A large built-in wardrobe took up the opposite wall, a full-size mirror on one of the panels. Beside it was a tall shelf that had more shoes than she owned. A few random pieces of art adorned the walls, adding color to the otherwise plain room. His curtains were a cream color that didn't look like it served any purpose other than to cover the windows. But Micah had to admit that the bed was positioned in such a way that it might not get any sunlight, irrespective of if the curtain was open or closed.

"Are you going to join me?" His voice floated from the bathroom and she made quick work of stripping off her clothes, tossing everything haphazardly on the floor. Looking at her naked body in the mirror on his closet, she grinned at herself and walked into the bathroom.

fletcher

I'll save the edging for another time.

"COOL YOUR JETS, ROCKSTAR," she said, laughter in her voice, as she appeared stark naked in the bathroom. "Sure there's room in there for me?"

He nodded dumbly, looking her over. It wasn't the first time he was seeing her naked, but he'd never seen this version of her and Fletcher had to admit that his imagination had been lacking. She was still curvy in all the right places, dips and arches shaping her beautiful body. Her hips were a little fuller, thighs a little thicker; but that was all proof of the human she'd brought into the world.

His eyes did a slow survey of her soft brown skin—the dandelion still tattooed on her hip, the gentle folds, rolls of fat and breasts that he was certain would still fit perfectly into his hands. When his gaze lingered too long on her chest, a smile ticking at the corner of his mouth at the sight of her dark nipples pointing in different directions, Micah cleared her throat.

"My body is a whole lot different from what you remember."

"A whole lot better is what I would say," he said, his voice scratching against his throat at how beautiful this woman was. She was aware of her beauty and perfection, but Fletcher liked to remind her as much as possible. He held a hand out and her face transformed with a grin and she took it, stepping into the shower with him. His fruit roll-up stained dick had been relaxed as he stood there, letting the cold water hit him, but with Micah in proximity, he was at attention again.

"Do you need help?" she asked, grabbing the soap and lathering it between her hands.

"Not with my cock, thanks."

"Aw, why not? That's my favorite part."

He grunted and took the soap from her, lathering it up as well before setting it aside. He let his mind run through progression chords and the track listing from the first ever Rescuers album as he soaped up his cock. His only priority was getting the sticky residue off him, otherwise he wouldn't be able to fuck Micah and that was not something that he was remotely okay with. He *needed* to fuck her.

"Fletch." He hummed in response and opened his eyes to focus on Micah. " I know I asked you already, but I can't remember what we discussed because you were distracting me with your mouth."

"I'm innocent," he said, soapy hands held up with a not-so-innocent smile.

She snorted. "Would you like to spend Christmas with Emery and me?"

"Yes," he said instantly, not even needing to think about it. The idea of spending the holidays with this woman and her kid set his soul on fire in the best ways possible.

"No Fletcher Claus duty that day?"

"Never getting rid of that name, am I?" Sighing, he soaped up the rest of his body. "I work until Friday and I'm done for the year."

"Okay." She nodded, turned around and gestured to her back. "Soap me up?"

"You're trying to kill me, aren't you?"

"No more than you're trying to kill me. Can't believe you're a fan of Christmas."

He chuckled and dragged his soapy hands over her back, down her sides and hips, and over her ass. "You didn't tell me *why* you don't like the holiday."

"I don't know. There's always so much false cheer, the music grates on my nerves and people spend so much money on gifts that we don't need."

"Ah," he said, hiding his smile when Micah turned to look at him. "You don't like the capitalism of the holidays."

She shrugged and set her hands on his chest, smirking playfully. "But I have to admit that seeing you as Santa tonight might have changed my mind a little."

He arched an eyebrow. "Oh yeah?"

"Absolutely. In fact, the Santa Kink is a long standing thing in romance novels."

"I'd prefer if it was a Fletcher Claus kink," he countered, hating himself a little for even using the dumb name Jensen started and Micah picked up.

"Well, you're the *only* Santa I know, so sure."

He laughed and leaned in to kiss her softly. "Thanks, that's very comforting."

Laughing with him, she poked his stomach and then pulled back to smooth down her wet hair. "Now I set up Christmas every year for Emery, because I won't be a Scrooge and take it away from her."

"You're a good mother, Mick. I hope you know that."

Her face softened slightly. "I do my best, but I'm also lucky to have a fantastic kid."

"You're responsible for a lot of that, in case you didn't know."

"I know." She tugged him under the water with her. "I can't imagine my life without her anymore, even though for so many years, being a mom wasn't even at the top of my list."

He remembered a 'list' of things she wanted to do in this lifetime. He'd teased her about it then, but if his memory served, she'd achieved a lot of it and then some.

"Remind me of what was on that list."

She narrowed her eyes, like she knew Fletcher remembered what she'd put down. But she still obliged him. "Travel the world, tour with my favorite band, fuck a rockstar, get my dream job, drive a truck, get a tattoo," she said, sticking her arm out to show off her gorgeous collection of random art. "Fall in love, get my heart broken…you know the usual."

"I remember there being more," he reminded her.

"Obviously, it was like two sides of a notebook page."

Fletcher smirked and turned off the water, grabbing a towel for Micah and one for himself. "Who broke your heart?"

"My parents," she admitted softly. "Twice, actually. Once when I got pregnant and then when I was divorced, they shut me out for a long time. They were disappointed and confused, but mostly they didn't know how to respond to everything I was going through."

"I'm sorry, Mick."

Nodding, she dried her hair and then patted her body down before wrapping the towel and knotting it on the side. "We're okay now. There are moments of tension, but they love Em and I think they deal with me because of her."

"You see them often?"

"One holiday a year, at the very least." Micah walked out of the bathroom, fingers dragging through wet curls.

Fletcher watched her as he finished drying his hair and wrapped the towel around his waist. When he walked out, he smiled at her folding their clothes and setting everything aside. It reminded him of the way she'd cleaned up his hotel room all those years ago—making sure not a single crumb or piece of clothing was out of place.

"Why are you looking at me like that?"

He shook his head, sitting on the edge of his bed. "When I woke up alone that morning in my hotel room, the place was spotless. Like housekeeping had come through while I was asleep."

She looked at the T-shirt in her hands and laughed. "It's always been something I did. My brother was messy, my ex was messy, my roommate in college was messy and now my kid is messy. Picking up after people is kinda my thing."

"That's not a bad thing to have."

She set all their clothes aside and dropped beside him on the bed, her chin resting on his shoulder. "I'd rather we do some*thing* else."

"Are you still the adventurous type?" he asked.

Micah smirked, looking up at him through her lashes as a finger seductively traced the lines of tattoos on his biceps. "Depends on the adventure."

His head spun with all the things they could do together. It wasn't even that he'd experimented a whole lot, but there had been a few women before and after his marriage that tried things with him. Fletcher had always been happy to take whatever they gave him, learning from them and returning the favor the best he could. But never in his life had he been the one to initiate something like that. Then again, never in his life had he ever felt this way about anybody before.

"Blindfolds?" he whispered, sliding an arm around Micah's waist. When she nodded, batting her eyes at him, he continued. "Ice cubes?" A shiver ran through her and she shifted to straddle one leg. "Hot wax?" Micah hesitated and then shrugged, bottom lip tucked between her teeth. "Vibrators?" She nodded slowly, pressing herself down on his thigh and he gritted his teeth.

"What kind of adventure is this?" Micah was breathless, her fingers curling into his arms as they held each other.

"A little bit of everything."

"Have you done any of that before?"

He nodded, his eyes fixed on Micah's. "Indulged in some sensation play before, yeah."

"And you own a vibrator?"

This time, he dropped his eyes and blushed. Because the vibrator had been an impulse purchase. "Years ago, I met this woman who used one of her vibrators on me and it was… incredible."

She rocked her hips against his thigh, drawing his attention to her dark gaze. "You want me to use it on you?"

"Maybe. But I was wondering if I could use it on you instead?"

Her eyes stayed on his and Fletcher felt like she could see into his soul. "Yes, please."

"Yeah?"

Nodding, she cupped his face in both her hands. "I'll go any *adventure* with you, Fletch. As long as hot wax isn't involved."

He laughed, nodding as he leaned in to kiss her softly. Micah's arms slid around his neck and she kissed him back, his hands moving around to grip her ass through the towel. When she rocked against him again, Fletcher growled into the kiss and pulled away.

"Get comfortable, I'll gather everything."

She nodded, kissing him again before she reluctantly slid off his lap and crawled to the center of the bed. He forced himself to his feet and glanced over his shoulder to find Micah rubbing her thighs together.

"Quit stalling," she teased, toying with the edge of her towel. "Or I'll get started on my own."

When he returned to the bedroom fifteen minutes later, the towel around Micah had ridden up and her legs were parted slightly. He swallowed back a growl at the sight of her pussy—pink, dripping and waiting for him. He moved further into the room and her eyes snapped to his, lifting her upper body onto her elbows as she watched him. It wasn't like he was doing anything she wasn't aware of, but he'd still draped a towel over the tray filled with the things he'd brought. Fletcher set the tray on the bedside table and from the drawer pulled out the vibrator (still in its packaging), fuzzy handcuffs and a dark eye mask.

"Handcuffs too?"

"Only if you want to use them."

She held her hand out and he set the fuzzy restraint in her palm. As Micah fiddled with it, he sat on the edge of the bed and opened the vibrator. Even before he knew she'd ask for it, Fletcher held the bright pink device out to Micah and they shared a grin. While she touched and explored the two toys, Fletcher lowered the lighting and connected his phone to the hidden bluetooth speakers he'd set up in his room. The soft sounds of Steely Dan filtered through and she looked up at him with an arched eyebrow.

"If we use the handcuffs, do I need a safe word? Maybe cactus."

"Sure," he said with a chuckle. "But nothing is going to hurt, I promise."

"You won't edge me either, right?" Fletcher tilted his head and Micah flashed him an innocent smile. "What? I'm plenty adventurous."

"I'll save the edging for another time."

"Good. Now, get restraining." She handed the vibrator and cuffs back to him, then lay down again and undid the towel, spreading it out on either side of her. Fletcher's tongue was heavy in his mouth as he took in her body. There were a few more tattoos he hadn't noticed when they were in the shower together—a long line of words on the left side of her breast, what looked like a panda hanging from under the other breast. Of course this woman would have a collection of totally unrelated tattoos on her body.

As he watched, Micah raised her arms over her head and gripped the slats of his headboard. His breathing was unsteady and his heart was racing a mile a minute. When they were talking about it, he convinced himself he was in charge. But he should have known that there was no way Micah wouldn't be calling all the shots. She smirked, wiggling her eyebrows and he nodded. Pressing one knee into the bed, he leaned over her and cuffed her wrists, but didn't attach the cuffs to the headboard.

"Now what?"

"Mask," he said, tugging it over her head, making sure it didn't snag in her hair. He let the mask rest on her forehead so she could still see him. "You sure about this?"

"I trust you, Fletch."

"Okay. I'm going to lower the mask and uh…"

"Drive me absolutely wild with whatever is on that tray?" she asked softly, her brown eyes sparkling at him.

"I love you, Mick."

"Love you too, Fletch."

He stared at her a moment longer, then kissed her before lowering the mask over her eyes. It was one thing to have someone do this to him, but to actually do it to *Micah* was so different. He knew that she trusted him and he also knew that because he was new to this, he would never overdo it.

Besides, everything he brought upstairs would only make *her* feel really good. He uncovered the tray and tossed the towel to the floor, reviewing the items he'd picked—a set of his drumsticks, an ice bucket, a small bowl of caramel sauce, and of course the vibrator.

"Fletch?"

"I'm here, sweetheart."

"Are you okay?" Micah was breathless.

"Admiring the magnificent beauty in my bed."

She scoffed and even though he couldn't see her pretty eyes, he knew she'd rolled them. When he increased the volume of the music slightly, Micah started to hum along, her hips moving to the song. The whole thing made him smile. He reached for the drumsticks, twirling them between his fingers before he tapped out a beat from the song on his thigh. He then dragged one stick down Micah's body, from her collarbone, down between her breasts and to her belly button. She gasped, arching against the hickory wood he always used for his sticks.

With the tip of one stick, he circled her navel and used the other around a nipple. Micah groaned loudly, but swallowed it down by biting her bottom lip. Her nipples hardened to stiff peaks and Fletcher put his entire focus on her breasts, making sure that his drumsticks were driving her wild. Smiling to himself, he lifted the sticks off and twirled them between his fingers before tapping out the beat to the song on her breasts. A choked laugh fell from her lips, before it turned into a moan as he used the tips to play with her nipples again.

Did every drummer dream of finding ways to pleasure their partner with their drumsticks or was that only Fletcher? Either way, watching her body respond to the way he teased her breasts with a tool he'd used for *years* got him going. He was already hard and aching, and he hoped that he would survive playing with *her*.

Dropping one drumstick to the bed, Fletcher used that free hand to scoop up some caramel on a spoon. Doing his best not to drop any, he brought it over her body and tilted the spoon. The sauce dribbled onto her stomach and Micah's body jolted. Fletcher set the spoon down and leaned over to drag his tongue through the caramel, taking his time licking it all up. She moaned and whimpered, her body arching and hips lifting for more. He made sure to keep up teasing with the drumstick around her nipples, stimulating her in more ways than one.

"Fuck," Micah muttered, moaning as he sucked a glob of caramel from her stomach, certain he was marking up her skin in the process too.

Sarah McLachlan's "Sweet Surrender" started up, making him smile against her stomach. He dribbled more caramel, this time thin ropes around her nipples and between her breasts. Fletcher straddled her legs, not putting any weight on her as he licked along the caramel trail. She arched up against him, cuffs rattling as she tugged. He dragged a hand up her arm, rubbing slow circles against her wrist with his thumb as he focused on licking every drop of caramel off her breasts.

"You're killing me," she moaned.

Instead of responding with words, he flicked his tongue back and forth across her nipple and then sucked it into his mouth. She cursed him, handcuffs rattling some more, and then to be an asshole he played with her nipple between his teeth. Micah cried out, hips bucking up against him and Fletcher chuckled softly as he used his thumb to wipe up the last of the caramel sauce. Sticking his finger in his mouth, he shifted off Micah to wipe his hands.

"Come back," she whined, stretching one leg out and bumping him in the side.

He gave her leg a squeeze. "You doing okay?"

"Yes. What else do you have for me?"

He opened the ice bucket and grabbed a cube. "This one might be a bit of a shock."

Micah started to speak, but he set the ice cube right under her breasts and she whimpered, body arching as the cube slid down to rest on her stomach.

"Holy fuck," she mumbled, quivering at the cold. He dragged the ice cube back up to her breasts and around each nipple, smiling as she squirmed under his touch. Every time he pulled away, she whined for more, so he obliged by adding another cube. Between her body heat and the temperature in the room, the ice was melting faster than he expected.

Popping a cube into his mouth, Fletcher shifted between Micah's legs and teased along her mound. Her hips canted, a low keening sound falling from her mouth as Fletcher dragged the cube along the insides of her thighs. Micah's legs parted some more and he almost swallowed the ice cube at the sight of her pussy bared to him. She was so fucking beautiful, it was almost unfair how perfect she was. Forcing himself to focus, he ran the ice along the inside of her other thigh while his fingers played with her seam.

"More," she whispered. He popped the cube out of his mouth and gently rubbed it over her clit. Micah clearly liked that, because her hips thrust up eagerly. One to please, he slid it along her clit and down her seam until it melted against her.

"More?" Fletcher asked, knowing what the answer would be already. She nodded and he obliged, grabbing another cube and rubbing it over her clit as his mouth worked her pussy, fingers spreading her open so he could taste her.

Her sounds, movements and reactions were everything he wanted and more. When the second cube melted, he used his mouth to tease her clit, warming her up as his fingers penetrated through her slit. Pumping two fingers into her, he sucked on her clit, sliding his tongue back and forth over the bundle of nerves as his fingers fucked her. Her hips practically levitated off the bed as he curled his fingers inside her, dragging the tips along her inner walls.

When he twisted his fingers and flicked at her clit with his tongue, Micah's body tightened and she came hard, a gasping moan falling from her lips.

As her body settled back into the bed, her chest rising and falling with her heavy breathing, Fletcher slid his fingers out of her and licked them clean. He moved over Micah and undid the cuffs, his fingers slowly massaging her wrists and the slight dents all the pulling and tugging had left behind. When he pushed the mask up to her forehead, Micah's unfocused eyes blinked up at him.

"I think you broke me," she mumbled and then burst into giggles, pressing her hands to her eyes. "In all the best ways, obviously."

He tossed the cuffs and mask to the side and watched as she stretched her body slowly. "You might need another wash."

"Yeah? What did you do to me anyway?" He nodded at the nightstand and Micah turned to glance at the items on the tray. "You know what…I had this fantasy once of being fucked by your drumsticks, so that's pretty great. Except, I also realize now that there could be splinters and that would be unpleasant."

He laughed and leaned over to kiss her shoulder. "I would never subject anyone to a drumstick fucking. That sounds painful."

"Caramel?"

"Favorite taste in the whole world."

Micah grinned and turned over to look at him. "What else tastes good?"

"You," he whispered, tugging her into his arms. She snuggled into him, their faces inches apart and he nudged his nose against her jaw, inhaling the vanilla and lavender scent that followed her everywhere. "You're better than anything I've ever tasted."

"And yet, you covered me in sticky sauce."

He grinned, his hands smoothing down her back as Micah's fingers teased over his chest and stomach. "Payback for covering my dick in sticky shit."

She snorted and turned her head to kiss him softly. "Totally worth it." And then she was rolling out of bed, heading to the bathroom. At the doorway, she glanced over her shoulder and smiled at him. "You coming?"

micah

I didn't get to fuck Santa Claus.

IT TOOK her a few minutes to process where she was when her eyes blinked open. The bright light confused her, followed by the warm body pressed against her. Inhaling deeply, she got a whiff of mint and a small smile tugged at her lips as she remembered where she was—Fletcher's bed. Everything about the night before had been pretty incredible, from meeting *Fletcher Claus* to the fruit roll-up blow job and the sensation play that followed.

She had to admit that she had never imagined she would get to enjoy something like that with him. Sex had become such a vague idea in her mind, so to have it with the man she *loved* was a big deal. God, she'd admitted to loving him the night before too. Micah pressed her lips together to stop from squealing like a little girl, because not only had she told him how she felt, he had reciprocated the feelings and they'd had the best night together.

Even though watching Fletcher sleep was at the top of her list of things to do, her bladder protested enough to drag her out of bed. Extracting herself from his arms slowly, so as not to wake him up, Micah walked to the bathroom completely naked. She'd made this trip a few times already and in that exact state of dress, which made her giggle softly. Once she'd emptied her bladder and washed her face, she tugged on her underwear and pulled on the flannel shirt hanging behind the bathroom door. He was still fast asleep and the sounds of his soft snoring infiltrated the room.

Downstairs, she fiddled around with his coffee machine and got a pot started. They'd cleaned up after dinner and the sticky blow job, so his kitchen was spotless. But being there brought everything back into focus. She remembered the way he looked when she told him that she loved him—the shock and adoration in his eyes, the confusion and frustration that she beat him to the punch. She recalled the way it felt to suck his cock into her mouth while it was covered in strawberry flavor and his fingers were tangled in her short curls.

While the coffee brewed, she found his Santa coat hanging by the door. Smiling to herself, she swapped the shirt for the coat, smoothing it down so it covered her breasts, but left most of her body exposed. Micah poured out the coffee, making it her way and hoping Fletcher would like it, then returned to the bedroom and found him awake. He was sitting up in bed, sheets pooled around his waist, hair in a topknot.

Even their first time together, she had noticed that he wasn't muscular and bulky like most men she met. Some would even say he had a 'dad bod', which was honestly really sexy. More than anything, he seemed so comfortable in his skin that all those other things didn't really matter. Besides, there was so much else about Fletcher that was *hot*. From the silver in his beard and hair, the way he looked in his glasses, the tattoos on his bare chest that called for her to explore them some more.

But it was his expression that had her attention right then.

"Fucking hell, Mick."

"Nice, right?" If her hands were free, she would have flipped the coat back, exposing as much of herself as she could, while setting one hand on her hip. Alas, coffee.

"You told me about your slightly concerning fantasy about my sticks last night, but I never told you mine." His voice was scratchy with sleep and gruff in the sexiest way. "You in my clothes. I dreamed about it countless times and I could never have imagined how fucking good it would be when I got to see it for real."

"*Technically*, these aren't your clothes. I did start this morning in your flannel, though. So I think it's a fantasy we can totally make come true. *A lot*."

"Oh, I intend to make it happen every chance I get," he said, eyes following her as she came around the side of the bed and held a mug out to him.

She climbed into bed and made herself comfortable, blowing on the hot coffee as his hand landed on her thigh, pushing the coat aside.

"I think I might like you in my Santa coat more than my flannel," he whispered and she laughed, resting her head on his shoulder. His fingers drew abstract patterns over her skin, goosebumps following in its wake.

Humming softly, she said, "So, last night was fun."

"I have my work cut out for me if you think it was *fun*."

She laughed and nudged him gently. "I didn't get to fuck Santa Claus."

"Maybe I'll get to fuck her instead," he whispered into Micah's ear.

"Yes," she moaned, eyes rolling back in her head, her thighs parting to allow him further exploration.

"Did you really have fun, Mick?"

"Could you not tell from the moaning and the triple orgasm last night?"

He chuckled, the sound making her lips curve into a

smile. "Good. I've read about how ice cubes heighten the whole thing, did it?"

Humming in acknowledgement, she clenched her thighs together, trapping his fingers between her soft flesh, as she took another sip of her coffee. The ice cube had been an interesting change from the drumsticks and the caramel poured onto her body. The sudden shock of cold had brought every inch of her alive and then when he used it on her clit and her pussy, everything else faded to exist.

"Shame we didn't get to use the vibrator, though," she whispered, not trusting herself to speak louder. "Maybe I can use it on *you* next time."

"Vibrators, fruit roll-ups and ice cubes."

"Sadly I don't have any appendages that you can wrap a fruit roll-up around."

He laughed loudly, shifting beside her and then she felt his lips against her forehead. "You already taste pretty fucking good, Mick, I don't need a roll-up when I'm eating you out."

She licked her lips, core pulsing because now she was imagining the brush of his beard against the inside of her thighs again. Right where his fingers were. The way his tongue lapped at her as she rode his face. She couldn't remember the last time she'd let herself go that way during sex. Maybe when they first met.

"What do you remember of our first time together?" she asked, glancing at Fletcher with a smile.

"Everything. Why?"

"Do you remember us trying to have shower sex and failing because you couldn't hold me up?"

He nodded, the corner of his mouth curved up in a smile. "Less about being unable to hold you up and more about being so nervous that I would drop you because I'd never done that before."

"I guess groupies weren't looking for shower sex if they could ride you into the sunrise after a show."

"Even after all this time, it's amusing that you're jealous of people I never indulged in."

She arched an eyebrow. "You never hooked up with a groupie?"

"Maybe in the beginning, but they got boring pretty fast. And when I was ready to hook-up with random strangers again, there was this curly haired stunner in the crowd who completely stole my attention."

"Damn her for taking away your chance to experience magic with groupies." Micah smiled into her coffee when he snorted.

"You know what I remember from that night? The four times you rode me."

"Was it four?"

He nodded. "Almost five, but you started yawning as you climbed into my lap and I could tell that you needed to sleep."

"You were so not the rockstar I thought you would be. Gentle and shy and nervous."

Maybe she'd watched too many movies about rockstars—*Sid & Nancy*, *Rock Star* and *Almost Famous* mostly—that she was convinced all musicians were sex gods who had alcohol running through their veins. She also liked to believe that everyone had the best hair too. Fletcher and his bandmates had erased that notion when she started following them around on tour. But still, she didn't expect him to be awkward. He hadn't tossed her around or manhandled her. In fact, he had been so fucking soft that night. Even the night before, he'd asked questions, he made sure she was okay and he touched her reverently. Like he was afraid he'd hurt her.

"I didn't want to come off as this horny asshole who only wanted you for sex."

She arched an eyebrow and he mirrored the expression. "What did you want me for?"

"At first, I wanted to have more long conversations with you. Then, I only *wanted* you. I was going to ask you to stay the next morning."

"Then I left before you woke up," she whispered and he nodded.

"You fell asleep in my arms, tucked against me, and all I could think about was how good it would feel to have you in my bed every day for the rest of my life."

"Fletch…"

He smiled, shaking his head as he finished his coffee and set his cup down. "You were the first person I had met who didn't treat me like a rockstar. You talked to me about music without giving a shit about my opinion, you challenged me at every turn and you made sure that I was aware that I had terrible taste in music."

"I said *questionable.*"

Laughing, he took her cup away and set it aside. Micah whined at the loss of caffeine, but didn't protest when he tugged her into his lap. The Santa coat spread out around them, keeping only her breasts covered.

"People, mostly women, I meet are always ready to agree with me on everything. They think that by supporting my suggestions and favorites, they're doing the right thing. You didn't give a shit about any of that. You tortured me about my list of the best female rockstars and believe it or not, I actually agreed with your list."

"I mean, we agreed on Stevie Nicks being the best, with Karen Carpenter and Bonnie Raitt a close second," Micah reminded him. "I know we couldn't agree on Grace Slick and Ann Wilson. What about Joan Jett?"

"Nope. We're not discussing anymore rockstars, unless

we're talking about me and this dick that's hard as fuck for you."

Her eyes widened and she smirked. "Someone woke up on the horny side of bed this morning."

Fletcher rolled his eyes, but was already running his hands up her stomach and under the coat to cup her breasts. "I can't decide if I want to fuck you in this or not."

"Only if you have a spare. Because we don't want to get bodily fluids on this," she told him as they worked together to slide the coat off her shoulders, leaving Micah in her underwear.

He tossed the coat aside and Micah used those few seconds to scoot backwards. He frowned as he glanced from his empty lap to where she was toying with the waistband of her underwear.

"Why are you so far away?"

"Middle of the bed, rockstar," she told him. Leaning back on her hands Micah pushed her underwear off and spread her legs, giving him an undisturbed view of her pussy. "Grab the vibrator too."

The corner of his mouth lifted in a smirk as he shifted on the bed, pushing the covers out of the way. He tossed her the vibrator from the nightstand and then slid out of his boxers, his very erect cock springing to attention. She whistled and Fletcher grunted, his cock twitching as he moved towards her. While messing with the vibrator, finding the setting that worked for her, she instructed Fletcher on where to sit, where his legs needed to go.

With his legs bent at the knee on either side of her, Micah slid her legs over his thighs so that she was half straddling him, even though both their asses were firmly on the bed. His eyes were firmly fixed on the spot between her thighs and that allowed Micah to admire him for a long moment.

"Should have asked you this before," he murmured and

Micah dropped a hand to stroke one finger through her pussy, "do we need condoms?"

"Definitely before I put your dick in my mouth. But I got tested a few weeks ago and everything came back all clear."

Because of Emery, Micah went through full check-ups twice a year to make sure that she was going to be okay. Everything from checking for STIs and breast cancer, she spent tons of her hard earned money making sure that she was healthy. No part of her imagined that she would be sleeping with the man of her dreams that year. That was the kind of stuff that was saved for Christmas hopes and wishes.

"Me too." He nodded, but his focus was fixed entirely on where their bodies were touching and rubbing. His eyes were dark as his tongue slipped out to wet his lips. "Do we need lube?"

Pushing herself to sit up a little more, she held the vibrator up and arched an eyebrow at Fletcher. "Not yet. You up for an adventure?"

His eyes widened and then he looked between them before nodding slowly. She turned it on the lowest setting and carefully ran the vibrator along Fletcher's length. He grunted, hands fisting in the sheets, which only spurred her on more. She kept the vibration at low and moved it around his tip, her body quivering in anticipation of how good it would feel to have him inside her again. Fletcher groaned, his cock jumping at every gentle touch.

Her core clenched and she bit down on her bottom lip as she slid a hand between her thighs. Dipping a finger into her pussy, her eyes shuttered for a moment as she slid the digit deeper. Forcing her eyes open when she heard a strangled sound come out of Fletcher, she slid the vibrator down and around the base of his cock. His hips jerked and he moaned loudly, head falling back. She added a second finger and pumped them both deep inside her. When her body started to shake, she pulled her fingers out and dropped the vibrator at the same time, drawing Fletcher's hooded eyes to hers.

"Look at me, Fletch," she whimpered, running her wet fingers along the length of him.

"You're dripping, Mick."

"This is what *you* do to me. Every single time."

Both of them sat there, legs entwined and panting as they stared at each other. The vibrator lay between them, still buzzing softly. When he'd caught his breath, he repeated, "Lube?"

Micah nodded and licked her lips to steady herself as he grabbed a bottle from his nightstand. Even though she was wet and primed for him, it had been a while since Micah had a human dick inside her. Her vibrator and the dildo were great sizes, but it was what her body was used to. Fletcher's dick? Bigger than her toys and *definitely* bigger than the last man she'd been with. Taking the bottle from him, she squirted a good amount into her hands and then tossed it aside. He watched her the whole time as she rubbed her hands together and then dragged them along his dick one at a time. She could hear him grinding his teeth as her hands circled his base and his head, thumb swiping over the bead of precum on his tip. Fletcher's head fell forward, chin resting on his chest as she stroked him from base to tip again and when he growled out her name, she knew he would take matters into his own hands if she didn't work faster.

"Fletch, look at me," she whispered, hand around his base as she lined him up with her pussy. His dark gaze met hers and she smiled at how his jaw flexed as she guided him into her. That first night they shared had been slightly messy and there was some fumbling. This was different. They were both in much better control of themselves and each other.

Her breath caught in her throat as she pushed her hips forward, taking Fletcher deeper. Her toes curled against the sheets and she gasped as his hips snapped against hers, filling her up completely.

"Oh, *fuck*."

"Jesus, Mick, you're perfect."

Her head lolled backwards, breathing a little unsteady as his dick twitched inside her. Her memories and imagination didn't do justice to how fucking good he felt inside her. Their eyes met and she bit her lip at the look Fletcher was shooting at her—love, adoration, desire, passion and a desperate need to possess her. With every shift of her hips forward, he did the same and before she knew it, they were moving together, his cock sliding through her wet and hungry pussy. When he shifted forward, hands sliding down her thighs, the angle of his thrusts changed and her head spun at how good even that felt.

Fletcher's lips landed on her jaw and she tilted her head away from him, giving him access to her neck as their hips rolled together desperately. His hands continued to wander along her legs, down to her hips as she met him thrust for thrust. It was the slowest kind of sex she'd ever had and shockingly enough, Micah was enjoying it.

Turning her head slightly, she caught his mouth with hers in a kiss that she felt all the way to her throbbing clit. His tongue swept between her parted lips and she moaned, clenching around him as he pushed as deep into her as he could go. A soft gasp escaped her through the kiss when his hand landed on the bundle of nerves, a finger teasing it slowly and seductively as their kiss deepened. When her walls fluttered around him, Micah leaned forward and gripped his biceps, on the edge of her orgasm. With one more gentle snap of his hips and a not so gentle pinch of her clit, Micah detonated with a loud shout of his name. The orgasm rocked through her, shivers wracking her body as she rode out her orgasm. Her grip on him loosened and she collapsed backwards, breathing heavily.

"Mick?" His voice broke through her orgasm haze and Micah hummed with a smile. He chuckled and his hands spread over her thighs and stomach. "You good?"

"Define good." She carefully propped herself up on her elbows and found him watching her with a smile. "Are you?"

"Almost."

Micah frowned and sat up fully, that's when she noticed Fletcher's dick was still hard and inside her. "Oh my god, you didn't come."

"Which is not the end of the world, but I would *really* like to come."

"How do you want me?"

"Just the way you are," he said softly and Micah rolled her eyes. He laughed and ran a hand up her stomach to tweak a nipple. "Lie back, please."

She lay back down and he pulled out of her, making both of them moan. She was so satisfied and and her muscles were loose that when he moved her around, slipping pillows under her hips, Micah didn't protest or question it. When he moved over her, she grinned and wrapped her arms around his neck. Their lips met as he settled between her thighs, his cock pressing against her slick entrance. She whimpered into the kiss, arching her back slightly to press against him some more. His hands steadied her hips and Micah playfully protested at not being able to move more.

She kissed him hungrily, one leg lifting to wrap around his waist. One minute she felt Fletcher's fingers sliding through her slit, spreading her open and the next his cock was pushing into her. An unidentifiable sound escaped her mouth as she broke the kiss and her head tilted back. He thrust into her fully, burying himself inside her and she wrapped her other leg around his waist.

"Eyes on me, love bug," Fletcher whispered as his hands landed on either side of her head. She blinked them open and found him smiling down at her. His hips moved steadily, first in slow rolls and then back and forth. Micah's legs tightened around him and despite every urge to close her eyes, she focused on his face as he rocked against her. When his hips rolled in slow figure eights, Micah's pussy fluttered and she fought against everything to come again. He rocked harder, hips moving in a slow thrusting motion as her hands wandered over his chest and up to his shoulders, back around his neck again.

When she thrust her hips up against his, she felt his cock pulse inside her. With a few more thrusts, he was coming, spilling into her as she clenched around him. His head dropped into the crook of her neck and Micah held onto him as they rode out their orgasms, bodies completely spent and wrung out from hours of sexual magic.

fletcher

I'm drink! And corny!

FLETCHER WAS SUPPOSED to be doing inventory, but his mind kept wandering back to his weekend with Micah. It had only been two days since he'd walked her out to her car before his shift as Santa. And in those two days, he replayed everything they'd done together. Sex on Sunday morning had been quite something, watching her body buck and roll against his, her pussy clenching around him so tight he was sure he'd black out. The rest of Sunday was spent pretty much the same way, except for bathroom and food breaks.

If that wasn't enough, he was also smiling at the fact that she loved him.

That first night they shared together sixteen years ago was imprinted on his soul and he'd accepted that not only would he never see *Mick* again, he'd never connect with anyone that way either. Then she waltzed back into his life looking like the best thing on earth and he took that as a sign. And the last three weeks were proof that he'd made the right decision to follow the sign.

Except, he was now so distracted, he couldn't get any work done.

When Emery and Nico had come in for their lessons the day before, Fletcher had let them go wild with their instruments. Which was a terrible idea, because despite being interested in learning, neither of them had any musical talent. He knew the right thing was to dissuade them from pursuing this any further, but at the same time, he felt bad about crushing their spirits. He would have to find a different method to get them into the right musical direction during their session later that afternoon.

"Why aren't you picking up your phone?"

Fletcher jumped at the voice behind him and knocked his head against the shelf that held all the cymbals. The sound of them clashing together echoed through the room and he groaned as he turned to glare at Erin, who smiled at him sheepishly. Fletcher didn't bother trying to steady the cymbals, he nudged Erin out of the room and closed the door, rubbing the top of his head as he blinked at her.

"What are you doing here?"

"Thought I'd spend Christmas in Sirena Beach."

Fletcher stuck a finger in his ear and wiggled it before opening and closing his mouth, like that would get rid of the ringing in his head. "I'm spending Christmas with Mi…"

"The *woman* from the photograph, I figured." Erin grinned and started towards his office, hand shoved deep into her large bag. "Speaking of which…"

He took the phone she held out to him and couldn't even fight back the smile that stretched across his face when he saw the photograph. It was from the night Micah found out he was Santa, they were standing below mistletoe, arms around each other, grinning like fools in love. The paparazzi had caught Emery in the shot too, but they didn't get her face, which he was grateful for. The thing that got his attention was how happy both he and Micah looked. The joy was practically blinding.

"So…who is she?"

"Micah George, local. The one that got away."

Erin sat in his office chair, leaving Fletcher to sit in the uncomfortable ones on the other side. "You mentioned that already."

"I met her *years* ago while on tour with The Rescuers. Best night of my life."

"Groupie?"

"Not even close. She was a fan I pulled out of the crowd and spent the night with."

Erin watched him curiously, head tilted to the side and he blew out a frustrated breath. Outside of Jack, Soren and Brandy he hadn't made a lot of close friends during his band years. And when he moved to Sirena Beach, it was hard to connect with people who were already part of friend groups. So when Hank set him up with Erin, Fletcher was happy to realize that the two of them were compatible as friends and not romantic partners. Since then, she'd gotten to know him pretty well and could read him like a book.

Which was why he didn't startle when she said, "You're in love with her."

He nodded, dragging a hand through his hair. "Have been since the night I met her. She's amazing, E."

"Do I get to meet her?"

"Sure."

She arched an eyebrow. "I expected you to protest or make excuses."

"No point," he said, using a pencil from the desk to tie his hair up. "She's important to me and you're my best friend, so why hide you from each other?"

Her eyes widened and she released a loud cackle. "Best friend?"

"I regret everything." He groaned, rubbing his temples. Between the clashing of the cymbals still in his ears and the force with which he hit his head, Fletcher was in some amount of pain.

She laughed, swinging her feet onto the table. "Tell me everything about her."

Fletcher smiled this time, because asking him to talk about Micah was the easiest thing in the world. He could talk about her *forever*. The flavor of ice cream she preferred, how she tucked her curls behind her ear when she was cooking or the different smiles she had for Emery. He could describe the details of her perfume and the number of freckles she had dusted over her nose.

Instead, he said, "Single mom and she raised the most incredible kid, who has great taste in music, but is tone deaf. Works as a speech therapist with the Haven Clinic, is the strongest woman I've ever known."

"That's not what I asked, Fletcher. Tell me *everything*."

He chuckled, combing a hand through his hair. "She's got tattoos that her daughter either picked or drew for her, she's badass and drinks wine like it's water. Micah is passionate about her kid and the people in her life. She fights me on who the best female rockstar is every single time, she cleans up as she cooks and you know how much I love that. She's tough as nails and wild in bed." Clearing his throat, he thought about the fruit roll-up blow job and the fact that she did it once more before they parted ways on Sunday. "She's also the woman who inspired "Mermaid"," he added with a shrug when Erin's eyes widened.

"Holy shit, you *have* been in love with her forever."

He smirked and stretched out his arm to drag his thumb over the cerulean mermaid tail. On their first *date*, Erin had asked about the tattoo and Fletcher told her that it was for a woman who inspired a song many years ago.

"Does she deserve you?"

Frowning, he looked at his friend. "Of course she does."

Erin smiled, shaking her head. "Take off your rose colored glasses and tell me the truth."

"She does, Erin. She's never been interested in me for my money or my fame, she doesn't want anything from me other than…me. Her kid too. They're nothing like so many of the women I've met over the years."

"Okay." Erin nodded, searching his eyes with a small smile. "And she wants to stick around even though she knows you're Santa?"

The corner of his mouth kicked up in a grin. "She's not a fan of the holiday, but definitely has a Santa kink and I'm happy to indulge her."

Erin made a gagging sound and waved her hands at him. "Please spare me the details of your kinky girlfriend."

"You brought it up."

Faking another gag, Erin leaned back in the chair. "So this means you're sticking around Sirena Beach for the foreseeable future."

"Or until she gets tired of me, yeah."

"Judging by the way she looked at you in the picture, I'm going to assume that she'll never tire of you. Besides, you're a pretty decent guy."

"Thanks?" Fletcher chuckled and patted his pockets before realizing he didn't have his phone. "Tell you what, why don't we do lunch or coffee tomorrow? That way you can meet Micah and Emery, if they're up for it."

"Kicking me out already?"

"Gotta finish inventory before the kids come in."

"Riiiiiiight, that's how you reconnected with your lady love. How's that going, by the way?"

Fletcher sighed. "The aforementioned tone deaf kid is going to make me get behind the drums one day just to show her how it's done. But, seeing them get excited about something and want to learn is pretty cool. Might keep it up if I can find the energy and time."

"Maybe next time you should do it when you're not playing Santa, because you're gonna need more time for your little family."

Your little family. He smiled at that, his heart racing a million miles. That's who Micah and Emery were to him, his family. He'd lost the closest thing he had to a father when Hank died and outside of Benson and Erin he didn't have anybody else. Until the George women welcomed him into their lives.

"I didn't realize that being in love made you look like a dumbfuck," she said, flipping her phone around to show him a picture she'd taken seconds ago. He was leaning back, totally relaxed and the most content smile on his face.

"Once you meet her, you'll get it."

Erin snorted and got up, grabbing her things. "Text me about tomorrow once you find your phone."

"Come by the Village tonight, I'll show you around."

"As long as you can score me some reindeer antlers."

Fletcher rolled his eyes and followed Erin to the front of the store as Benson walked in. His friends paused as they looked the other over. Then with a playful handshake he couldn't track, they laughed and walked past each other. Fletcher frowned as he glanced between the two of them and followed Erin outside. He would get to the bottom of that look eventually.

"Stay out of trouble, E."

She turned to him with a wicked grin. "Where's the fun in that?" And then she strutted off on her high heels to a cherry red SUV. Fletcher watched her climb in and drive off before walking back into the store to finish his job for the day. His phone started ringing before he got too far and found the device buried under piles of sheet music.

Swiping it open, he went through the notifications—five missed calls from Jensen, a bunch of texts from Emery about being late for lessons, a few missed calls from Erin and a text from Micah. He forwarded the mistletoe picture to Micah and grinned as he leaned against the wall and texted her.

FLETCHER

Maybe we should redo the whole 'I Saw Mommy Kissing Santa Claus' thing for the newer generation.

MICAH

heart eyes emoji

I love this! The picture, not us redoing or recreating anything.

FLETCHER

So you're not upset that the paparazzi are following us around?

MICAH

At least they're taking pictures of me at my best, can't hate them for that.

And she was right. When he'd seen her in that red dress, he'd almost abandoned his Santa duties and dragged her into a dark corner. Her legs were on display and the way it cinched at her waist made his mouth water. Now that he'd seen her completely naked and knew every inch of her body with his eyes shut, he needed to see her only in dresses.

FLETCHER

You always look your best, Mick.

Micah

Aww, look at you being the best boyfriend.

FLETCHER

I thought we agreed on Stallion.

MICAH

We agreed on nothing of the sort.

FLETCHER

You're still my love bug, though.

MICAH

eyeroll emoji

FLETCHER

kissy face emoji

Been thinking about you all day.

MICAH

Oh yeah? What have you been thinking about?

FLETCHER

Everything. All of it. Fruit roll-ups and caramel sauce and ice cubes and drumsticks.

Fucking hell, I have a lesson with your kid this evening.

MICAH

Don't think about drumsticks, Fletch.

FLETCHER

Well, thinking about you while she's here isn't any better.

MICAH

That's true. How about you think about…

FLETCHER

My best friend wants to meet you.

MICAH

Who is your best friend?

FLETCHER

Erin Decker. She's based out of San Diego, but she's in town for a few days and was hoping to meet the woman that has me smiling like a loon.

MICAH

Did you tell HER about the drumsticks and fruit roll-ups?

FLETCHER

I thought we were trying to stop me from thinking about that?

MICAH

monkey covering mouth emoji

But I'd love to meet your best friend. What did you have in mind?

FLETCHER

Coffee tomorrow?

MICAH

Mrs. Hershey booked a session for tomorrow afternoon, but I've got a late start. So breakfast?

FLETCHER

Bring Emery too.

MICAH

Oh wow, full court press.

FLETCHER

Hardly. I told her about Em and she wants to meet both of you.

MICAH

We'll be there, Fletch.

FLETCHER

Have fun tonight, Mick.

MICAH

You know I will. *kissy face emoji*

Since Micah was out with her friends, Fletcher had every intention of working until the Village closed. He'd promised Jensen that he'd say for clean-up a few nights of the week and it worked out for the evening. He'd already texted Erin about breakfast with the George girls, so his best friend could plan her day around that. Instead, he focused entirely on being Santa that evening. Even though memories of Micah from over the weekend filtered through every so often, Fletcher was determined to hang out with all the kids.

But he was starting to feel the exhaustion. Every year, towards the end of his Santa run, Fletcher would start to wilt. The combination of running the store and functioning like a normal adult, along with being Santa felt like a lot. This year, he'd also added music lessons and dating; it was more than he was used to. But he wasn't complaining. And he wouldn't walk away from Santa duty unless it was absolutely necessary.

It had been another evening of squatting and bending to talk to kids, having them whisper in his ear about their hopes and dreams. So when he and his elves—Portia and Kyle had finally taken their respective shots and were now going on a date—packed up for the evening, he was ready to crawl into bed. Except, the minute he climbed into his truck, his phone rang and Micah's name flashed on the screen.

Swiping to answer the call, he smiled. "Love bug."

"Fleeeeeetttttch," she squealed and then giggled, the rest of her words a garbled mess.

"Hey sweetheart, you okay?"

"I'm drink! And corny! Horny!"

He chuckled at the slurring and fumbling. "How corny are you, babe?"

"So fracking corny. Wanna come to me?"

"Where are you?"

"Dunno, stallion. But find me."

Before the call dropped, he heard someone say Loose Lasso. Not that he expected a western themed bar to exist in Sirena Beach, but when he pulled it up on the map, he was proven wrong. Even though he was exhausted, his girl was clearly drunk and Fletcher wasn't going to let her climb into someone else's car and get herself home. It took him less than ten minutes to reach the bar and when he pulled up in the parking lot, he heard someone call out his name.

Fletcher hopped out of the truck and grinned at the sight of Micah and her friends holding each other up as they giggled and waved at him. The other two were beautiful, he was sure. But his focus was entirely on Micah wearing a white lacy top with a deep neck that was tucked into high waisted jeans and boots. She was an absolute vision.

"It's my stallion!" Micah squealed and her two friends joined in on the weird sounds.

Tatum wiggled her fingers at Fletcher and offered him a sloppy smile. "Fletcher."

"Love bug. Tatum. How are you ladies doing tonight?"

Micah scrunched up her nose and leaned against the one with brightly colored hair. "Is that a good nickname?" When her friend shrugged and both of them swayed, Fletcher reached out to steady them. "You found me," she whispered, hands resting on his arms.

"Yeah, honey, I found you," he said with a smile and

chuckled when Micah stumbled into his arms. Brushing a kiss over her sweaty temple, Fletcher looked at her friends. "Can you three wait here? I'll bring the truck closer."

Micah settled between them again and shot him a drunken smile, along with a messy wink and he laughed as he went to get his truck. He brought it right up to where they were standing, and one by one helped Micah and her friends into the backseat. He knew there was no point trying to figure out where any of them lived, so he figured he'd take them back to Micah's place. But on the way, they insisted he stop and get them greasy food.

Parked outside Stacked Buns—the only place in Sirena Beach that was open that late—Fletcher made sure that Micah and her friends were well hydrated and fed. Sadie and Tatum stayed in the backseat while they stuffed their faces. Micah and Fletcher sat on the tailgate as she inhaled her food. He picked at his fries, watching her not give a shit about anything but eating.

"I didn't mean to get drunk," she said, mouth stuffed with food.

"As long as you had fun, nothing else matters."

She nodded, glancing at him for a moment. "Thanks for coming to get me."

"Always, Mick."

She looked sad and also a little worried, which he put down to her coming down from her high. But it was in the way she refused to meet his eyes that had him worried.

"Hey," he said softly, touching her chin to draw her attention to him. "What's wrong?"

"You're not mad, right? I know you're tired after your day and looking after your drunk girlfriend is not fun."

Frowning, he shook his head. "I'm glad you called me, Mick. I'm glad I could be here for you. No matter what I was doing or where I was, I would have shown up for you. And as for being mad? Not in a million years. You trusted *me* to be there for you, that's all that matters."

"I love you," she whispered, sounding so small and scared. He tapped her nose with a finger and then scooted close enough to wrap his arms around her shoulders.

"Love you too, Mick."

micah

Fucking perfect, love bug.

"OH GOD."

The heavy metal band in her head would not quit and Micah groaned as she turned onto her back, stretching an arm out. While the bed was empty, it was still slightly warm and a small smile floated over her lips at the memory of Fletcher being in bed with her. But then everything else about the night came flooding back and she groaned again.

Given that it was a Tuesday and they had work the next day, she had been surprised to get a text from Tatum about needing a drink. It was only when all three of them were seated at the Loose Lasso that they understood why Tatum needed them. Having spoken to Tatum about the whole Benji-Ambrose kerfuffle, Micah knew that her best friend would be struggling. But never in her wildest dreams did she think Benji would come back and make *demands*. They'd been divorced for three years and he was now asking for all the things they'd laid out in their settlement. And it had right-fully shaken Tatum up.

So they went drinking.

At first, Tatum was angry and knocking back tequila shots

faster than was good for her. Then they switched to pitchers of margaritas, which wasn't as smart as they thought at the time. Of course when men saw three gorgeous women out and about, having the time of their lives, they *insisted* on buying them drinks. None of them would ever turn down free alcohol, even if it was a bad idea.

So they continued drinking.

They went from tequila to margaritas to beers and then more tequila shots. With a small break to eat and line their stomachs. Then back to the margaritas. By which time the Loose Lasso staff had set up the mechanical bull riding competition. And nobody was going to stop the three of them from participating. However, they did *not* participate in throwing themselves into the arms of the hot cowboys— though Micah was certain Sadie was disappointed in their decision. The bull riding prompted multiple restroom visits after which they ate more food and *then* Micah called Fletcher.

Mostly prompted by Tatum and Sadie laughing about how he was her stallion.

Apparently drunk Micah was okay with their silly nicknames.

And Fletcher had shown up.

More than that, he'd helped her best friends into his truck, got them food and waited until they were all a little more steady and sober before driving them to her place. He tucked her friends into the guest bedroom and then helped her out of her clothes before wrapping her up in her bed. *And* he stayed the night, judging by the delicious scent of him still lingering on her sheets.

She grinned through her pounding hangover, right until her brain reminded her of the vague mumbling while they were eating burgers. Wincing, she turned over and buried her face in the pillow. When they were married, Geoffrey would give her so much shit for drinking with the girls and having a good time. On the rare occasions she'd call him for a pick-up after a night out, Geoffrey would show up begrudgingly and berate her the whole drive home—*You're a mother, you need to behave that way. What will Emery think when she finds out her mother's a fucking lush? What is wrong with you, you can't get drunk on a week night.* Micah would sometimes fight back, but when you're slurring through your rebuttal, it's hard to really make a point.

So she obviously freaked out that Fletcher would feel the same way. In her drunken state, that was the only thing that made sense. Because she knew that she was *really* drunk and it wasn't entirely the most attractive thing. Except, he hadn't seemed to judge her and when she brought up her worries in the most vague way possible, he'd been confused. *You trusted me to be there for you, that's all that matters*, was all he said, but it was the way he said it that made her realize she'd underestimated how wonderful Fletcher Kelley was.

After a few more minutes of silently grumbling at herself, she slid out of bed and found two Advil and a glass of water on her nightstand, along with a note that said 'this goes in your mouth, love bug'. She popped the pills and on wobbly knees, walked to the bathroom, brushed her teeth and rinsed her face. Then with a big headband, she pushed her hair back. She grabbed the silk robe from behind her bathroom door and tugged it on over her camisole set before heading downstairs.

Apparently everyone else was already awake, judging by the laughing and talking *and* the delicious smells of breakfast food coming from her kitchen. Micah hugged herself, smiling as she hit the bottom step, attempting not to get too giddy over this development.

"I still can't believe Mick's dating Santa," Sadie said loudly, drawing laughs from Emery and Tatum.

"For a few weeks a year. The rest of the time, I'm…"

"Fletch, former rockstar," her daughter supplied and Micah snorted out a laugh as she stepped into the kitchen.

Her best friends looked fresh as daisies, perched on stools at the kitchen island. Emery was standing with Fletcher while he made breakfast. The sight of all her favorite people in one room made her heart swell.

"Morning," she greeted them, wincing at the way the word grated on her throat.

"We were getting to know your *stallion* a little better," Tatum said with a smirk and Emery shuddered. "And we're still processing the fact that you're dating *Santa*."

Fletcher rolled his eyes playfully, shooting her a smile as he held out a mug. "They keep skipping past the fact that I'm also a regular guy."

"With platinum albums and awards *and* a Santa hat to his name!"

Micah shot Sadie a smirk and then sidled closer to Fletcher as he flipped pancakes. Her friends had never liked Geoffrey and they'd never seen her be affectionate with him either. When it came to Fletcher, she liked being able to touch and hold him as much as possible. Pressing a kiss to his shoulder, she sighed softly and leaned against him as one arm came around her shoulder. "You feeling okay?"

"The Advil helped, thank you," she whispered and then took a sip of her coffee.

"Have a seat, I'm almost done."

She nodded and tipped her head back as he dropped his lips to hers for a quick kiss. Smiling against his mouth, she patted his stomach and sat down, inhaling the coffee deeply.

"I thought you three were past the point of black out drunk or whatever," Emery said, slurping on her water loudly, making everyone groan.

Tatum shrugged. "We did not black out, we...had too much fun."

Then her friends were pushing to their feet, stretching as they stood up. "On that note," Sadie said through a yawn, "we're heading out. Thanks for the pick-up and the coffee, rockstar."

Fletcher tipped his head towards the women and Micah waved as they let themselves out of the house. She was halfway through her coffee when Emery and Fletcher joined her, plates loaded with food. For a long moment, nobody said anything. The only sounds in the kitchen were the light scraping of cutlery against their plates.

"Did you have fun, Mom?"

She nodded, glancing at her daughter then at her boyfriend, before smiling. "There was a mechanical bull riding competition and as you can imagine Tatum and Sadie wanted to participate."

Fletcher's lips twitched, but she was glad he didn't say anything. He'd said enough about her penchant for *riding*. If he'd seen her last night, he would have most definitely been impressed with her skills.

"Did you win?"

"Not even close." She laughed, recalling how many times they fell off the bull. "Pretty sure I've collected more bruises."

Emery shook her head. "It's crazy how the three of you have stayed the same my whole life."

"The magic of lifelong friendships."

"You have any friends like that, Fletch?"

He shook his head at Emery's question and Micah frowned. "What about the band?"

"We're friends and I love them with my whole heart. But we're not the kinds to go drinking or bull riding together."

"Erin?"

Emery's head snapped between the two of them. "Who is *Erin?*"

"Another friend," he explained. "But also, no. Maybe you and Nico will have that kind of friendship when you get older."

Emery blushed as she shook her head. "Maybe."

Micah smiled and slid off her stool to refill her coffee. Standing on the other side of the counter, she watched her two favorite people. "I like this. Three of us having breakfast together."

"Does this mean more sleepovers?" Emery asked, glancing sideways at Fletcher.

"Uh..."

"I'm not saying it's a bad thing."

"Em," Micah sighed and her daughter grinned.

"I'm glad you're here, Fletch. Thank you for breakfast."

Then she was gone, leaving them alone in the kitchen.

"She's going to give me hell about this for a while, isn't she?"

Micah laughed and came over to give him a quick kiss. "I managed for fourteen years, you'll be fine."

And not once did she think about how those words might sound.

An hour later—they made Emery help them clean up—the house was empty of friends and teenagers. With Emery on Christmas break, she had already grabbed her things and left to go see Nico. That meant Micah and Fletcher standing on opposite sides of the kitchen island, smiling at each other, letting the silence wrap around them.

"Now that we're alone—" Micah twirled towards him, aware that her robe was flaring open to flash her mostly bare legs and delicious cleavage "—what can we do with all this time?"

"A shower, for starters." She gasped as she came to a halt and put her hands on her hips, staring at Fletcher. "What? You might look edible as fuck right now, sweetheart, but you do not smell that good."

Huffing at him, she undid her robe and let it fall to the floor as she walked out of the kitchen, fully aware of Fletcher's eyes fixed on her retreating form. She smiled to herself when she heard him swear and when she was halfway up the stairs, his arm wound around her waist, pulling her against him.

His warm breath brushed against her shoulder as he said, "I didn't say shower alone."

"Considering I don't smell so good, I figured you didn't want to be anywhere near me."

He released her when they hit the top of the stairs and she glanced over her shoulder and found his jaw tight as his eyes stayed on her ass. "I want to be near you all the time, not so good smells and all."

Smirking to herself, Micah walked into her ensuite bathroom and turned on the shower. A peripheral glance in her mirror showed that Fletcher stood a few inches shy of the doorway, so she stripped her clothes off, tossing them into the hamper. And then without looking at him, she stepped into the shower, tipping her head forward to let the warm water soak her hair. When she felt his hands slide over her hips and his front press against her back, she smiled.

"I want to talk to you about something," he whispered and Micah's heart stuttered. She slowly turned to face him and Fletcher brushed the wet hair out of her face. "What was going through your head last night when we were getting burgers?"

Of course this man was astute enough to know something

was going on and she was grateful that he hadn't brought it up the night before. Sighing heavily, Micah turned off the water and reached for her shower gel and squirted some into her hands. Fletcher held his hands out and she did the same for him.

"I should preface this by saying I don't get drunk very often. It happens maybe once a year, if anything. But there were a few times after Emery was born and I was still with Geoffrey when I'd go drinking with the girls," she told him, lathering the soap in her hands before working it into Fletcher's chest and stomach, over his shoulders and biceps. "He would always criticize me and make me feel guilty for having a little bit of fun. He'd get mad, say some awful stuff which would get me worked up.

"But I know that when I'm under the influence, the things that come out of me might not always be nice or said the right way. So I kept my mouth shut countless times and he'd keep giving me shit." Resting her hands on his chest, she closed her eyes as his fingers massaged her shoulders and neck. "As you can tell, I didn't date a lot or have a special someone who'd answer my call when I needed some help. When I called you, I was only thinking about how I wanted *you* to hold me. Then we were sitting in your truck and I kept waiting for you to question my decisions and tell me I was being foolish and irresponsible."

He grunted and she smiled to herself, turning the water back on. "I know it's silly to be hung up on something that happened years ago, something that *someone* did to me. But you're the first serious relationship I've been in since the divorce and my brain was processing it that way."

He didn't say anything as he brushed his hands over her body, washing the soap away, lips pressed to her forehead. Micah knew that the comfort, love and safety she found with Fletcher would never be found anywhere else. Or with *anyone* else. He didn't expect her to be anything but herself or change who she was. In fact, he liked all of the parts of her that Geoffrey didn't. Not that she needed to keep comparing the two, because they were like oil and water.

"First of all, fuck your ex. I hate that he made you feel guilty for finding joy in the little things. Secondly, I love when you're happy and having the time of your life. Last night was a new side of you, but your eyes were so fucking bright and that's how I want you to always feel."

She looked up at him as he turned off the water and then reached past the shower curtain and pulled a towel for her. This man. She patted herself dry and wrapped the towel around her body as Fletcher did the same thing. Stepping out of the shower, she finally looked at herself in the mirror and smiled when Fletcher stepped up behind her.

"And most importantly, I was serious when I said that I appreciated you putting your trust in me last night. It might not have been how you wanted me to meet your best friends, but you called *me* when you needed me and that's enough." He pressed his chin against the side of her head and wrapped his arms loosely around her shoulders. "I will never hold you back, curb your joy or put out that light in your eyes. I will stand by your side and behind you, tell me what you need and I'll make it happen. Okay?"

With her heart ready to leap and emotions clogging her throat, she blinked back tears and nodded. "Okay."

He pressed a kiss to her temple, against her cheek, down to her jaw and her neck. With one more soft kiss to her shoulder, he released her and took a step back, smiling at her through the mirror. "Luckiest son of a bitch to be yours, Mick," he said and stepped out of the bathroom, leaving her gasping for air as she gripped the counter.

She was never under any illusions that what she and Geoffrey had was love, but like so many people in the world, it's what Micah craved. To love someone and be loved by them in such a way that every thought of them left you breathless. Fletcher did that by infiltrating every waking thought, but by also being present in her life at all times.

Even when she didn't know she needed him, Fletcher was there. He was *hers*.

Once she caught her breath, she dried herself off fully and chose not to add any product to her hair. Instead, she let it air dry and figured that Mrs. Hershey could say whatever the hell she wanted at their session that evening. When she stepped out of the bathroom, wearing only an old Rescuers t-shirt, Fletcher was sitting on the bed and waiting for her.

"Have you been sitting there this whole time?"

He nodded, smiling softly. "Thought you might need a few minutes, so figured I'd wait here."

"You are…" she trailed off, stepping between his spread legs and cupped his face in both hands. How could she put into words the way this man made her feel? Safe, secure, loved, cherished and like herself. She'd accepted that not every relationship would make you feel whole, then Fletcher came back into her life.

"*I* am the luckiest person in the world to have you love me. Your heart and soul are mine, Fletch. And I promise to take good care of them. I can't believe I get to be yours and have you in my life again. For real this time."

"It was real the last time too."

"You know what I mean."

"I'm yours, for real, for as long as you want me."

She carefully climbed into his lap, knees pressing into the bed on either side of his hips. "Don't want to make big declarations and all that yet, but how does forever sound?"

"Fucking perfect, love bug."

A sound that was a mix between a growl and a scoff came

out of her and she shook her head. "I am not calling you my stallion."

"You already did. Multiple times. It's such a good title."

"Fiiiine, but only in the bedroom."

He grinned, leaning in to brush his mouth against hers as he said, "Does that mean I can't call you *love bug* in public?"

"Oh, you must. It's growing on me, shockingly."

He laughed against her mouth and Micah smiled before kissing him soundly, their arms winding around each other. The kiss seeped into every inch of her soul, it was in the way he held her—one hand cradling the back of her head, the other wrapped tightly around her waist. It was in the way his tongue swept into her mouth, searching, giving and taking. It was in all of their love for each other that lingered between them, the deep seated passion and hunger they'd held onto for sixteen years that had finally bubbled to the surface.

She had never put much stock into second chances.

Until Fletcher.

fletcher

You're too obsessed with me.

IN THE WEEK leading up to Christmas, both Fletcher and Micah were busy. Between his Santa duties and the sudden influx of customers at Big Wave, he was swamped all the time. Micah was wrapping up sessions for the year and that meant she worked pretty tirelessly every day. But there were a *few* windows of freedom that would open up.

While Fletcher thought it would be filled with quickies and orgasms in his office, they actually spent most of that time talking. Sure, there was a lot of kissing and touching, cuddling even. And he fucking loved it. One afternoon, they inhaled street tacos while sitting on his tailgate; late one night, they stuffed their faces with burgers and fries by the beach; and after a particularly grueling day, they drank milkshakes and walked down the promenade hand-in-hand.

There had been one night when he got home after his Santa shift and found Micah waiting at his house. After a hot, knee-shaking kiss at the front door, they barely made it to his bedroom before clothes came off and she rode him until she'd had two orgasms. Then she sucked and swirled her tongue around him until he was a collapsed heap on the floor. Afterwards, they showered, cooked together and ate their meal standing at the kitchen counter.

Sex wasn't their primary objective and Fletcher loved that. It had been a long time since he'd *dated* someone, but every minute spent with Micah was pretty fucking special.

While their original plans were to meet Erin the morning after the Loose Lasso night out, with Micah's hangover firmly in place, they pushed it to another day. His girls were excited, even though he was nervous as fuck about having the three most important people in his life in the same space. But he knew that Micah and Erin would get along, and that Emery would be fascinated by yet another badass boss babe.

Sleepily stretched out in a large booth at Stardust Diner— Emery had mentioned her favorite all-day diner enough times that Fletcher didn't even think twice while picking it as their breakfast spot—all four of them sipped on their hot beverages while waking up.

"We're all definitely setting great first impressions this morning," Micah said around a yawn that made Erin laugh. "Sorry, we're so much better behaved than this on a regular day."

Erin echoed Micah's yawn and waved a hand. "I get it, trust me. It's not even that early, but I feel like I've been running a marathon."

"Quit it," Fletcher mumbled, covering his mouth as he also let out a yawn. "It's 11 a.m. and everyone's been awake for hours."

All three women glared at him before Emery turned to Erin with a slight frown. "So you and Fletch are best friends and nothing more?"

"*Em.*" Micah poked her daughter in the side and he caught Erin's amused smile. She had sounded just as skeptical the first time he mentioned having a female friend.

"What? Making sure that this is not some kind of second

family situation or whatever," Emery said, frowning even deeper as she rubbed her side.

He didn't know if he was amused or concerned that Emery thought there was something else going on. But he liked that she was protective of her mother and maybe a little bit of him? The variety of expressions around the table amused him and Fletcher used his coffee cup to hide his smile.

Erin finally straightened up beside him and leaned over the table with a smile. "A few years ago, Hank tried to set us up. It didn't work out."

"I was too grunge for the likes of Miss Polished here," Fletcher offered with a chuckle.

Erin rolled her eyes and added, "Besides, we're better off as friends."

Emery looked between them, nibbling on her bottom lip and Fletcher gently tapped her foot with his. When the teenager looked at him, he smiled. "Just friends, kid."

"*And* I'm pretty sure the reason we didn't make sense is because he's been in love with your mom all along."

Micah cleared her throat and he watched as the blush spread over her cheeks. But she met his gaze and winked when he smirked. He *had* been in love with Micah for a long time, even when he wasn't sure what the feelings were. Then again, Emery didn't know the details of their history. Not that he wanted her to know about their epic one night stand or how for a split second he thought Emery was *his* kid.

"I mean, my mom's pretty awesome," Emery said, grinning at Micah before looking at him. "So you have great taste."

"I have to agree," he told her, clinking his mug against Emery's filled with hot cocoa.

The rest of the breakfast went smoothly as Emery asked Erin a million questions about what it was like to be a lawyer and a partner at a big law firm. The whole time, Micah shifted between watching her daughter with love and adoration and shooting Fletcher grateful looks. He'd spent so many years wanting this, but never finding it. His ex-wife hadn't been the kind of person he could have had a solid life with and they both knew it. And now that he was closing in on fifty, Fletcher definitely didn't expect everything to look this good.

To be sitting at breakfast with his family.

Afterwards, Micah and Emery left to do last minute Christmas shopping before Micah went into work. Fletcher and Erin grabbed coffee from his favorite shop and walked along the promenade silently. He'd known her long enough to know that Erin had *thoughts* and sitting quietly with her for a few minutes was part of the process. Finding a bench—not too far from where he and Micah had discussed nicknames not too long ago—they sat down and Erin leaned back with a sigh.

"Hank would be proud of you." Erin nudged him gently and Fletcher smiled. "She's great. Both of them are."

Knowing that Erin approved and that she knew Hank would too made this all the better. "Apparently Hank knew them."

"For real?"

Nodding, he sipped on his coffee. "When Micah came home the first time, she mentioned visiting him there. Surprised the old man didn't try to set me up with her."

"Maybe he was protective of her and the kid. I mean, I get why he would be."

"Yeah. They're pretty fucking special. Best thing to ever happen to me."

She shifted on the bench, straddling it so she was facing him. "I'm happy for you."

"But...?" he said, dragging the word out as he glanced at her.

"Have you been planning a future with her?"

"What do you mean?"

"Like…you always talked about how you never wanted to get married again or have a kid. But she's different, right?"

He sighed, pondering the question with his head tilted back. If he hadn't met Alice and married her, his answer might be different. But he knew that if he got to spend his life with Micah, he would be the happiest man alive. And that didn't mean marriage. *Though*, as he closed his eyes, he could see Micah in a wedding dress clearly and suddenly it was all he wanted.

"Yeah," he whispered, opening his eyes to stare at the sky for a long moment. "I don't think either of us wants to raise a baby, but everything else? I want that."

"Emery adores you, I hope you know that."

He smiled, remembering how quickly he took to her. Maybe it was because she reminded him of Micah or because she was that great a person.

"I love her too. From the minute she walked into my store and sassed me about teaching her the drums, I knew that she was someone special."

She was funny, smart and despite being tone deaf, she was determined. The passion that flowed through Emery when it came to music was something Fletcher connected with. He'd been like that too, falling in love with music and then wanting to be a part of it. Emery would eventually have to either give up learning drums or keep going batshit with her sticks, and he would be there every step of the way.

"And Micah…" Erin trailed off, making Fletcher smile. He waited for his friend to continue, because he knew she saw what he did. "Those pictures didn't do her justice. But she also seems like someone with her head screwed on straight."

A laugh burst out of him and he raised his coffee in a

silent toast. "She's the best, E. I don't think there are enough ways in which I can express how fucking perfect she is."

"I can also see *why* you've held onto your love for her."

"She sees me, always has," he admitted softly. "Sixteen years ago, she looked at me and didn't expect anything other than what I had to offer. She still does that and it's amazing."

Erin nudged him again and he grinned. "I never thought of you as a sap, but I guess the man who wrote a love song for a Mermaid would wear his heart on his sleeve."

He groaned loudly, aware that Erin would never let it go. Laughing as he straightened up, he gently tapped his coffee against hers and then let himself relax into the bench.

"She's always been the one."

"Well, I'm happy for you. You, of all the people I know, deserve this."

He gave his friend a nod and took a long sip of his coffee. Then turned to face her, one eyebrow arched. "Speaking of which…we need to talk about you and Benson."

"What? No. Who's Benson?"

"Decker."

"Kelley," she countered, rolling her eyes. "It was a while ago and it was nothing."

"Clearly. Judging by that silly handshake the other day."

Erin sighed and made a face. In the whole time he'd known her, his friend had been single. She wasn't against relationships and she wasn't celibate, but she very rarely talked about her personal life that way. The more Fletcher thought about it, the more he realized that the two of them never really talked about their pasts. They didn't know about each other's families, they knew about almost all the surface-level things. Sure, some would say that's not how friendships were built, but if you asked him, that was how some of the best bonds were created. History didn't define everything, it was enough to know the other person would be there for you in the present.

"Couple of years ago, before you moved to town, Benson and I had a friends with benefits thing going on."

"Huh."

She held a hand up and shook her head. "This was before he got married and became a dad. We hooked up for about six months while I was in the process of becoming partner, it was a stressful time in my life," she explained and he nodded, because he wasn't going to judge her for the choices she made. "While I was gone, he met his ex and when I came back, we knew that it was over."

"And now…?"

"I sometimes forget that he still works at the shop, so whenever I see him, it's a shock."

He tilted his head to catch Erin's eye. "Did you have feelings for him?"

"Not really." Erin made a face, one side of her mouth going up and the other sliding down. "He's a handsome man and the sex was *phenomenal*, but it was never more than that. He does this thing with his to—"

He covered her mouth with one hand and said, "Nope. Don't need that in my head before I go back to work."

"You asked." She pushed his hand away, laughing at his expression.

He sighed dramatically and finished his coffee, setting his cup aside and then caught a look of confusion on her face. "There's something else."

"I'm queer," she said softly. He shifted so he was looking at her properly. She searched his eyes and added, "You're the only person I've told."

He smiled and held a hand out, watching as Erin hesitated before setting her palm against his. "Thank you for trusting me with this."

"You're my best friend, remember?"

"Am I? I didn't know it went both ways."

Erin snorted and poked his palm. "Don't be an asshole."

"Love you, Decker," he mumbled and pressed a kiss to her temple.

"Love you too, you grunge rocker."

After another walk along the promenade where Erin complained about work, but reminded him that she had finally found her dream job, Fletcher dropped his best friend off at her hotel. When he returned to the store, Emery and Nico were already causing havoc with their instruments. Well, Nico was at least *attempting* to make music. Emery liked the noise. He watched Benson try to corral the teenagers to no avail, but didn't bother to step in and help.

Replaying his conversation with Erin, he realized that he never wanted to know what his life would be like without Emery or Micah. This kid changed him almost as much as her mother had.

"What do you think, Fletch? Am I getting better?"

He narrowed his eyes at Emery's smug expression. "Maybe I need a proper demonstration."

"Hell yeah!" Emery cheered and stood up behind the drum kit. "What do you want me to play for you?"

Running through the songs they'd worked on together, Fletcher pursed his lips. Emery couldn't read music and she either went too fast or too slow. But what she lacked in musical ability, she made up for in determination. So the only way to not completely destroy their hearing was to give her a track with an easy progression to follow.

"How about some AC/DC?" Benson offered and Fletcher shrugged. You couldn't go wrong with Phil Rudd.

Emery beamed and sat down, stretching her arms and rolling her shoulders, which made Nico and Benson groan dramatically. Nothing this kid did could be simple. And honestly, he loved how everything was a little more dramatic every time. Benson waited for her cue and then through the speakers, pumped "Back in Black" without the drum backing and nodded to Emery.

As expected, she came in a few seconds late and then rushed through the opening to catch up. Then fell back again, before she finally leveled out. But even then, her rhythm was a little off and she couldn't work the kick and snare at the same time. Emery didn't give up though. With the tip of her tongue peeking through her teeth, she smashed through the song until Benson turned the backing track off. Emery stumbled as she came to a stop and then grinned at him while she panted from all the exertion.

"So, what do you think?"

He could feel Benson and Nico's worried glances on him, but he shrugged. "You've improved. A little more work on the timing and you'll get better."

"Seriously? Does that mean I can come back next year?"

"Maybe."

Her face fell. "What, why?"

"I meant *maybe* I'll have classes next year, maybe I won't."

"But if you're dating Mom, you can still gimme lessons, right?"

This kid. Fletcher snorted and shook his head. "No preferential treatment."

"Ugh, fine. I'll make Benson teach me."

Fletcher patted his friend on the back and shot Emery a wink before heading to his office, pulling his phone out of his pocket.

FLETCHER

What's the nicest way to tell someone
they're not good at something?

MICAH

You suck.

FLETCHER

...

MICAH

Not you! That's what you tell someone.

FLETCHER

What about when the someone is your kid?

MICAH

Oh god, how bad is she?

FLETCHER

Well...

Before he could type out the rest of his message, his phone started to ring, Micah's name flashing at the top of his screen. He chuckled and settled behind his desk as he swiped to answer.

"Love bug."

"*How* bad is she, Fletch?"

"She's a little tone deaf." *Among other things.* But he kept that to himself for now.

Micah groaned and he could picture her rubbing her forehead. "Maybe I should tell her to give it up."

"No, don't do that. We'll find a way through this."

"Is that her?" she asked and Fletcher winced at the sudden clashing and banging. He got up to close his door and leaned against it. "She's so bad, Fletch. Save us all."

Laughing, he pushed his hair behind an ear. "She's

passionate and determined. There are some things we can try and teach her, but let's not discourage her yet."

"Maybe she'll find something new to get excited about and music is not the thing for her."

"Maybe. But for now…we're not giving up on her."

"Why not?! Save Benson and Nico, that poor kid."

He smiled and sat in his chair. "Love bug."

"*Fiiiiiiine*," Micah said, dragging the word out. "In other things…I'm glad we got to meet Erin. She's not the kind of person I would have picked as your best friend."

"She's pretty great. She liked you too."

"Maybe we'll run away together one day." He clenched his jaw and smiled to himself, glad that she couldn't see him. "Oooh, is this silence you being jealous?"

"Fuck no. Erin's awesome, but I know you'd never leave me."

"Is that so?" He could hear the smile in her voice.

"You're too obsessed with me."

She gasped and then burst into laughter. "You're not wrong."

Smirking, he settled back in his chair. "Love you, Mick."

"Aw, I love you too. I'll see you later?"

"Yup. I'll drop Em off before I head to the Village."

After another round of 'I love you', Fletcher hung up and closed his eyes, letting the chaos of Emery's drumming wrap around him. He could teach her how to hone those skills. It would take longer than expected. But it would be worth it to see Emery happy.

fletcher

Have you really loved her forever?

TWO DAYS LATER, it was Emery's last music lesson and Fletcher was doing final inventory for the year. It was also his last night as Santa and he was ready to spend the rest of the month wrapped around Micah. Because the George women weren't traveling for the holidays, Emery was the only one of her friends still in town. But that also meant she got to damage his eardrums a little more. Fletcher knew that she wasn't *bad*, she was just not the best. Emery enjoyed music and he had caught her dancing and head banging to everything playing through her earphones. But loving music and knowing how to play it were two very different things. And yet, she never gave up.

After his phone call with Micah, the two of them had sat down and talked about it further. Both their families had clearly tried to curb them from doing things they loved, and yet they made it work. His parents didn't understand his fascination or interest in being a musician and even after The Rescuers went platinum, won Grammys and traveled around the world; they still thought he was going through a phase. He knew that Micah's parents belittled her life decisions too.

And in that vein, he never wanted to make anybody feel like their hopes and dreams were not worth it. Even when they weren't good at something.

He was going to give Emery one more shot, teach her as much as he could and then if it still felt like she wasn't able to play music, he'd ask her to give it up. It would hurt like hell, but he knew that lying to the kid wasn't a good idea. Same way, discouraging her was also pretty harmful.

"I don't want other kids to tease her about it," Micah had said as they sat on the couch in her living room the night before.

"Nobody else knows about this."

"Yet. I know how awful teenagers can be, my poor baby doesn't need to suffer that."

He kissed the side of her head and smiled. "Okay, how about this. We've got one more lesson tomorrow and then I'll talk to her."

"Are you sure that I shouldn't be the one talking to her?"

"You can, but as her music teacher maybe I should do it first."

Micah nodded and tilted her head back to smile at him. "You know you're not *only* her music teacher, right?"

"I know, Mick." He tightened his arm around her, lips brushing against her hair. "But seriously, your kid is a badass and won't let anyone take her down."

That morning, she had very politely reminded him about their conversation before she left to go read with Mrs. Hershey. Safe to say, he was nervous about having that conversation with Emery. His whole career as a musician, someone else had done the 'serious talks' with people who were fired or otherwise. He'd never had to deal with confrontation or tears. And while he believed that Emery would be understanding, he was still pretty worried.

Until she walked into the store, twirling her drumsticks

like she was ready to take on the world. Fletcher was glad Benson and Nico were off on their respective holidays, because he definitely didn't want Emery to feel embarrassed later. Not that she'd been embarrassed the last month of lessons, but there was a first time for everything.

"So…what do you want me to do today?"

Setting his clipboard aside, he gestured to the second drum kit he'd set up for himself and smiled. "We're going to play together."

"For real?" Her eyes were wide in shock or awe, he couldn't tell.

"I'll be honest with you, Em," he started and pulled his hair out of his face. "You've been working really hard, but you still have a long way to go."

Emery's mouth dipped and she nodded, shuffling on her feet. "I know."

"Hey—" he squeezed her shoulder and smiled when their eyes met "—you've got this. Come on, settle in. Pick a song and let's do this."

She nodded, a small smile on her lips. He settled behind his drum kit, sticks twirling between his fingers. She stopped at the music player plugged into the store speakers and went through the list. Once she had a song selected, she rushed to her seat and tied her hair back as well. Glancing at him, her face brightened and she hit play on the remote. The open beat started and Fletcher smiled at the choice—"Billie Jean" by Michael Jackson—and nodded at her to hop in when she was ready. It was mostly kick drum, toms and hi-hats, but he could see Emery struggle to match the beats.

"Deep breath, Em. Go with me," he told her and then joined in. It took her a few more fumbles before she was able to match his beat. He kept it steady, eyes on her so that she knew he wasn't going to leave her behind. For most drummers, this was an easy song to play, but it was also a really good starting point for new drummers.

When the backing track ended, she groaned and waved her sticks in the air. "Why do I suck at this?"

"Will it help if I say that I was terrible at it too?"

"Nobody will believe that," she mumbled, setting her sticks down.

He smiled and gently tapped a stick against the snare. "The reason I taught myself the drums is because every instructor I met told me I sucked. Yeah, they used that word. It was hard for me to hear it and I refused to let them be right."

"Are you saying I suck?"

"No, but you're also not very good."

She huffed and crossed her arms over her chest. "Rude."

"Em." Fletcher sighed and pushed back from the kit, moving to stand in front of her. "Do you want the truth or do you want me to sugarcoat it?"

"Which will make me cry less?"

He laughed and picked up her sticks, holding them out to her. "I guess we'll find out. Okay, let's play this without the track. You know the basic progression, play it, but follow the beat I set. Got it?"

She hesitated, but took the sticks and Fletcher snapped his fingers at a much slower pace than the backing track. She took a few minutes to start playing, but once she did, she was going at his beat. Gradually, he increased the speed and she matched him. But then when the snare came in, she fumbled. This time, Emery let out a cry and threw her sticks to the side before burying her face in her hands.

Fletcher came around the drums and kneeled beside her. "Hey, hey, come here," he whispered and Emery collapsed into his arms. He wrapped both arms around her as the teenager dissolved into quiet sobs. Leaning against the wall, he held her, letting Emery go through the motions. Maybe Micah was right, telling her upfront would have cut back a lot of this pain. But he also didn't want her to give up because someone else told her she couldn't do it. Besides, Emery had the drive and passion, the interest and determination. She lacked the musical ability.

"I'm sorry," she mumbled and slid out of his lap, sitting beside Fletcher. "That was embarrassing."

"I happen to think crying is good for the soul."

A laugh escaped her as she wiped her face and then she turned to him. "I suck."

"You don't suck."

"Yeah yeah, I'm not very good," she echoed his words from before, putting quotes around them. "Does that mean I should give up?"

"I'll answer that question, but I want to know what *you* think you should do."

Emery pursed her lips, pulling her knees up to her chest and shrugged. "Give up."

"Why?"

"Because drums are clearly not my thing."

"Okay." He leaned back, head resting against the wall. "I agree with that assessment. I'm glad you were excited about the drums and wanted to make it your thing. I love that you were raised on my music and maybe it inspired you. But I'm also proud of you for powering through even when it wasn't working. *And* admitting that maybe it's not your thing."

"When I was a kid, Mom told me I could be anything. So I tried everything and some of it felt weird, some of it felt really good. Being a drummer *sounded* good. You know that when I was growing up, she talked about you a lot? How The Rescuers made some of the best music of her generation."

He smiled as he glanced at Emery, his heart racing at the knowledge that Micah talked about him and his band to her kid when she was little. "That made you want to become a drummer."

"Mom loves me more than anything in the world, so I wanted to do something else she loved and I hoped that I'd be good enough."

His heart ached for Emery and Fletcher bumped her shoulder with his. "You know that you didn't have to do that, right? You are your mom's whole world and she will support you no matter what you do."

"She said that too," she whispered, picking at invisible lint on her pants. "Maybe I'll focus on Drama Club instead. Could be fun."

"Oh, you would be *perfect* in Drama Club." Fletcher laughed when Emery whacked him with the back of her hand. "What else do you like?"

She shrugged, a slight blush rising up her neck and cheeks. Fletcher had seen some of the longing looks Emery shot at her best friend, but he didn't want to ask about it. It was none of his business after all.

"Maybe instead of *playing* music, you and I can talk about it?"

Fletcher smiled at her effectively changing the subject and nodded. "Absolutely. Micah and I have this long-standing discussion about who the best female rockstar is. Do you have any opinions?"

"Alanis, duh."

He barked out a laugh and shook his head. "Your mom said the same thing."

"Have you really loved her forever?"

His breath caught at the question and he looked away from Emery, eyes focused on the ceiling. "We met in the early 2000's, when I was on tour. I wasn't expecting her, but she changed my life," he said softly, not wanting to share too much. "She inspired our greatest hit."

"Whoa, "Mermaid" is about *Mom*?"

Nodding, he smirked at Emery's shocked expression. "I have loved her for a long time, even when I didn't realize it. I think on some level, everything in my life always came back to Micah."

After a long moment, Emery said, "You're not going to vanish on us, right?"

"What?"

She sighed and he watched as she untied her hair, fingers working through the tangles in the dark blonde locks. Emery seemed to be considering what to say and Fletcher nudged her gently with a nod.

"My dad, *Geoffrey*, was an asshole. He didn't love us enough. He didn't even want me," she spoke softly, but given that they were sitting close together, he heard the hitch in her voice. "He hurt Mom by being the worst person on the planet and I know that not everyone is like him. But he was awful. He wasn't worthy of Mom and I'm glad she left him.

"She's also been really weird about dating. Like, I know she's gone out with a few people, but she's never introduced any of them to me. Whenever Sadie and Tatum come over, they gossip and they're not as quiet as they think. So I've heard them talk about their…dates," Emery said, shuddering on the last word. "And Mom hasn't been this happy, like ever. So clearly that's your doing. And I'm glad. She deserves someone who loves her the way you do."

His heart clenched at how open and emotional she was being. He never imagined that this would be how they'd spend their last music lesson.

"That's why…I want to make sure you won't hurt or leave her."

"I won't. I don't want to make promises, but I intend to be right here for as long as your mom wants me."

Emery nodded, sniffling loudly as she said, "What if *I* want you to stay forever?"

The world stopped and he sucked in a sharp breath as he replayed the question. *What if I want you to stay forever?* This kid wanted him to stay forever. He looked at her and found Emery staring up at him, worrying her bottom lip. Nodding slowly, he smiled, not wanting her to take his silence as anything but a promise that he *would* stay forever.

"I'll stay forever, if that's what you want."

She released her bottom lip and smiled, turning quickly to hug him. The awkward way they were seated made it hard for him to hug her back, but he rested his cheek against the top of her head the whole time she held him.

"Thank you, Fletch. For showing up in our lives. For loving my mom. For being there for me."

He forced back the tears that were blurring his vision and he smiled as Emery pulled away. "Easiest thing I've ever done in my life," he whispered, bumping shoulders with her. "I'll always be here for you. Okay?"

Emery nodded and quickly swiped at her fresh tears. Then with a soft laugh, she pushed herself to her feet. "So, since music is not my future, maybe we should wrap up today?"

He got up as well and took a moment to catch his breath as she put everything away, humming softly under her breath. How had they gone from talking about Emery's music skills—or lack thereof—to diving into the emotional aspect of him being in their lives? Fletcher was glad that they'd talked about it, because he knew that the only way he and Micah were going to have a solid relationship was if Emery was also on board.

❄

Once everything was straightened up, Emery climbed into his truck and Fletcher drove them home. *Home.* He was still living in Uncle Hank's house, but every night of the last week had been spent at the George house. They hadn't talked about the future in big terms or said anything more than what they were right then, but after this conversation with Emery, it was clear they needed to have a more serious discussion. He pulled into the driveway and Emery was out of the truck before he'd even parked fully. Smiling, Fletcher checked to make sure his Santa gear was in the back, then followed the teenager into the house.

Emery was hugging Micah so tight, she was staring at him with wide eyes. When she pulled away, Emery kissed her mother and mumbled something before rushing off. Micah turned to him as he closed the door and arched an eyebrow.

"What the hell happened?"

"Hi, love bug," he said and kissed her softly, wrapping both arms around her. "Your offspring and I had a heart-to-heart today."

"About what?"

He pulled back and walked into the kitchen to fill a glass of water. Leaning against the counter as he sipped, he smiled at her staring at him, arms crossed over her chest. All she was missing was the tapping of her feet.

"We discussed how maybe music wasn't for her. Had a bit of a breakthrough."

"Oh god, how did she take it?"

"Pretty well. There *was* crying, but we talked it out." He pushed off the counter and moved to stand in front of her, hands framing Micah's face. "We also talked about you and me."

"Fletch…"

"She was making sure I wasn't going to up and leave one day."

"What?"

He smiled at her wide eyes and brushed her hair back. "She wants you to be happy and she also wanted to make sure I wasn't going to hurt you."

"Did she bring up her dad?"

"Yeah. The guy really pulled a number on her, didn't he?"

Micah groaned and pressed her forehead against his chest. "He broke her heart over and over again, so now she's obviously scarred for life."

"She told me. If I ever meet him, I might stab him with a drumstick." Micah laughed softly, arms winding around his waist. He took a minute to gather himself before saying, "She also asked if I would stay forever."

She pulled back to stare at him. "What?"

"Yup. So I guess you're stuck with me forever."

Her eyes searched his and Fletcher smiled, thumb stroking back and forth across her jaw. "You promise?"

"Well, I told your kid I wouldn't make promises…"

"Fletcher."

He saw the tears well in her eyes, so he nodded, dropping his forehead to hers. "I promise, Mick. For as long as you want me, if that's forever, then yes."

"Forever, Fletch. You and me."

"You, me and Emery," he added before her mouth crashed into his, her arms winding around his neck. He tightened his grip on her sides and sank into the kiss, letting her know how much he wanted forever with her.

"I love you, Fletch."

"Love you too, Mick."

micah

Eating you for Christmas dinner.

IT WAS Christmas Eve and three days since Fletcher had come home with Emery after their heart-to-heart, and Micah was still reeling. She loved that her daughter trusted Fletcher enough to talk to him about things that weighed on her. But she hadn't known how much worry Emery was carrying in her heart. The three of them spent a lot of time together—even if it was just eating breakfast before responsibilities got in the way, or movie night. She was glad for it. Fletcher Kelley's return to her life hadn't been on her bingo card for the year, but it was the only box she wanted to cross off. Micah was happy. She was with someone who didn't expect her to be anyone but herself. Someone who loved her daughter and was loved in return.

Santa duties and music lessons were over, so while they played board games and cooked together, the three of them also found ways to do their own thing. Fletcher had all but moved into her house, and she was waiting for the right moment to ask him to make it official. She knew that she loved him and would do so for a long time to come, but she hadn't wanted to put that kind of pressure on him. Now knowing the things he and Emery had talked about, she was ready to ask him to move in with her. Or hell, they'd move into Hank's old house together, if that's what he wanted.

Except, she was rushing through the bedroom getting dressed for one last session with Mrs. Hershey. The old woman had improved in her reading, but that only meant she wanted Micah to help her with a few more chapters before the book club discussion. Micah knew that book cover-to-cover and Fletcher was benefiting from this newly developed Santa kink in a big way. So much so, the night before, Micah had tied Fletcher's wrists to her headboard using Christmas lights and rode him like the stallion he was. Afterwards, when his dick had twitched awake again, she'd dropped his Santa hat over it and collapsed into fits of laughter.

Her feelings about Christmas hadn't changed, it was still a capitalist holiday where all the cheer felt manufactured. *But*, she had a new appreciation for Santa. And she still liked seeing the holiday through Emery's eyes.

"Hey, twister," Fletcher's voice broke through her thoughts as she adjusted her belt. "Come here."

She barely had a moment to respond before Fletcher's hand was in the waistband of her pants and he was tugging her towards him. He pulled the belt out through the loops and started the process again. She was a *little* frazzled. And the bedroom did look like a tornado had swept through. Micah sighed and dropped her hands, looking at him as he perched on the edge of the bed in nothing but his pajama pants. His hair was tied back in a ponytail—he and Emery did this quite often and Micah thought it was cute as fuck— glasses were on and his chest shimmered thanks to the water droplets clinging to his skin after his shower. God, she loved this man. More than she thought it was possible.

She'd been so complacent in her marriage to Geoffrey because he treated her as such. But not Fletcher. He offered her smiles and kisses, touched her every chance he got and reminded her constantly that she was his. If you'd told her sixteen years ago, when she'd snuck out of that hotel room that she'd be with the same man again, Micah would not have believed you. She was a realist and that meant reconnecting with the man who rocked her world seemed unlikely.

Smiling, she cupped his face and tilted it up to look at her. "You are the best thing that's happened to me in a really long time."

"That's my line," he said softly.

"Tough shit, stallion. I'm so grateful for you, in ways that I might not always be able to put into words."

He leaned into one hand, his cheek resting against her palm and beard scratching against her skin. "Me too, Mick. Me fucking too."

Dipping her head, she brushed her mouth against his and Fletcher's hand moved from her waist to her ass, pulling her against him. Laughing into the kiss, she let him gently tug her into his lap so she was straddling him. With her thumbs tracing the apples of his cheeks, Micah pulled back and sighed. "Thank you for loving my kid too, Fletch. *That* means the world to me."

"You never have to thank me for that, Mick. It's my honor to love and be loved by the George women."

She kissed him again, forehead resting against his until her phone started ringing again. Groaning, Micah slid off his lap and held the screen up to face him. "I think she's taking me for granted," she whispered before answering Mrs. Hershey's call. After confirming that she would be there in thirty minutes, Micah stole another kiss from Fletcher and finished getting ready.

"You have the list, right?"

Fletcher arched a playful eyebrow. "*Your* list or something else, love bug?"

"Fletch…"

"I've got the list."

"I hid my list, so if you found it, then we're in trouble."

He laughed and stood up as she slipped earrings on, his eyes meeting hers in the mirror. "I know where your list is, but don't worry, I won't look."

Micah rolled her eyes and grabbed the brown sweater off the clothes horse and tugged it on. "How do I look?"

"A hot, sexy teacher I'd like to be punished by."

She gently punched him in the arm and turned to her reflection. *Okay, maybe he's not wrong.* Light brown pants, white t-shirt and brown sweater paired with white sneakers and simple earrings. She was an off-duty speech therapist, helping out the old lady who had once been her childhood neighbor.

"Well, if I come home to an empty kitchen, you *will* be punished," she threatened, voice low but playful.

"And I'll like it?"

She snorted and shook her head, stepping around him to grab her things. "I'll see you in a few hours," she told him, stretching up to kiss him and then darted out so she wouldn't miss her appointment with Mrs. Hershey.

As she predicted, the session with Mrs. Hershey ran late. Micah had planned for it, but she hadn't expected the old woman to drag the whole thing out that much. It started with a trip down memory lane and her favorite Christmases, then how her late husband used to dress up as Santa and "maybe that's where my kink started, you know?" to how the Santa in the book was not doing enough to get her blood pumping. By the time she had put the book aside, Micah was a bundle of emotions. She was exhausted from lack of sleep and incredibly horny—see: riding her Santa boyfriend like a stallion—and she was desperate to get home because it was Christmas Eve.

However, the upside was that Mrs. Hershey was able to read an entire chapter without fumbling. She might have been going slower than expected, but that didn't stop her. Micah loved working with her because of that. The old woman might be stubborn and difficult, but when it came to doing what she wanted, she powered through. And it was an absolute treat. Even if she sometimes said *puzzy* instead of pussy and *cawk* instead of cock. It was still quite entertaining.

Walking into the house, she dropped her things by the door and was hit with the scent of toasted cinnamon. "Oh my god, what is this glorious smell?" Micah groaned as she moved through the kitchen and wrapped her arms around Emery.

"Ugh, *Mom*, I can't breathe."

She tightened her arms around her daughter and looked up at Fletcher briefly only to have him join the hug. Emery whined again, which turned into a laugh and the three of them held each other for a long moment before pulling apart.

"Sorry I'm late. Mrs. Hershey is dangerous," she announced and then looked around the kitchen, smiling at the little stations Fletcher had set up for each dish. "Honey, this is way more organized than I expected."

"Figured we could cook together and Em could help too."

"The only station we didn't make was one for dessert. Fletch said that you—"

She groaned loudly, interrupting Emery's words and then touched her elbow in apology. "Sorry, kid. I didn't make it to the store. Told you, Mrs. Hershey is dangerous." She gathered her hair into a tiny ponytail and looked around the kitchen with a sigh. "Okay, let's get started on dinner and then I'll see what can be done."

Her plan had been to whip up a Yule Log, because Micah loved it and it was a dessert she'd made many times for Emery. But with how few of those ingredients existed in the house, she was going to have to figure something else out. Grabbing aprons for her family—*her family*, Micah's heart exploded at the sight of Fletcher and Emery putting on their aprons and laughing together—she turned to her boyfriend.

"Okay, chef. Put us to work."

Fletcher's eyes flashed with something naughty before he started assigning duties. Micah was working on the tarts while Emery handled the salad, and Fletcher was making the roast chicken. At some point, someone had turned on Christmas music and the soft sounds filled the kitchen. Despite her lack of interest in the holidays, she had to admit that Christmas music was sometimes pretty catchy. She found herself humming along as she made the tarts, until she realized the song—"You're My Christmas" by Double Toned. After talking about Ambrose a few weeks ago, Tatum hadn't brought him up again. Even when she was talking about the mess her ex-husband was now starting to cause. Micah made a mental note to check in on her best friend later and then got back to cooking.

"Mushroom and feta tarts are in the oven," Micah announced, closing the oven door with a proud smile. "What's next, Santa?"

He growled and she grinned at the realization that simple things like this got him all hot and bothered. Emery was singing and dancing along to the music, so Fletcher sidled over to Micah and dipped his head low enough that only she could hear.

"If your kid was in a different room, I'd be spreading you out on this counter and eating you for Christmas dinner," he whispered, eyes blazing with lust and she swallowed at his words.

"Jesus, Fletch."

His face softened and he smiled. "Was that good? Picked up a Santa erotica the other day, thought I'd get to the bottom of this kink."

"I love you so much," Micah said, laughing as she tugged his mouth to hers. "And I loved *that*. Make sure you use that voice on me later tonight."

"Anything for you, love bug."

The rest of dinner prep went smooth and while Fletcher and Emery plated everything and set the table, Micah worked on putting together dessert. She might have learned very few things from her mother—the right way to fold a fitted sheet, how to *not* comb curly hair, why coconut oil is better for your skin than anything else—but she had definitely learned the magic of Desperation Pie. Thankfully she had more ingredients than vinegar and water, but it was still a bit of a hodge-podge of things that came together to make dessert. She had some condensed milk and cocoa powder, which she whipped together and used the remaining flour from the tarts to make the base. Then managed to scrounge up some pecans and walnuts in her pantry that were also tossed into the mix. It wasn't going to be a spectacular dessert, but it would provide enough sweetness to round out their Christmas meal.

With the pie cooling, Micah joined Fletcher and Emery at the dining table and was shocked by how beautiful every-thing looked. They'd *finally* finished decorating the house, including hanging a stocking embroidered with an F. The tree was sparkling and Emery had made sure to hang up mistletoe everywhere. Then there was the table itself, that Emery insisted on decorating. They so rarely sat at the dining table, always choosing to sit at the spacious counters in the kitchen, so the fact that her daughter worked her magic was wonderful. Red linen and crockery that was 'saved for a special occasion', wine glasses and holly leaves, sparkles and stars—the table was set beautifully. Emery handed her and Fletcher paper crowns, which they slid onto their heads as they sat down.

"I know we usually do this at Thanksgiving, but I'd like to talk about the things I'm grateful for," Emery said as Micah served everyone. "If that's okay."

"Of course, sweetheart."

Emery beamed and looked between her and Fletcher, before dropping her eyes to her lap. "I'm grateful for Mom. For doing this every Christmas even though it's not her favorite time of year." Micah's heart jumped and she glanced at Fletcher who shrugged with a smile. "I'm grateful for Fletcher. For coming into our lives and making it even better than it was before, which I didn't think was possible." When Emery looked up at them, her eyes were brimming with tears. "I'm grateful for your relationship, too. For showing me that two people can truly love each other in all of the weird and beautiful ways. Gives me hope that one day I'll have that too."

Micah set a hand over her heart and reached across with the other to grab Emery's. Tears slipped down her daughter's cheek and Micah smiled. "I am so grateful for you, kid. You are the best thing in my life and watching you grow up? Nothing beats that. I admire you and am inspired by you constantly. You are my heart and my soul."

"Don't make me cry more, *Mom!*"

"You started it with those ridiculously sweet words!"

All three of them laughed and then Fletcher was reaching for both Micah's and Emery's hands. "May I?" At Emery's nod, he cleared his throat and smiled. "I love you both, that's the first and most important thing. I am *so* grateful that I was welcomed into your home and your lives, because this is exactly where I was meant to be. I hope that this is the first of many incredible holidays we'll spend together, because you two are everything to me."

Sniffles went around the table and then Emery was on her feet, arms wrapped around Fletcher. Micah blew out a shaky breath, using her free hand to wipe away her tears. Once her daughter was seated again, she shook her head and smiled at her family.

"I don't remember Christmas being a time to cry," she teased.

"I was making up for the lack of tears at Thanksgiving," Emery said with a smug grin. "Besides, Fletcher should know that us George women cry very easily."

Fletcher snorted out a laugh and Micah squeezed his hand. "Okay, after all that hard work of shopping and cooking, we shouldn't waste this delicious meal."

Emery cheered and as Fletcher poured out the wine and finished serving the food, they dug in. Micah moved her food around the plate as she watched them, talking and laughing, teasing each other. *This* is what she wanted for Emery. She wanted her daughter to have someone who loved her so much that they would be honest when they talked to her. Someone who would give her the opportunity to speak her mind and have opinions. Someone who wanted her as much as she wanted them in her life. Micah knew she was a good parent and she'd provided Emery with a lot of good things. But she could see that Emery had been *craving* a second parental figure to guide her through everything else in life.

Micah knew that there would never be enough words or ways to show Fletcher how grateful she was that he came back into her life. But she would try. Every single day, for the rest of their lives.

fletcher

The family that burps together, stays together.

FLETCHER'S HEART hadn't stopped its little happy dance since the day Micah said 'I love you'. But it was doing twirls and jumps now that he had both the George women in his life. *Forever, if Emery has anything to say about it.* He couldn't believe that this was his life. A woman who was way out of his league, but everything he ever wanted. And a teenager that was funny and charming and beautiful and sassy, and certainly kept him on his toes. The past week had been a test of his emotional capabilities and he was happy to say that he'd survived.

Growing up, he was told that 'men don't cry'. Men were supposed to be strong and silent, stoic in the face of sadness. But that was a whole lot of bullshit. When he met Jack, Soren and Brandy, and they started The Rescuers, there were a lot of tears. And nobody joked about them being 'manly tears', they just cried. Happy tears over a successfully recorded album. Sad tears over the loss of a family member. Ecstatic tears when their tour was sold out. And so much more. Crying was therapeutic, or at least Hank said so.

So when Emery opened herself up and told him she

wanted him to stay, when she said she was grateful for him, he let himself cry. Because if there were two people who would appreciate his tears in this world, it was Micah and Emery.

But that also brought to mind the fact that he hadn't had such an incredible Christmas in a long time. His last memory of a big and fun Christmas was with the band before they took their sabbatical—if you could still call it that. It was before any of them got married, so the four band members, their entire crew and every single person who helped them on that last tour got together and had a wild time. Booze was flowing, celebrations were loud and chaotic. Everyone was happy. The Rescuers had made more than enough albums to keep their bank accounts full, they had gone on tour for years at a stretch and it was finally time to hang up their instruments. That Christmas played on loop in his mind regularly, because it was the last time he'd smiled so much while sitting around a table surrounded by his favorite people.

What did it say that the Christmases when he was married to Alice were boring in comparison to that or to what he was experiencing now? Since his relationship with his family was non-existent, Fletcher would go with Alice to see her folks and dinner would be a quiet affair. Everyone would do their own thing around the Christmas tree. Gifts would be exchanged quietly. It *was* dull. He liked Alice's family fine, but they didn't enjoy the little things. Back then, he didn't know what he was missing.

Until now.

Micah's house was dressed up far more than he thought possible for someone who had zero interest in the holidays. But it was clear that she'd done everything for Emery. From the beautifully decorated tree—seriously it was almost as good as what he'd seen at Rockefeller Center in New York— to the lights strung across the windows, even the faux fireplace had something including a stocking with his initial on it. This was the kind of Christmas you saw in movies, but it wasn't for show. The George women took everything they did seriously and while it might not be Micah's favorite time of year, she didn't hold back.

More than all of this, it was the way he felt when he was with them. Welcomed and wanted. *Loved*. Which wasn't totally unbelievable, but it had been a while since he'd felt like he belonged. He'd sent pictures to Erin—who had returned to San Diego for her firm's holiday party—and his best friend had reminded him that he was the luckiest son of a bitch in the world. Which was the absolute truth. He had everything he never thought he'd have—a partner he loved with every fibre of his being and a kid that he would protect and love for the rest of his life.

"Fletch. You okay?" Micah's voice broke through his thoughts and he turned to find her looking up at him with concern.

"Yeah." He nodded and leaned into her slightly. "Still thinking about how lucky I am."

"You looked angry there for a minute."

He handed Micah a plate so she could slide it into the dishwasher. "I didn't have holidays like this, you know. Maybe when I was a kid, but Christmas never looked this good."

She nodded and gave his arm a squeeze. "Well, better get used to it. Because this is what Christmas will be like until Emery gets sick of it."

"I'm absolutely okay with that," he told her, pressing a kiss to the side of her head.

And he was. He was excited to see what kind of stuff Emery would conjure up next year, what new hobbies she'd pick up by the time Christmas rolled around again. The fact that he would get to see that for another year—and then some —made his heart do somersaults.

"Are you two done making out?"

"I thought you were grateful for our weird and beautiful relationship?" Micah countered and Fletcher laughed at Emery's fake gagging.

"Please don't…I have regrets."

"Did you clear the table?" he asked and Emery pouted at him. "Come on, kid. That's all you've gotta do. Bring every-thing in here and then we'll stop making out."

With an epic eye roll and a sigh that could shake even the strongest building, she stomped off to clear the table. Micah shot him a smirk and bumped her hip against his.

"You've already got this whole *stern dad* thing down."

Dad. The term lodged in his brain and Fletcher stared as it pulsed slowly. "Is that what I did?"

"And you didn't even realize it." Micah laughed and walked away. He shook his head as he tried to process what was going on.

When he first met Emery, Fletcher was terrified that he'd never know how to talk to teenagers. He was forty-seven and his experience with kids was in the meet and greet line at concerts and when he was Santa for three weeks. Then he met Emery and Nico, and suddenly he needed to know how to talk to younger people. People who had never heard his music or knew who he was. And it was an adjustment. He was lucky that Emery was more of an adult than most people her age, but still.

Dad was never a role he saw for himself. Yet, he liked the way the word fit him.

❄

"Can we please eat dessert now? It's melting," Emery whined as she gestured to whatever Micah had made. And to be honest, it *was* melting.

"Oh fuck, what the hell happened to it?" Micah stared at the dessert, which made Emery giggle. But then instead of losing her mind over it, Micah grabbed spoons and held them out to the two of them. "We're gonna stand here and eat, dig in."

He didn't have to be told twice, leaning over the counter, he scooped up a large piece of the dessert and shoved it into his mouth. He groaned at the melted chocolate and caramel as Emery made a similar sound on the other side of the counter. He ate another piece and another before finally turning to his girlfriend. "What is this deliciousness?"

She beamed, smug and proud of herself. "It's called a desperation pie, you cobble together ingredients you have and make it work."

"God, Mom, it's *soooo gooooood*!"

"We've got cocoa, pecans, walnuts, salted caramel, condensed milk, graham crackers and a regular pie crust," Micah said as she ate some more of the pie.

The whole thing was seconds away from collapsing onto the counter, so Fletcher was glad that they'd found a way to keep it standing up right, at least for a little longer. But once they were halfway through the pie—"why did I make such a big one for the three of us?"—everyone dropped their spoons and leaned away.

"Chocolate overload," Emery groaned and Fletcher rubbed his stomach as he straightened up.

"But it's worth the sugar rush that's going to hit me very soon." Fletcher released a burp and smirked when his girls released matching ones of their own.

"The family that burps together, stays together," Micah added, winking at him.

She had to know what she was doing with all these big words. First, she called him a *dad*. Now, she was tossing around *family* like it was totally normal. He agreed with all those words, but he was already so emotionally charged by these two women, those terms were amplifying his feelings. While Micah and Emery put the rest of the dessert away, Fletcher fixed them tea. He listened as the two of them giggled and talked about messy dessert memories, about how there was one time when Micah made a birthday cake that collapsed as soon as she set it down in front of all the other kids. By the time he'd turned around with cups filled with hot apple cinnamon tea, his girls were lying on the kitchen floor hooting and howling as they laughed.

"Do you need help?" he asked, looking down at the two of them.

Micah nodded as Emery shook her head, both their hands stretched out to him. He set the tray down and held out his hands, smiling as they reached out and he pulled them to their feet. But instead of thanking him and moving away, both of them hugged him, arms tightly wrapped around him. His heart skipped and his breath caught at the feeling. He hugged them back, squeezing them against him, kissed the tops of their heads and then stepped away.

"It's almost bedtime for this old man, so let's go unwrap those gifts." At the mention of gifts, Emery released him and charged for the living room.

"I love you," Micah said, tilting her head back for a kiss.

He dropped a soft kiss to her lips and smiled. "I love you too."

Armed with their tea, they sat snuggled together on the couch while Emery went through her stack of gifts. Even though he and Micah had decided not to buy each other any gifts, Fletcher got Micah something. After all, she said "don't spend any money on me, okay?", she didn't say anything about no actual gifts. However, they did discuss and buy Emery a bunch of gifts that were thoughtful and what she wanted.

He'd wrapped a pair of his old drumsticks for her, not to use, but to hold onto. There were tiny cracks from being used so much and a faint outline of his hands still lingered on the base, but he knew that Emery would appreciate it. Especially when she started crying as she unwrapped it. Even though they'd decided she was done with drums, he still bought her a book that helped her read sheet music. In some part of his mind, Fletcher believed that Emery could play music. Just not the drums. At Micah's suggestion, he'd also bought her a pair of star-shaped earrings and a gift voucher to get another piercing in her ears—this was accepted with much squealing and hugging.

Then Emery moved onto Micah's gifts, which were a lot more in line with what she wanted—a makeup kit, a pack of suspenders with skulls on them, a poster of The Rescuers that Fletcher had gotten his bandmates to sign and send over. Emery was over the moon about all her gifts and Fletcher was glad for it. Once she was done, she carried her loot up to her bedroom and closed the door. Leaving him and Micah alone on the couch, with wrapping paper strewn around everywhere.

"I got you something," she said, sliding out from under his arm to retrieve an envelope from behind the tree. "But this also depends on whether or not you opened your birthday gift."

"I uh…forgot," he replied, looking apologetic.

Micah laughed and returned to the couch. "Of course you did."

He took the large envelope from her, realizing that it was the same size as the one she'd given him for his birthday. Carefully opening it, he tipped it sideways and glanced at her as a bunch of photographs slipped into his hand. He didn't know what to expect, so when he flipped the pictures over, his eyes widened.

"Holy shit," he mumbled, drinking in the photoshoot of Micah dressed up like a mermaid in dangerously sexy and provocative poses in front of and around a drum kit. The tail matched the tattoo on his arm, a tiny bikini top held her breasts up and whatever makeup she was wearing added to the sexy allure of the pose.

He pressed the photographs to his chest and glanced at Micah, who grinned from her position beside him on the couch. "You like?"

"You did this for me."

"I'm your mermaid, right? Figured I'd make it official."

"Fucking hell, Mick," he breathed out, chest heaving and heart racing as he held the pictures out to stare at them again. There were six in total and in every single one, she was in a slightly more sexy pose. The final one had her topless, sultry eyes boring holes into his even through the printed image. When he could finally function, adjusting his hard dick and shifting around a little, Fletcher nodded. "I got you something too."

"Next year, we're seriously sticking to the 'no gifts' rule, no matter what."

He grinned as he set the photographs face down. "Next year, huh?"

"You're stuck with us, Fletch, might as well get used to it."

"Nowhere else I'd rather be, love bug."

Getting to his feet, he rummaged around in his bag and pulled out a messily wrapped gift. Handing it to her, he dropped to sit beside her on the couch and smiled as she attempted to be gentle with the wrapping paper before giving up and ripping it apart. Her fingers brushed over the frayed Moleskin notebook, tracing his name that was carved into the center. When Micah's eyes met his, Fletcher nodded, and she carefully opened the notebook, landing on a random page.

"This is a notebook filled with you," he said softly. "Memories, dreams, thoughts and lyrics. I wrote "Mermaid" on hotel stationery, but I put everything else into this. Songs I thought we could record, but never talked about. It became my Mick Journal."

"Fletch…" she whispered, shaking her head as she turned the pages slowly, stopping every so often to touch a doodle or a word.

"I want you to have it. It's as much a part of you as it is a part of me. Besides, I get to have you now, so I don't need to write about pining for you from a distance."

She laughed softly, a tear sliding out of her eye. Fletcher caught it before it followed the curve of her cheek. "A part of me is still in shock that you thought about me all this time. That I made such an impact on you that night."

"Before or after you, I'd never eaten every morsel of room service in a hotel bed while wrapped in bathrobes while a beautiful woman called me out on my taste in music."

"For a musician, you really do have questionable taste."

"I stand by the fact that Grace Slick was a legend of her time."

She rolled her eyes and closed the notebook, setting it in her lap as she turned to him. "Thank you, Fletch. This is the most precious gift I've ever received."

"Better not let your daughter hear you say that."

"I heard that!" Emery yelled as she charged down the stairs. Fletcher hurriedly put the mermaid pictures away and looked up as Emery slid into the living room. "If you're done being romantic, can we watch a movie now?"

"Yup. Fletcher's on popcorn duty, you're picking the movie and I'm going to put everything away."

He shook his head and shot Emery a pointed look. "You

pick the movie, babe. Em and I are going to clean up and work on the popcorn."

"What he said," Emery responded, pouting playfully at him.

With the teenager by his side, Fletcher gathered all the discarded wrapping paper. Then they worked together to put away all the leftovers, wiping down the kitchen while the popcorn did its job in the microwave. With two large bowls filled to the brim, they returned to the couch and sat on either side of Micah as she cued up *The Nightmare Before Christmas*.

This life, he could totally get used to it.

micah

Now come here and tie me up.

EVERY MORNING SINCE CHRISTMAS, Micah would open Fletcher's notebook and read a page of what he'd written. She never went in order, picked a random section and read. The first few times she stumbled across little notes he'd written addressed to her—*We drove past a field of dandelions this morning and I thought of you. Thought of that tattoo I loved to trace on your hip.* Then she read a few lyrics, all of which were far more innuendo filled that she expected. There was even a sloppy sketch he'd done of her in the margins of one page.

It blew her mind that all those years ago, while they fooled around in his hotel room, Fletcher had fallen in love with her. Not an infatuation or a crush. No, that's not how he'd do it. He fell, without a parachute or any hope of being caught when he landed. For sixteen years, he held onto those thoughts and feelings, loving her from a distance. Like it was the most natural thing in the world.

If he knew about her new routine, he didn't say anything. Falling asleep and waking up in his arms, the scent of him wrapped around her was exactly what she wanted every day. They'd drink coffee and make breakfast, then while Fletcher was at the store, Micah would spend the day with Emery and they'd do all kinds of random things that ranged from watching a movie or shopping to attempting a new recipe. The holidays were always a time for mother and daughter to be together, because with school and her clinic closed for the break, they had loads of hours in the day to do nothing.

Today, however, was going to be different. After their last session together, Mrs. Hershey had *insisted* that Micah stop by their book club that evening. While she wouldn't do this with her clients, her entire relationship with Mrs. Hershey was different. Besides, she knew the book like the back of her hand and she figured it might be fun. When she'd told Fletcher about it, he'd been so excited. Ever since they uncovered her Santa kink, he'd been doing research on books to read. His nightstand had a few paperbacks with shirtless men in Santa garb and she knew that he had some ebooks on his phone as well. The man was committed to finding ways to drive Micah wild. She showed her appreciation just as enthusiastically.

The book club pick, however, she'd forbidden him from reading, because she wanted it to be a surprise.

"Think they'll read out all the filthy bits?"

She chuckled at Fletcher's question, swiping mascara on. "I'm sure if *you* ask Mrs. Hershey, she'd be happy to provide. But knowing her, she'll improv most of it."

"I'm really looking forward to meeting this woman, especially with all the stories you've told me." Fletcher stood beside her in front of the bathroom mirror as he rolled up the sleeves of his black shirt.

"She's going to flirt up a storm, so please let me down gently if she works her magic."

Chuckling, Fletcher nodded. "That's why we're doing dinner after, so I can break up with you and find my joy with the infamous Mrs. Hershey."

Smiling, she straightened up and put her mascara away, blinking at her reflection. "It's such a shame that our second proper date out of the house would be the end of it all."

"The heart and body wants what it wants, love bug."

Their eyes met in the mirror and she shook her head, playfully smacking his butt as she walked out of the bathroom. There had been a time in her life when she would have been insecure in this relationship—or any relationship, for that matter—but now she knew that anybody would be lucky to be with her. She knew her worth, her power and her beauty, she knew what she brought to the table and how good of a partner she was.

Which was why joking about Fletcher running off with Mrs. Hershey had become a thing over the last few days. It was always fun to see how he responded to her ribbing. He never disappointed either.

Shrugging out of her bathrobe, she tugged on her shape wear. It was a constant battle, pulling the damn thing up her hips and worse taking it off after wearing it all day. But it was worth it, because she needed a little assistance now and then when she wore certain dresses. Because it was also a date night, Micah had whipped out one of her newer thrift store purchases and slid it on. The full length floral wrap dress was soft against her skin and fluttered around her legs as she held everything together, thanks to the buttons in all the strategic places.

"Fletch, need your help."

He stepped out of the bathroom and froze, his eyes doing a full sweep of her. "Fuck me, love bug, you look incredible."

"I know, now come here and tie me up."

"You know the way to my heart, Mick."

She rolled her eyes, laughing at the way he stared at her. "The dress, Fletch. And maybe if you play your cards right, I'll let you tie me up when we get home."

"Guess I'm ignoring Mrs. Hershey tonight then."

Laughing, she turned around and gave Fletcher her back. He tugged on the thick bands at her sides, slowly wrapped them around her front and then fiddled with it in the back for a minute. "There you go," he whispered, pressing a kiss to her neck as his hands slid down over her hips. "Wet dream come to life."

She smiled and leaned back against him, his arms sliding around her waist as they swayed slowly. "Some days I'm still shocked that this is my life."

"Having your very own stallion?"

"Having *you* as my stallion." Micah turned in his arms and set her hands on his shoulder. "When I first saw you perform, I decided that drummers were my type. Shockingly enough, there aren't all that many great or handsome drummers in the world."

"We're a rare breed," he agreed, brushing a kiss over her cheek, down to her jaw and neck.

Micah hummed and tilted her head. "And then you called me backstage, took me to your hotel room and I had the best sex of my life."

"Best sex of my life too, Mick."

"Took us sixteen years, but we found our way back to that."

He leaned back and searched her eyes. "For the record, I am only with you for the sex."

"Same," she said, blowing a raspberry. "I mean, calloused hands, scratchy beard and magical dick are exactly the reasons I keep you around."

He nodded, but Micah could see the smile in his eyes. "Good, wouldn't want you to think this was about anything else."

"Wouldn't dream of it. Best sex is enough at our age."

"I'd definitely rather blow out my back than anything else."

"Great," she said with a firm nod, pressing her lips together to hide her smile.

"I might also love you a little."

"Don't blame you, sweetheart. I'm fucking irresistible," she teased as a soft growl built in his chest. She held his face in her hands and grinned. "Now, let's go see Mrs. Hershey, read some smut, eat great food and then you can put that magical dick to good use."

She stepped out of his arms and stepped in front of the full length mirror to fluff her hair and straighten out her dress. Micah watched him through the reflection and smiled as his eyes did a slow trail of her body. When he finally looked up and met her eyes, he unleashed his beautiful smile and her heart stuttered.

"Hey Fletch."

"Mick," he replied.

"I love you a little too."

"Don't blame you, honey."

There was something to be said for sitting in a book club with a bunch of septuagenarians as they read and discussed erotica. Even though she'd read the book and *every* sex scene, listening to Mrs. Hershey and her friends discuss penis size, shape and girth while gesturing to the few male members of the book club was weird as fuck. Especially when Fletcher became a target. It didn't surprise her that he pretended to be innocent about what they were doing as they made him twirl in place slowly, stretch out his arms, spread his hands and legs—like he was some kind of doll for them to play with. She was incredibly glad that he hadn't brought his Santa coat to rile them up further.

When he sat back down, Fletcher flashed her a wide grin and dusted off his shoulders.

Then there was the reading itself. She should have known that despite working tirelessly with the old woman, Mrs. Hershey would pretend like she couldn't make sense of the words. She kept batting her eyes at Fletcher and Micah, hoping one of them would save her. The more they ignored her, the more she tried until finally the woman who organized the book club cast her as the heroine and Fletcher as Santa. Which made her boyfriend lose his mind.

It also made Micah lose hers, because the more they read together, the more her clit throbbed with need. Halfway through one particularly naughty scene—Santa was licking a candy cane that he intended to use on the heroine later—Micah crossed one leg over the other to stave off the aching between her thighs. The action made her dress part at the slit, giving Fletcher an eyeful of her bare thigh. Before she could straighten out her dress, he dropped a large hand on her leg and squeezed. With every *cock* and *pussy* and *thrust* they read out, her body responded to Fletcher's touch. And she knew that if they weren't surrounded by those people, he would have taken her right there without a second thought.

"With his cock buried deep inside me, I knew that there would never be anything more I needed in life. Santa and his candy cane were all I would ever want," Micah forced out, feeling hot all over. She slammed the book shut and the book club cheered, everyone praising them for their reading skills. Fletcher's hand flexed on her bare thigh and Micah swallowed back a moan before gently nudging his hand away.

"Oh, sweetheart, you were so wonderful." Mrs. Hershey shuffled over, hands stretched out. "You two should consider getting into reading those audiobooks. With voices like that, I bet you'd have all the listeners reaching for their battery operated devices."

A choked laugh escaped Fletcher and Micah shook her head, feeling the heat rush through her whole body as she gave Mrs. Hershey a hug. "I'm really proud of you too. You read that whole chapter without any hesitation."

"You taught me well. But, I was hoping that I could keep coming back in the new year?"

Micah smiled and nodded, squeezing Mrs. Hershey's hands. "Of course. Make sure you bring your next book club read too."

After another round of quick hugs, Mrs. Hershey hurried back to her friends and Micah sank into Fletcher's embrace. While she was still very turned on, she was finally able to stand steadily, even if she was leaning into Fletcher like she couldn't.

"In case you were wondering, I'm open to dirty voicemails of that nature in the future."

"You'll be lucky if you get anything at all from me in the future," she shot back with a laugh.

He smirked and wiggled his eyebrows. "At least I know you had a good time while it lasted."

Shaking her head, Micah smoothed down her dress and pushed back her shoulders. No, she *loved* how easily he turned her on. The potent combination of Fletcher and the erotica had gotten her so hot and bothered, it was a miracle she'd gotten through reading all of the scenes they kept assigning to her. He reached for her again and Micah didn't even protest, she let him sweep her into his arms while surrounded by books.

"Does this mean you want to go home and—" he dropped his voice to a whisper, lips brushing along her jaw "—have my candy cane buried inside you, right where I'm meant to be?"

"Fletch," she moaned, smacking his chest as she turned her head to catch his mouth in a kiss. His hand drifted down to her ass and pulled her against him. Arching into him, she gripped his hair in one hand and let him hitch one of her legs up around his waist. But then reality set in and Micah gasped as she pulled away, steadying herself against him as she dropped her foot to the floor.

"You're the worst." She laughed and brushed her hair back, shaking her head. "Stop seducing me."

"You started it, with this erotic book club and that dress and that reading and by existing." She growled and Fletcher's lips kicked up into a smirk. "That sound too, love bug. Gets me going."

Huffing out a breath, she held a hand up to stop him from getting closer. "We're going to dinner like people who can control themselves. And *after*…we'll see how I'm feeling."

"I'll show you how I'm feeling," he said, taking a step towards her, but they were interrupted by one of the book club biddies.

"Are both of you attempting to create your own little erotica in the stacks?"

"We were trying to find our way out, actually," Micah said, shooting Fletcher a glare.

"Of course you were, darling. Come on, I'll show you out through these very complicated stacks." The old lady flashed them both a smile and winked at Fletcher before leading the way to the front and out of the bookstore. "We hope to see you both next time too!"

They rushed out to Fletcher's truck and the whole way to the restaurant, they were cracking up because this kind of thing would only happen to them.

❄

The Italian restaurant Fletcher had picked was a lot fancier than the places Micah usually went, so she was glad she'd put effort into her clothes for the evening. Even if her stallion was dressed like a rockstar, looking completely out of place in his dark jeans, black shirt and scuffed boots. He'd handed over his jacket and her coat as they walked in, but he still looked so good.

The table they were seated at was tucked away from the rest of the crowd and despite looking small, seemed to hold all of the food they kept ordering. But it was also the perfect size for them to lean in and steal kisses every now and then, for her legs to be tucked between his under the table. She couldn't remember the last time she'd been on a *date* that she was excited about. He was really changing things in all the best ways.

Much like the night they shared in his hotel room years ago, they had made their way through every dish that was brought over. They talked about making plans with her friends, maybe flying out to see his bandmates in the new year and the conversation moved to music that they were listening to. It fascinated her that for two people who loved music and spent so much time together, they hadn't once discussed their current musical tastes. So to hear Fletcher admit that he was an Adele fan was a treat for Micah.

Then he brought up Emery and what the future looked like with her, which made Micah's heart soar. This man loved her kid completely and was willing to do whatever it took to make her happy. For that, Micah would forever be grateful.

"Speaking of, there's something I want to ask you," Fletcher said as she bit into an arancini ball. She nodded, hand over her mouth as she watched him cautiously. "You're sure, right?"

"About what?"

"You, me and Emery."

Micah stared at him a moment and nodded, because hadn't she already been clear on that? Had she not told him she wanted that future with him? He watched her, smiling as she processed his statement. He'd been doing that a lot that evening, smiling and watching her, not saying a damn thing. She liked being looked at by him, which was another thing that was exclusive to Fletcher Kelley.

"I am more than sure, Fletch," she finally said. "Even if you and Em hadn't had that conversation, *we* would have. I want you. I want *us*. I've never been more sure of anything in my life than knowing I want you with me permanently."

Fletcher released a shaky breath, head dropping forward slightly and Micah reached out to brush her fingers through his hair.

"Okay, good. Because I am fucking serious about you and me, Mick. Serious about Emery being a part of my life for as long as she wants me. You two make all the calls here. If at any time I'm not needed, I'm gone. In case it wasn't clear yet, Micah, I love you and your kid. I love being a part of your life and want you two to be a part of mine."

He lifted his head and she saw the certainty there. Of course she'd known that. Fletcher had said so in many different ways over the last few days, but it never hurt to hear it again. Or with so much surety.

"So forever. You, me and Emery."

He nodded, stretching a hand across the table with a smile. "The George women and me. I was never going to be the kind of musician that had a million kids running around the country, or have multiple ex-wives. I resigned myself to being alone and I was honestly okay with it. Even after I had and lost you, I was okay with living life in simple terms. But I get to have you again, Mick, and if I'm being honest, there's nowhere else I'd rather be."

Her shoulders sagged with relief and she offered him a

smile. "Forever, Fletch. I wasn't expecting you and certainly didn't plan for you, but here you are. And honestly? I don't want to go back to life without you."

Forever was a long time, but when you met the right person, you just knew. Emery already told her that she smiled more and looked happier now that Fletcher was in her life. Plus, he'd proven to be a good guy in so many ways—helping her and friends when they were drunk, looking out for Emery, introducing her to his best friend and most of all loving the heck out of her.

"There is no life without you, Mick. But glad we're on the same page."

She laughed and blew him a kiss that Fletcher caught and pressed to his chest. This man was definitely the most unexpected part of her year, and that's why he was also the best part.

They finished their dinner and despite her protests, he paid the bill. Hand-in-hand, they drove back to her house and found all the lights on. Even though Emery was supposed to be at Mrs. Cannon's house, she'd clearly come home early. Which was a bit of a dampener on her plans to ravage Fletcher and scream her heart out while he fucked her. Letting them into the house, she got a strong whiff of chocolate as she walked down the stairs.

"You're back!" Emery greeted them with chocolate all over her face and hair. "We made cake."

Looking past her daughter, Micah found the kitchen in absolute chaos and Nico also covered in chocolate. Fletcher came up behind her and let out a loud snort at the sight. "Did Willy Wonka come through here or something?"

Emery stuck her tongue out at him. "We were in the middle of cleaning up, okay?"

"Ms. George. Mr. Kelley." Nico offered them sheepish smiles and went back to loading up the dishwasher. Micah glanced at Fletcher, who pulled a stool out for her at the counter and then sat down beside her.

"Okay, this is the best cake ever and you both should have some," Emery said, slicing the cake up and putting a big piece on a plate, sliding it in front of her and Fletcher. "You can share."

Fletcher swiped his finger through the layer of icing and held it out for Micah. She didn't hesitate to wrap her lips around his finger and suck the icing off, drawing disgusted sounds from the teenagers in her kitchen. She knew that was exactly why he'd done it, because moments later, he cut himself a piece with the fork Emery handed over and took a bite. Micah followed suit, her eyes on the kids as they cleaned up.

"This is good," Fletcher mumbled, cutting off another piece. "So *fucking* good."

"Really?" Nico asked, eyes wide as they looked between Micah and Fletcher.

Micah nodded and licked her spoon clean before going in for another bite. "I must agree, best chocolate cake ever."

Nico and Emery squealed and bounced around the kitchen, sharing a quick hug before they returned to cleaning up the space.

fletcher

I want all the days with you.

"RIGHT THERE," Micah panted, hips rocking back against him, his thrusts slow and shallow to get her warmed up. They'd been alternating between sex and lazing around all day and if he was being honest, it was definitely the best way to spend the last day of the year. They were sweaty and the sheets definitely needed to be changed, but they were having too much fun to stop.

He dragged his hands up from her waist to cup her breasts, his lips pressed against her shoulder as he thrust deeper into her. On her knees, hands stretched out to hold the headboard, Micah was a beautiful sight. She'd woken up that morning prepared with various positions and things she wanted to try and Fletcher would never deny her anything; even when it meant twisting his body in ways that made no sense. But the pleasure he got from those moments? Nothing quite like it.

"Fletch…stop playing with me," she whined, a hand reaching back to grab at his hair as her hips kept pushing back, seeking more from him. Tweaking her nipples, he smiled against her warm skin and did exactly what she didn't want him to do—he played with her. A low growl came from Micah and she tugged on his hair, then before he could make another move, she was pulling away completely, his cock sliding out of her as she turned to face him.

"You wanted slow."

"That was *not* slow," she huffed and pushed him onto his ass, her hands mapping his chest and stomach before wrapping around his dick that was wet with her arousal. "That was excruciating."

Gritting his teeth, Fletcher stared at her hands as they moved up and down his cock. The words were on the edge of his tongue, but he couldn't speak. Not when she was torturing him that way. When she squeezed his tip, his head fell back as he groaned. She was going to kill him. Not because he had taken it *slow*—as per her wishes, he might add—but because she knew exactly where his weak spots were. When a finger dragged down the length of him, tracing his vein, Fletcher quivered. Only she had ever figured out how to do that to him and what it was about that stretch of skin that got him so tangled up.

"Fuck, okay," he finally forced the words out, supporting himself on one hand, while using the other to pry her hands off him. "What would you like me to do instead?"

A saccharine smile lit up her face and she moved forward, hands pressing into the bed on either side of him. "Sit there, look pretty and let *me* show you how it's done."

Fletcher nodded, eyes dipping to her full breasts as they swayed with her movements. When one of her hands cupped his jaw, he focused on her face. Her pupils were dilated and the evil things she had in mind for him flashed through her eyes. Oh, he was more than ready to be devoured by her.

"Are you comfortable?" she asked, sitting back on her heels, hands resting demurely on her knees like she wasn't completely naked, looking well fucked and flushed.

He swallowed hard and nodded again, but then quickly scooted backwards so he could stretch his legs out. Micah watched him like prey and it was probably the hottest thing ever. "Yes, ma'am."

"I love it when you want to make me happy," she whispered and his heart bloomed at the words. He only ever wanted to make her happy, whatever form that took. Sex, love, food; he'd do it for her. She crawled forward, hands brushing over his thighs and teasingly against his dick as she finally settled in his lap. Fletcher touched her hip gently and she shook her head. "No touching the merchandise."

He pulled his hand away and licked his lips, eyes drinking in every inch of this woman. Their first night together, they might have fucked like animals in the shower and in his insanely soft hotel bed. But there had been an hour or so when Micah touched and teased him, never giving him what he wanted. When she did finally slide a condom on and ride him, he was so overcome with pleasure that he came within seconds of being inside Micah. He didn't want that to happen again, he wanted to enjoy every minute with her. Except, she'd clearly gotten better at the torture.

Turning around in his lap, she leaned forward slightly to rest her hands on his knees and looked over her shoulder at him. "You can only touch me when I say and *where* I say," she instructed and he nodded dumbly, not even bothering to protest or ask why. His mermaid wanted things a certain way, he'd do it however she wanted.

Eyes fixed on her delicious ass, Fletcher grunted and clenched his jaw as her hand wrapped around his dick again. He breathed slowly, needing to stay steady and hold himself together as Micah rocked her hips back and forth, rubbing her pussy along his cock. "Mick," he breathed out, fingers curling into the sheets as he ached with need.

Her body lifted, hand sliding down to his base and

through the lust haze, he watched as Micah slowly lowered herself back down. The minute his cock made contact, a strangled growl fell from his lips and his head dropped back. He could feel her pussy stretch and spread around him as she slid lower, taking him deeper. And when he was buried all the way inside her, she let out an unidentifiable sound that vibrated through her entire body.

"Ah *fuck*," he mumbled.

She clenched around him briefly and moaned. "You're so fucking perfect, Fletch."

He forced his eyes open, drinking in the curves of Micah's body as she started to move. He wanted to touch and *fuck* her; but he knew that she was in charge. This was her game and he was the lucky son of a bitch who got to participate.

Her hips rocked slowly, back and forth, her ass bumping against him with every shift. He couldn't even thrust up into her with the way she was clamped around him. A soft keening sound came from her and Micah sat up, taking him even deeper and making him groan.

"Hands….on….breasts." The words came out between gasps and he didn't even wait for her to finish the last word before he covered her ample breasts with his palms. She moaned, head falling back against him as he kneaded her breasts, making sure to rub his palms against her nipples.

Her hips undulated against his, moving faster and clenching around him hungrily. Fletcher continued to tease her, hand surrounding one breast as he massaged it, while fingers plucked at the nipples of the other one. Her hands came up and around the back of his head, her fingers sliding through his hair. Even though his lips were inches away from her neck, Fletcher didn't push his luck. Not that she would stop what she was doing, but he was following her lead.

When her head fell to the side, moaning so loud it reverberated through the room, Fletcher pinched both breasts and the sound was amplified.

"I love how well you take me," he growled, letting his breath brush against her skin.

She hummed and with the hand on the back of his head, pulled him forward so his mouth was against her neck. He inhaled deeply, the intoxicating scent of apples, coconut and *Micah* filling him up. Dragging his nose up and down her neck, he took his time giving her what she wanted. Micah made an impatient sound and he smiled, pushing her breasts together as he clamped down on the spot where her neck met her shoulder and sucked.

"Fuck!" she shouted, pussy clenching tightly around his cock. He loosened his grip on her breasts and her back arched, but he didn't stop his assault on her neck. The fingers in his hair gripped harder and he felt her body shudder against him.

Finally pulling away, he licked the spot he'd marked, already seeing the redness reflected back at him. Smiling, he kissed around the spot, watching goosebumps spread across Micah's skin. She leaned back against him, her hips moving slower, but taking him deeper with every shift. He kissed along her shoulder, one hand now resting on her stomach while the other toyed with her nipple.

When her hand covered the one on her stomach, Fletcher opened his eyes to watch the descent until their hands were between her thighs. "Touch me," she whispered and Fletcher nodded, lips still pressed against her shoulder. With two fingers, he spread open the hood and pressed a third to her clit, smiling when her head fell back against him. Rubbing her slowly, he felt how that slight touch was getting her pussy worked up. Increasing pressure on her clit slightly, he peppered kisses along Micah's exposed neck and licked the spot behind her ear. The combination of everything made her body spasm, but she caught herself with one hand gripping his forearm and the other clutching her breast.

He could feel how close she was, teetering on the edge of her orgasm, and he knew exactly what it would take to make her come. He pinched her clit and smiled, feeling her body tense up for a brief moment before she exploded. Her back arched and pussy clenched around his cock, as she came hard, soaking him. He continued teasing her clit until she was unable to sit up straight. When she fell forward, he planted his feet on the bed and shifted enough to thrust up into her, making them both moan. Fucking her through her orgasm, he groaned as he came as well, spilling into her.

"Holy…fuck that was good," Micah said between big gulps of air and slid off him.

His hands settled on her hips, steadying her as she turned onto her back and smiled up at him. God, this woman. She was his everything. She would have been his everything even without the mind-blowing sex, but that added bonus continued to remind him how lucky he was to have her in his life.

"I think you broke my vagina."

"Let me take a look," he teased, spreading her legs to drink in the sight of her wet and dripping. *They* did that, together. "You look absolutely fucking perfect."

Giggling, she swatted his hands away and pressed her legs together. Fletcher squeezed her knee and then held both hands out to lift her up.

"As much as I want us to stay in bed and fuck each other's brains out for the rest of the evening, we shouldn't."

"Aw," Micah said, pouting as she followed him out of bed. "I thought we were banging in the new year."

Fletcher turned on the shower, glancing over at her as she stripped the sheets off. His mermaid, always cleaning up after herself. Rolling his eyes, he walked back to the bedroom, scooped Micah up and carried her into the shower.

Almost two hours later, they were sitting on Micah's back porch furniture, with their legs kicked up waiting for the fireworks. With her head tucked against his shoulder and body pressed firmly against his, he was happy and content and satisfied. All the wild sex aside, they'd had a pretty good day together, and this was the best way to end it all.

Emery had graced them with her presence for breakfast and they'd dropped her off at Nico's house before going for a drive around Sirena Beach. Micah had made him stop at The Mermaid Mart, where they'd met one late night in the bread aisle, so she could pick up baking ingredients. Fletcher made sure to snag a bouquet of flowers as well, and when they got home, clothes came flying off. It had been a while since they had her entire house to themselves and usually when they wanted to fuck on every surface, they picked his place.

After the first few rounds of sex, Micah made a fluffy chocolate cake and licked icing off of him. She almost slathered some over his dick, but there was a line to what he would allow her to eat off his penis. Fruit roll-ups were the limit. They made lunch together—what started out as burritos turned into bowls instead—and ate in silence while soaking up each other's company.

That was another thing he'd never done before, eat without some kind of noise or distraction. With Micah, he didn't have to fill silences. They talked and laughed together, but they also found peace in the quiet moments together as well. However, when they were eating their cake, his girl got super excited about the things she had planned for the new year. Everything from new hobbies—she was going to finally learn how to surf and ride a bicycle—to the new methods she was going to implement at work to bring in more senior citizens who needed help. She even talked about holidays and things to do with Emery, while also including him in every plan.

They hadn't really talked that deeply about the future, besides saying they were going to be together. He hadn't asked about living arrangements, she hadn't offered any either. But she was talking about trips to Disneyland with Emery *and* Fletcher, doing a wine country trip with the girls, skiing and snowboarding and attending Comic Con. And in every exciting thing she mentioned, she asked him what he thought about the place or if it excited him too. And truthfully? It did. Being able to be a part of Micah's life was a big deal and he wasn't taking it for granted.

So Disneyland, skiing and snowboarding and Comic Con as a family? Sign him up.

"More wine?" Micah's soft words broke through his thoughts and he nodded, holding his glass out to her. She topped it up and filled hers before turning to him again. "What's on your mind?"

"You."

"Besides me, obviously."

He chuckled, pressing a kiss to her forehead as he tightened his arm around her shoulders. "Thank you for including me in all your plans for the new year." He knew she was going to protest, so he shook his head before continuing, "I know we said we were going to be together, but I didn't want to assume that meant we'd be doing *all* the things. I also know that this is a serious relationship and we're meant to be together and all that other good stuff you're going to tell me, but it still means a lot that you included me."

She leaned back, resting her head against his arm with a small smile. "Why do all the words that have to do with two people choosing to be together sound so strange and child-ish? Relationship, boyfriend, girlfriend…it's so weird."

Only Micah would focus on that instead of what they were talking about. A smile tugged at his mouth as he shook his head, sipping on his wine.

"Can you imagine me going to Disneyland without adult supervision? I'd probably lose my head if it wasn't attached to my body," she said, still continuing with her joking tone. "But in all seriousness, I wanted to do these things with someone. With *you*. And sure, Emery and I can have a ball at Disney and skiing and snowboarding, but I want *you* to do it with us too."

She clinked her glass against his and continued, "I didn't believe in soulmates or fate or destiny or whatever people say in their vows and big declarations. But seeing you again, falling in love with you *again* and knowing that you are everything I didn't know I was waiting for maybe changed my mind."

"Did you say vows?"

"Oh my god, that's not the important part of what I said." Micah slapped his chest and Fletcher laughed. She sobered quickly, sitting up as she stared at him with wide eyes. "But is that what you want?"

"To recite vows? Yeah. Hell, I'll do it right now."

She put a hand over his mouth and shook her head, eyes glassy as she smiled. "Save it for the big day, Fletch."

He gently tugged her hand down and arched an eyebrow. "The big day, Mick?"

"Yeah, when I walk down the aisle and say 'I do' and we're surrounded by our friends and fam—" He leaned in and covered her mouth with his, cutting off the rest of her spiel. Her lips curled against his and he felt her arm wind around his neck as she kissed him back. Their tongues tangled and danced, his free hand sliding into her hair as he pulled her even closer.

The sound of fireworks bursting broke them apart and he watched as the pink, yellows and blues reflected over Micah's face. She stroked his jaw with her thumb and said, "Does that mean you want the big day?"

"I want all the days with you, love bug."

"All the days it is," she whispered and kissed him again.

epilogue. micah.

How will everyone know I'm yours?

One Year Later | *Sirena Beach, California*

"FRIENDS AND FAMILY, I present to you," Jack, of The Rescuers, announced, his voice filtering through the speakers set up around the spacious backyard, "Micah and Fletcher George-Kelley!"

Micah grinned as she and Fletcher stepped through the beaded curtain, presenting themselves to their closest friends and family. Everyone was on their feet, whistles going through the crowd, shouts and cheers. And then there was Emery, who was still so teary eyed, Micah wondered if her daughter would ever stop crying. Squeezing Fletcher's hand, Micah shot her *husband* a wide grin and nodded towards Emery. He gave her a quick nod in return and they walked down the short stairs and wrapped Emery into a hug. Her unshed tears were suddenly streaming down her face, one arm coming around Micah's neck as a loud sob exploded from her mouth.

"Honey, you're starting to scare me," Micah whispered, squeezing Emery around the waist.

"I'm...so...fucking...happy." The words came out between sobs and Micah fought the urge to laugh at how adorable this moment was. Emery finally pulled away and wiped at her cheeks aggressively, like that would hide the evidence of her tears. Her heart was bursting at how much love she felt for her teenager. Well, Emery was now a high school freshman. Where did all the years go?

"You okay, kid?"

Emery nodded at Fletcher, flashing him one of her broad smiles even though her eyes were still brimming with tears. "Thank you for staying, for choosing us, for choosing *me*," she whispered and Micah blinked back tears at the words. Fletcher shook his head, fighting back tears of his own before he pulled Emery into his arms again. Stepping away from the moment, Micah let Sadie and Tatum engulf her in their arms.

When Fletcher told her about the conversation he and Emery had at Christmas, about him staying with them forever, Micah had been so emotional. She knew how much Emery craved having a father, how much she hated that her own father hadn't claimed her or wanted her. In the short time that Fletcher had been in her life, Emery had gotten attached and that was even before Micah's relationship with him came to light. Besides, Fletcher was the kind of guy you loved at the first meeting so to know her daughter felt that impact said a lot.

Watching her husband and daughter hold each other, both crying and laughing at the same time made Micah's heart swell.

She'd made it fifteen full years as a single mother. She'd found the job of her dreams. She had the best friends a person could ask for. She had a home that was constantly filled with love.

Most importantly, she was now married to the only man who'd ever had her heart.

A year ago, when they'd talked about writing vows on their *big day* while fireworks burst above their heads, she hadn't believed they were going to be planning a wedding. That was before they spoke to Emery about their plans a few weeks later. Micah wanted something small and simple, and if it were up to her, they would have eloped to Vegas and let Elvis marry them in one of his many chapels. But one morning over breakfast, Fletcher asked Emery if she wanted to go ring shopping with him and then all hell broke loose. Her daughter was excited at the prospect and dragged him out of the house as soon as she was ready. When they came back, Emery also announced that Fletcher was moving in with them and spent an hour giving Micah a run down of what ring shopping was like.

Of course her daughter also insisted that Fletcher put the ring on Micah's finger right there. So without ceremony or a big fancy speech, Fletcher said, "Let's get hitched, love bug. Let's make this damn thing official."

There was no part of her that believed she would get married again. She was closing in on forty, raising a kid all on her own and working her ass off every single day. A husband and a marriage never factored into the way she planned her life. But for Fletcher Kelley? She'd make all the adjustments necessary to have him look at her *that* way for the rest of their lives.

They started off the new year moving Fletcher's stuff into the George household. Then did some work to Hank's old house so Fletcher could put it up on Airbnb—Emery made sure to update the listing to mention that it was owned by a former rockstar. When Valentine's Day rolled around, Emery started dropping hints about a wedding. She was quite subtle about it at first—asking about flowers, the best time of year for a backyard wedding, what kind of cake Fletcher liked. When neither of them took the bait, she got more aggressive;

wedding magazines started popping up all over the house and Micah knew that a Vegas elopement would never happen. Not when Emery was set on being part of the whole thing.

To be fair, Micah's first wedding wasn't much to write home about either. They'd exchanged vows in front of thirty of his family members, her parents, Sadie and Tatum. So a bigger celebration, with more people and all the fanfare wasn't the worst idea. When she agreed with Emery's suggestion, she saw Fletcher flinch. He would never deny her daughter anything. But, the poor man was already thinking of what it would be like to be the center of attention for a whole day and he clearly hated it.

Emery worked her butt off for six months, planning every tiny detail to make sure that it was the best day ever. Micah and Fletcher only got involved when payments had to be made—if Sadie and Tatum hadn't taken over that part already—and let Emery handle everything. For the first time in her life, Micah was completely hands-off when it came to something her daughter was doing. Because after raising her for fifteen years, she knew what Emery was capable of. And watching her little girl grow into this young woman was completely blowing her mind.

Just like she predicted, Emery had planned the most gorgeous wedding. She'd invited Micah's parents, people from Haven Clinic and even sent out personalized invitations to Fletcher's bandmates—Jack, Soren and Brandy—insisting that they be there for the big day. Because they didn't do anything traditionally, Micah and Fletcher planned to walk down the aisle together. But they did have bridesmaids and groomsmen. So when they came down the stairs and the members of The Rescuers were waiting for them, Micah saw Fletcher tear up for the first time that day. Hugs went around and all three of them laughed about how they *knew* she and Fletcher would end up together.

And the day itself was absolutely beautiful.

Emery had transformed Hank's backyard into a stunning venue, using the big tree in the middle as the backdrop for the whole thing. Edison bulbs were strung up along poles scattered across the space. Tables had been set up in clusters, allowing guests to sit wherever they pleased. A long table was being used as the bar—which Micah was assured had been Sadie and Tatum's department—while caterers had commandeered Hank's state-of-the-art kitchen to prepare the meal. There had been no rehearsal, there was no time to get cold feet (though Fletcher promised her he would never think twice about marrying the love of his life) and definitely no time for her mother to ask her a million questions about whether or not this was the right decision.

Micah might not have wanted it soon after her divorce. But when she looked into Fletcher's eyes and thought about how much he loved her, there was no doubt in her mind— spending the rest of her life with him was vital. They didn't need any of this or a marriage license to have that, but Fletcher was already talking about adopting Emery and for that they needed all the paperwork and bureaucracy that came with it.

As for their surnames? Micah had never taken Geoffrey's name and even though his name was on Emery's birth certificate, they'd hyphenated it for their daughter. The minute the divorce was finalized, Micah filed all the paper- work necessary to remove the hyphen from Emery's name. Along with getting Geoffrey to hand over his parental rights.

"What do you think about Fletcher George? Do I sound like an old man yelling at kids to get off his lawn?"

Micah had laughed at his expression—face all screwed up

and lips turned sideways—and shook her head. "Like Boy George, without all the glamor."

"So that's a yes?"

"I love you, honey, but we're not changing your surname."

He'd pouted, scooting closer to press his nose against hers. "But how will everyone know I'm yours?"

"The fact that you call me *love bug* in public? Or we can get my name tattooed on your forehead," Micah had suggested, brushing her hand over his bare chest. "Or maybe by the fact that my ring is on your finger."

"I can't wait to wear your ring."

She'd hummed, pressing her mouth to his. "How about we hyphenate?"

"Can we do that?"

"As long as we file the necessary paperwork, we can change our names to whatever we want." He'd grinned and Micah covered his mouth with one hand. "We're not changing your name to Stallion."

"You're killing my buzz here, babe."

"Mr. and Mrs. George-Kelley?" she'd suggested, completely ignoring his pout as she pulled her hand away. He nodded and they filled out all the paperwork necessary—including the adoption papers for Emery—and decided to file it after the wedding.

Now all they had to do was tell Emery about the big plan.

The reception party was in full swing and everyone was having the time of their lives. Micah and Fletcher had found chairs away from the dancing and laughing to sit down and stretch their legs. Her wedding dress—a simple white strapless dress with a tight bodice and a tulle skirt—was fluttering in the light breeze as Fletcher massaged her feet. Her matching white pumps had come off as soon as they'd been announced as husband and wife by the officiant. Her husband was talking to Brandy while Micah watched Emery flit across the dance floor, laughing and dancing with random people.

Tatum and Ambrose drew Emery into their huddle even though they were clearly having a *moment* and Micah's heart leaped at that. Her best friend had finally done something about those pesky feelings and she was so happy for her. Emery then moved onto her parents, who performed their famous dance with their granddaughter without a care in the world. Micah used to hate it when her parents did that, but clearly Emery loved it. Beyond them, Micah caught Sadie and Erin standing close enough for everyone to ignore their 'just friends' statement from a few months ago.

Not that it mattered to Micah, because as long as her friends were happy, she was happy.

"As much as I was looking forward to doing this without fanfare, I gotta admit that this is the best party I've ever been to," Fletcher said, drawing her attention away from the dance floor.

"Our kid did good, didn't she?" Fletcher nodded, tears filling his eyes again and Micah smiled. "Are you going to cry every time we talk about Em, Fletch?"

"Until I can fully process the fact that I belong with you, yeah."

"Aw, sweetheart, we're so honored to have you."

He nodded, eyes in his lap where he was pressing his thumbs into the balls of her feet. "How do you think she's going to react when I ask her?"

Micah watched her husband for a moment, seeing how nervous he was about talking to Emery about the adoption. He'd whispered it to her one night while they lay in bed listening to Emery sneak into the house—"If she was my kid, I'd teach her to sneak in and out silently. Oh fuck, can she be *my* kid?"—and that was all it took for Micah to find the necessary papers. They had no intention of forcing Emery to make the choice, but they had everything ready in case she said yes. At fifteen, Emery George had way more personality than they knew how to handle. So they were approaching things slowly. Differently. *Her* way.

"I wish I knew Em the way you think I do, but I think she'd cry."

He frowned as he lifted his head to focus on Micah. "I don't think I can take anymore crying, babe. Not from her."

"Good tears, stallion. They'll be good tears."

He nodded, smiling a little brighter as a soft voice said, "Mama, may I have this dance?"

"Hell yes." Micah smiled at her daughter in a beautiful white tulle and Chantilly dress that matched hers. Getting to her feet, she blew Fletcher a kiss, grabbed Emery's hand and the two of them walked onto the dance floor barefoot. Emery's arms slid around Micah's waist as her head dropped to her shoulder. Jack was crooning while Soren and Brandy played guitars on either side of him, and it really set the mood for the evening.

"You doing okay, kiddo?"

"I'm doing great." Emery leaned back and Micah smiled, tucking some of her daughter's hair behind her ear. "Did you have fun today?"

"Absolutely. I knew you had good taste, because I gave birth to you, but this wedding? Em, it's beautiful."

"Maybe I can do this for a living."

Micah laughed softly and kissed Emery's forehead. "Fletch and I will be there cheering you on every step of the way."

"He's the best, isn't he?"

Glancing over her shoulder, Micah smiled when Fletcher stopped to talk to her parents. "He's pretty great."

"He said you're the love of his life, is he the love of yours?"

She smiled at the wistful look on her daughter's face. "When I first met him all those years ago, I didn't realize that he was so much more than my favorite rockstar. He was everything I'd been looking for in a partner," she admitted and then shrugged. "Now every time I look at him, I'm reminded that I got so lucky to find the person of my dreams *twice* in one lifetime. But he's not the love of my life, you are."

Emery rolled her eyes, but Micah saw the smile tugging at her lips. "I love you too Mama."

"Good, because I didn't spend eighteen hours in labor for nothing."

A snort escaped Emery and Micah hugged her again, swaying as the song came to an end. As Emery started to pull away, Fletcher appeared by their side and after a kiss to Micah's forehead, held his hands out to Emery. Leaving her two most favorite people in the world together, she turned to find her best friends having their own little sob fest on the sidelines.

"You two are ridiculous," Micah said, pulling them into a three-way hug.

"We're happy that you finally got your happily ever after."

"I was happy as fuck with the two of you and Emery, that was what I believed was my happily ever after."

Tatum snorted and pulled back. "But we can't make you happy the way Fletcher can."

"Well..." Micah laughed and turned to watch as Emery burst out laughing with Fletcher. "You made me plenty happy, girls. But that man..."

"He's special, Mick. I'm so happy for you."

Nodding, Micah smiled as Fletcher's eyes drifted her way. *I love you*, he mouthed and blew her a kiss.

Seventeen years ago she'd fallen in love with a rockstar within seconds of them being left alone in a hotel room. One year ago, she'd allowed herself a second chance with the man of her dreams. And now, Micah George-Kelley was living the life she never imagined she could have. With her Rockstar Santa.

what's next?

Micah's best friends—Tatum and Sadie—do get their *Holiday Remixes* too! But that's not going to happen anytime soon.

In the meantime, sign up for my newsletter, and you'll be the first to know about bonus content.

The final two books in my debut series—Love in Wildes—are also coming soon. *Almost Love* (Book 5) releases September 20th, so make sure you follow me on Instagram to stay updated!

acknowledgments

Mom and Dad, for instilling an intense love for music in me since I was a kid. I'm so grateful that you introduced me to the greatest hits from the 60s, 70s and 80s. Thanks for the song guessing games on road trips and continue to fill my life with the best music the world has to offer. PS. I forgive you for never understanding my boyband obsession.

Xenia, for THIS BEAUTIFUL ILLUSTRATION. You are not only one of the most talented people I've met, but you're so kind and generous. So glad we got to work together, here's to more art in the future!

Jordan Burns, for saving me from making a complete mess by working your magic to bring this gorgeous cover to life! I am so glad that we worked together and I can't wait to do more with you!

Kristen, for being the best cheerleader for me and other indies out there. Thank you for finding the time in your busy schedule to hang out with Micah and Fletcher and to help me fix things I never even considered before.

Erin Thomson, for putting the idea about Rockstar Santa in my head last year. Also for beta reading this and catching my messy bits. Erin Decker is in honor of you.

Cristina Santos, for taking the time between prepping for your own release to read this one and love it. And also for all the numerous DMs we've shared about everything under the sun. Including the awesomeness of Dave Grohl.

Julia Goodwin, for being an incredible source for all information about stuttering. Thank you for taking the time to read the scenes and give me valuable feedback. I appreciate you!

Taylor Epperson, you are the kindest and most generous soul. I appreciate you beautifying the inside of my book with your generous touch.

Jessi, for always being the most supportive and excited human in my life. Thank you for being so amazing. I am honored to be your friend. Here's to more secret projects that you get to read months before everyone else.

Kiira, for being you. We both know that our friendship drives my day and I love you to the moon and back! Also, thank you for giving me your extra booking with Xenia last year that pushed me to write and finish this book.

Also, Dave Grohl (and the Foo Fighters), for being the best rockstar of my lifetime and for being a generally awesome human being.

And YOU, dear reader. For taking the time to read this book, even though it was never on my public schedule, and (hopefully) loving these two wild people that came from my brain.

xo
Anna

about the author

Since she was a child, Anna has lived in a world of imagination—teaching in a classroom to being an astronaut, she's done it all.

With a Masters in Creative Writing, and a love for music got her jobs with Rolling Stone India and Sony Music. After a couple of years of selling her soul to advertising, she's finally following her dream of writing books.

Currently living in South India, she rocks out to Foo Fighters and reads 300 romance novels a year. She works as a copy consultant and book editor, while sipping on copious amounts of black tea.

annawriteshere.com | hello@annawriteshere.com

instagram.com/annawriteshere
goodreads.com/authorannap
threads.net/@annawriteshere
amazon.com/author/anna-p

also by anna p.

love in wildes

Almost Maybes

Almost Forevers

Almost Home

Almost Yours

Almost Love

www.ingramcontent.com/pod-product-compliance
Lightning Source LLC
LaVergne TN
LVHW041452170726
843492LV00005B/1202